Ink

Ink

ALICE BROADWAY

SCHOLASTIC INC.

ISBN 978-1-338-33169-1

10 9 8 7 6 5 4 3 2 1   19 20 21 22 23
Printed in the U.S.A.   23
This edition first printing 2019
Book design by Elizabeth B. Parisi

To the Inkwell.

chapter 1

I WAS OLDER THAN ALL MY FRIENDS WHEN I GOT MY first tattoo.

My mother loves to tell the story. I wish she wouldn't. At two days old you're meant to get your birth mark, but I got sick instead, and Mom canceled the ceremony.

Mom's friends said, "You need to get her marked, Sophie. What are you going to call her?"

But Mom told them she would wait until I was better. I would be named and inked then. She ignored their whispered warnings of what happens to babies who die unmarked. And so for twenty days I remained formless and void until one day my mother said, "Let her be Leora."

And I was Leora. The word was punched with minuscule needles into my flesh. Tiny letters that have grown with me for sixteen years.

. . .

We are not afraid of death. When your marks are safe in your book, you live on after you die. The life story etched onto your body is kept forever—if you're worthy. When we preserve the words, pictures, and moments imprinted on our skin, our story survives for eternity. We are surrounded by the dead, and, for as long as their books are still read and their names are still spoken, they live.

Everyone has the skin books in their homes: Our shelves are full of my ancestors. I can breathe them in, touch them, and read their lives.

But it was only after my father died that I saw the book of someone I'd really known.

. . .

We were lucky really, seeing death walk up from a distance. It meant we could be prepared. We massaged his skin with oil; he told us the stories of his ink and smiled when he showed us the tree on his back with our names on it. He was ready when he went, and his skin was prepared too. I watched his strong arms deflate, leaving the skin wrinkled like an old apple. I watched his straight back bend as though he'd been hit in the stomach. He stopped looking directly at us after a while; the pain was all he saw. It seemed like the sickness sucked him away, just leaving his shell. But the shell is what counts.

People had brought us flowers and food to make those final days easier. Little love tokens for Dad when there was nothing else they could do. We weren't the only ones whose hearts were breaking; Dad was precious to so many. The kitchen smelled of wilting petals, stalks moldering in stale water, and the casserole we hadn't gotten around to eating. It was like death was catching. Mom wrapped the blankets more tightly around him and wiped sweat from her brow. Dad shivered and his breath sounded crackly.

Yet when death came that bright day, in late autumn, I was not ready. I could still taste the coffee I'd drunk at dawn after Mom woke me with a frantic whisper.

"Sweetheart, wake up. I don't think he has much time left."

I hurried to his side. The gaps between his breaths grew longer. Mom and I leaned close and held his hands. I wondered which would be the final gasp, the last silence before he woke in the afterlife and breathed again. Suddenly, with a gasp, Dad's eyes opened and he looked straight at me. His hand gripped mine. He eased his other hand from Mom's and grasped the pendant he always wore around his neck. It was a slender, rough-hewn wooden leaf with a suggestion of veins etched into it that hung from a leather string. It was as much a part of Dad as his ink; I'd never seen him without it.

"Leora." His voice was hoarse. "This is for you. Leora, don't forget. You won't forget me, will you? Please, don't forget me."

Tears came to his eyes as he begged me. "And promise me you'll watch out for the blanks. Be careful, my little light, my Leora."

I nodded and, through sobs, whispered, "I promise." I looked at Mom, her lips tight and her face strained. She reached up and untied the leather that circled his neck, and Dad passed the pendant to me. I rubbed the smooth wood, and tears fell from my eyes as I blinked. He turned to Mom and made certain hers was the last face he saw. He went from the land of the living hearing Mom's "*I love you, I love you, I love you*" and feeling her kisses on his hand.

And he left us. Just like that, he went. The sun dimmed. A source of true goodness had gone from the world, and it was colder and darker without him.

After he died, the embalmers came to our house. They dripped oil over his body and rubbed spices into his skin. They wrapped him in blue cloth and took him away. He looked like a king. He'd always seemed that way to me. For days after, I would go into the room and inhale the fragrance of his anointing. Maybe if I could breathe him in he would burst out of my lungs, fully formed and laughing.

But the next time I saw him, his life had become pages. He would come home to us once the weighing of the soul ceremony had found him worthy. For now, we had to go to the museum if we wanted to be with him. We walked there in the light of an amber sunset, permitted to enter the museum after normal opening hours for this intimate viewing. In a private room that smelled of ancient wooden furniture and the perfume of whoever had been for a viewing before us, we were presented with my father in his new form. We placed the small casket with his skin book inside on the table. Mom appeared at my shoulder, her eyes wide. She had been tense and on edge ever since his death—less sorrowful than snappish and distracted. Sometimes I'd come into a room and find her staring into space, her hands clasped so tightly together the knuckles gleamed. I was starting to feel irritated by it; I didn't want to have to think about her, not just now. I wanted my Mom back—my calm, capable Mom, who always knew the right thing to say.

As we lifted the lid, a smell of wax and spice wafted through the room, raising a toast to him. And there he was. His skin taut, smooth, and slightly shrunken. With each page we turned, we touched him again and remembered the roughness of his forearms, the smoothness of his back. Every stiff page told his story. Mom seemed nervous at first; her shoulders were tense under my arm, but she became calmer the further we read. The cover of his book, which was made from the skin from the back of his shoulders, showed a picture of us and the ink from his birth showing his name—Joel Flint. A good title. A good man. A good introduction. We turned a page and saw the tree from his back telling the tale of his family—me and Mom; the girls who captured his heart. I saw my name there and traced the letters with my finger. There were marks I hadn't seen since I was a child. They looked much fainter now, blurred with time.

We turned a page and Mom laughed and closed her eyes. "You might want to look away, Leora," she said with a blush and pursed lips that hid a smile.

She was right, I didn't want to see it, but the flower that had been on his buttock was intricate and delicate. Stretched into the page of his book, it looked like any other part of him, but it was secret. It was their marriage mark—added to each year, getting more and more beautiful as their love grew. Mom's laughter suddenly blended with tears and she put her palm across her mouth as if stopping the sadness and reminding her of the kisses she missed.

We turned the page.

chapter 2

THE MORNING AFTER WE OPEN DAD'S BOOK, MOM goes back to work. She says that it is time, that we need to go back to our normal lives, or, at least, work out what our new normal is going to be. *Normal* is very important to Mom; she's always been effortlessly popular, sociable and busy, committed to the community, and I think she's always been a bit bewildered that her own daughter is such a loner. I decide to get out of the house too, but head to the market; there is no school today; my year are all on study leave. I know I have to engage with all that again, with revision and final exams. I will have to work hard to make up for the time I've missed if I am to be an inker—which is all I've ever wanted.

I walk along the sidewalk, rippled by tree roots beneath, and I wonder when we'll get a date for Dad's weighing of the soul ceremony. The most time-consuming part has already happened in this last month since Dad died: the flaying, the tanning, the binding of his skin into a book. Now the people at the government need to study his finished book and prepare his case before the ceremony can happen. And then he can come home. Back with us, where he belongs.

The weighing of the soul ceremony is where the leaders announce their final decision about the destiny of your soul. They will have studied Dad's book and judged whether he has led a worthy enough life. The worthy go home with their family, are placed among their ancestors, and are read and remembered forever. Their soul is safe in the afterlife. If you're found unworthy, your soul is destroyed in flames along with your book. I've never seen it happen, but they say you never forget the smell of a burning skin book. That won't be Dad, though; no one could have led a better or purer life.

Closer to town the road narrows, until the sidewalk is just wide enough for one person. Walking down the dusty street, I sneak looks into the windows of the terraced homes I pass. The higgledy buildings are each painted different colors and face right onto the sidewalk. When I was little I used to tell myself stories about the streets like this; I used to imagine a giant had squeezed the row of houses, making each one skinny and creating wobbly roofs of different heights. Now, I tell myself different stories as I peep into the leaded windows and wonder about the lives within. When people don't close their curtains, I take it as an invitation to guess at who lives there and what their life is like. I am so engrossed in looking that I almost bump into a man picking the dead petals from the red geraniums in his window box. I step around him quickly, one foot in the road, inhaling the sharp bitterness of the dying flowers.

I keep walking, and, in my mind, I turn the pages of Dad's book. I feel my shoulders relax. It was a beautiful relief to see him last night. Mom seemed like a different person when we left the museum; she sighed so loudly when we reached the final page I thought at first that something was wrong, but when I turned to look she was smiling. She was right to: His skin tells such a good tale. When someone reads your book, they should be able to read your life story; they can weigh the good against the bad and know if you're worthy. Everything important goes on our skin, because otherwise it stays in our soul, and no one wants their soul weighed down, either by pride at their good deeds or by guilt at their transgressions. We mark our bodies to keep our souls unfettered. Only the worthy attain remembrance, and to do that your good must outweigh your bad and your soul must be free.

I smile at the thought of Dad's pure soul ready to be counted worthy. I am longing for the day of his weighing to come.

Dad was a flayer—his friends at work will have been the ones to slice his skin to make it ready for the tanners. He did the same for their loved ones and for the countless unknown people who came their way each day. Mom is a reader; it's more of a calling than a job, I suppose, but it does pay—not everyone considers that a real job. It's hard to explain what makes someone a reader, but the best way is that some of us can read the meanings behind marks—we can see beyond the immediate message to what the ink expresses about that person's heart. My mom can look at your family tree and tell who is the favorite child. She can look at the age marks on your hand and tell which year almost broke you. She can look at the marks that describe your qualifications and tell whether you cheated. People admire readers, but they also fear them. Mom once told me that everyone has secrets they want to keep.

We shouldn't really have secrets, though. That's the whole point.

I have the gift too. I've been able to read people since I was a child. Mom says she worked it out when I got into trouble in my first week at school; I had asked a boy why he didn't live with his real dad. When his angry mom showed up at the door demanding to know who had been gossiping about them, Mom knew I must have read between the lines on the boy's skin. But just because I can do it doesn't mean I want to do it as my job. I love the glimpse it gives me into people's marks and lives, but sometimes I get tired of ink shouting out the inner world of strangers as they pass by. I don't think I could bear their anxious faces if they were sitting across the reading table from me, knowing that if their marks chose to reveal the truth, I could see everything.

No, my dream is to be an inker. All I can hope is that I do well enough in my exams, which aren't looking as straightforward as they once were. I've missed so much time with Dad not being well. I've always gotten good grades at school without having to try too hard, so being anxious is a first for me.

As I near the center of town, the houses turn into rows of shops. I pass the bakery, a florist, and the leather worker's place, where we get our shoes and bags mended. The dusty path becomes cobbles and the narrow street I'm on takes me to the town square. In the middle of the large square is a small comfort-blanket of green, standing out bright against the stone and timber of the buildings surrounding it. And at its center is the statue of Saint, the most important leader in our history.

He stands in the middle of our bustling town, a tall figure in bronze: smooth, robed, and watching us. I've always loved his story—the tale we tell to remind us of his faithfulness, the power of stories, and the soul-freeing necessity of flaying the dead. And, of course, he stands there as a warning to us about the despicable ways of the blanks. Footpaths cross the square, corner to corner, and people stroll along them chatting and trying to find a patch of grass between the footpaths where they can sit and drink their coffee.

The square is where you can really get a sense of what matters in Saintstone. And if things matter here, they matter everywhere. All the towns around depend on us: Saintstone is where the government is based and where all the decisions of any importance are made. I like living in the center of things. I'm not sure how it would feel to be in one of the smaller towns where everyone thinks they know you even before they've seen your ink.

Depending on which way the wind is blowing, you can usually smell the smoke from the hall of judgment. It's a large circular building made of stone and colored glass that tapers up to the wide chimney. The fire is always lit, the smoke creating permanent gray-brown clouds over the town. It's where the soul ceremonies happen and where Mom and I go when it's our turn to speak the names of the dead. It's also where matters of faith are taught and upheld. Our schoolteachers train there; our spiritual education and formation is just as important as our academic attainment.

On this side of the square, behind me as I walk, is the museum—my favorite place. It's raised high, with stone steps all around it. It towers over us, all stone pillars and arched windows. It looks dark and imposing from here but when you go inside it's bright and cozy. Dad used to take me there all the time. I swallow, feeling a sudden chill in the shadow of the building, and hurry on.

Across the square, beyond the grass and trees and benches, I see an unexpected bustle and commotion. People are setting up loudspeakers on a temporary platform that has been constructed outside the government building, which is a giant L-shaped box taking up two sides of the square. People are gathering round, some are getting up from their benches to get a closer look, and there is a low hum of conversation. There must be a meeting I've forgotten about.

Seeing the government building makes me realize I've not been called for my truth-telling test in a while; I should expect it soon, I suppose. We're meant to have one every few years to allow us to confess. The image of Dad taking me for the first time, when I was nearly fourteen, flashes brightly in my mind.

Dad had assured me it was nothing to worry about, but that hadn't stopped me from being scared. We'd all been told about the machine that reads your pulse and temperature and beeps if you're lying, but I'd never seen it. My imagination had convinced me it was definitely going to hurt. I was certain that this would be the moment that I would be found out; I thought of all the little lies I'd told my parents and times I had snuck an extra cookie when I'd been told I'd had enough. I even had nightmares about accidentally confessing to a crime I hadn't committed.

It was an anticlimax when we were shown from the main reception and led into a small, completely plain room with white walls, two chairs, a wooden table, and a small contraption that was nothing more than a dull and battered-looking metal dome with a light attached and wires coming out of it. A man with a notebook was waiting and gestured for me to sit down, but when Dad saw how nervous I still was, he asked if he could go first. He sat in the chair, placed his left hand on the dome, and looked at me with a smile and a roll of his eyes that said, "This is a breeze."

He answered all the questions calmly and the machine did nothing. I was relieved that the questions weren't too hard, just general queries asking about new marks and a list of crimes Dad had to confirm he hadn't committed. The man wrote down the odd note, and when he was done, he smiled at Dad and told him he could stand up.

"Your conscience is clear, Mr. Flint. Good, good." He smiled as though this was all a bit of fun and then looked my way. "Your turn now." He chuckled. "I promise, you won't feel a thing."

I sat down and took a deep breath, but the moment I put my hand on the machine it began to screech. I snatched my hand away in horror.

"What happened?" I remember wanting to cry and looking at Dad incredulously. He was trying not to smile.

The man was smiling. "Don't worry. I hadn't reset it properly."

Dad was really laughing now.

"Maybe you've got more to hide than I thought, Leora," he said. I turned to him and scowled.

In the end the whole thing was fine; I was asked the same things as Dad, plus a couple tailored for someone my age, like whether I'd ever cheated in school. The machine remained blissfully silent and Dad bought me cake on the way home to make up for laughing at me.

Cutting through the path between the hall of judgment and the government building, heading toward the market stalls beyond it, I realize I'm smiling. I wish he were here.

It's cool today. The first day with a chill in it this winter. The shock of it has made everyone wrap themselves in extra layers.

It's strange to see less skin—I feel a little cut off, walking past people when I can only see the marks on their faces and forearms. It feels good, though; I feel less naked today, and not simply because of the linen shawl wrapped around me and buttoned at my shoulder. Just sometimes—and I would never say this out loud—it feels nice to hide my marks.

The market is here most days, and I plunge into a mass of striped canopies, yells, and people. I try not to breathe in as I walk past the butcher—the smell of the meat hanging there makes me feel queasy. I gasp air once I reach the fabric stall. The earthy fragrance of the cotton and the spiciness of the dyes are alluring. Inhaling the colors, I imagine my breath coming out in rainbow puffs. I walk among the crowds, watching the ground ahead of my feet—it's easier this way. Just for today, I want to tune out the snippets of conversation and let people's marks become background noise. I feel content to have only Dad's marks in my mind while the memory is still fresh.

I follow my nose until I can make out the fruity tang of the grocer's stall. Wooden boxes hold the grocer's wares, propped up so we can be tempted by their deliciousness. The grocer is smiling, his green apron dusted slightly with dirt. He's holding a paper bag open and waiting to take my order. His sleeves are pushed up—we're always supposed to have our forearms on display—and I can see so much of him from them. He's thirty-six and bright—the smartest in his class, clever enough to have had the pick of trades, but there's death in his marks. I read of a youth cut short by the passing of his older brother. He looks happy now, though, and his marks twist to tell me he has a family. I read joy in his ink—there's abundance in his life beyond the glut of apples and beans in the boxes around him.

I ask the grocer for onions and begin to fill a brown paper bag of my own with grubby potatoes. The carrots look good and the tomatoes smell fresh and sweet.

"Do you know what's happening in the square?" I ask. "There's a stage set up and lots of people are gathering."

He shakes the bag of onions and swings it closed, holding the corners tightly.

"Haven't you heard? There's going to be a public marking," he says as I pass the bag of potatoes for him to weigh while I choose some pears. I hear suppressed excitement in his voice, and something else too; is it fear? "There's not been one for years."

A lot of things have passed me by recently; I've been so caught up with Dad. I glance down the street, hesitating. I've only ever heard about public markings in school; I'm intrigued. I pay the grocer, pick up my bag, and join the crowd heading toward the square. Someone's shoulder bumps mine in their rush to get by me. Voices rise, and as I get closer the path is packed with everyone drawn to the center of town to see what's going to happen.

By the time I reach the square, a large crowd has already clustered around the stage, and I'm stuck near the back. A woman next to me nods and leans toward me. Her eyes are bright with excitement. "They say Mayor Longsight is coming here today!" she says breathlessly.

I'm not the type to pay much attention to politics, but there's something about Dan Longsight that seems to have made everyone take a little more notice, even with the kids in my class. He became mayor about six months ago, and he's totally different from the doddery old men we've had before; he's handsome, for one, and younger than most other politicians. For the first time in a while, people are excited about change. I remember the excitement we all felt at his inauguration when we recited the words that invested him with our hopes and trust: *He is good, he is wise, he is the best of us. He is not cruel, he loves us, we will not fear. He does all things for our good.* I believed those words so strongly my heart nearly beat out of my chest.

He's brought in changes too, which we studied in history class with Mrs. Oldham. We needed these changes, he said; it was like we'd got lost somewhere. We used to know who we were and we used to be sure of our strength. That seemed to get more and more diluted with each weak leader who preceded Longsight. His government wanted to bring us back to our roots—to a society where our marks matter, where their power is taken seriously, and where we truly see they have the power to change our eternity. So, Mayor Longsight and his supporters wear as little as possible, to show that they have nothing to hide. Anyone can see their marks and can know their lives. Mrs. Oldham looked embarrassed when she explained this to us; I assume she is the type who feels our marks should be private. After seeing him on the screen, and studying him so much at school, the idea that

I might actually get to see him sends an excited shiver down my spine. I'm relieved that none of the old mayors shared his views—I don't think I'd have liked to see too much of their skin. Mayor Longsight, from what I've seen so far, might not be too bad.

Some people say he is Saint reborn, come to purify our hearts and our community. All I know is that it feels like change is coming: change for the better.

Everyone is pushing, trying to edge closer to the stage so they'll get a good view. There is constant chatter; it seems everyone else is just as intrigued as I am. There's a strange intensity, and I hear small arguments break out over feet that have been stepped on and latecomers pushing in. The staging is made of wooden sections and there are speakers on each end of it. Thick black fabric encloses the stage at the back and sides, flapping in the breeze. There's a wooden block in the center of the stage and I wonder what it's for. The murmur of the crowd builds and builds, but moments later, when a tall, dark figure walks onto the stage, the atmosphere changes. No one needs to tell us to be quiet. It feels like even the birds are taking a moment of silence to stop and gaze in awe of him. A long minute passes, and then cheers start, and we clap and whoop as Mayor Longsight steps toward the microphone. He raises his hands and eventually the noise subsides, becoming a bustling murmur as we wait for him to speak. He clears his throat, and his ineffable authority seems to resound through the square. He moves closer to the large microphone. He's even taller than I expected, and he stands so composed and straight, his confidence shining from him like rays of warm sunshine. I can't believe he's here—right here in front of me.

"Thank you," he says, and the crowd falls completely silent. "Thank you for being here on this momentous occasion." Underneath the tinny quality of the loudspeakers, his voice is rich. I wonder what it would be like to hear him speak without amplifiers. "What an honor it is to gather in this way; to stand together as a community united against evil. United," he hesitates for a moment and then goes on, "against evil."

There is an uneasy murmur from the crowd, and I feel cold despite my shawl.

"Yes, against evil," he goes on. "For I am here to tell you what many have suspected—these are dark times."

He pauses and looks around at us all. He's wearing nothing more than a simple loincloth, but he doesn't shiver in the chill air. Despite this, from this distance it's hard to read him; I wish I could see the elegant tattoos on his shining black skin more clearly.

"You are gathered here to witness something that will be new to many of you—the first public marking in many decades. Some of you—the respected older members of our community—might remember seeing public markings like this before. You know what to expect. You remember those days—better days, I would say. But for the rest of us, this is something we've only read about in our schoolbooks."

He's right; we've all studied markings, but no one I know has seen another person marked.

"You know that I honor and admire the leaders that have gone before me—and they, in their ... wisdom"—he pauses briefly, and we all know he means the opposite—"chose to do away with certain parts of our tradition. But it's time. It's time we returned to the old ways—for all our sakes, in these dangerous, dangerous days—we *must* recover our heritage, and not forget the decisions our ancestors made."

At this, he is interrupted by an enormous cheer. He signals for quiet and smiles broadly. I can see his white teeth even from where I'm standing.

"For too long, my friends, we have seen truly abhorrent crimes treated as mere misdemeanors. This must stop. Punishment must be meaningful once more. And so, although today is momentous, soon it will be more common to see a marking in the square. Not frequently—a public marking is not something to be given lightly—but for the most heinous crimes, yes. We cannot continue to gloss over the sins happening within our own society."

There is more applause, and he waits a beat before continuing. He doesn't seem to crave applause; he looks almost embarrassed by it.

"For too long we have allowed ourselves to slip into apathy, but now we cannot afford not to be vigilant. There has always been a threat from the blanks. No one believed that they really went quietly after the great expulsion—but we chose to think that they were living peacefully, posing no risk to us. And yet I am here today to tell you that we are paying the price for our apathy."

Another murmur, almost a groan, rises up from the crowd, and I feel my heart thudding hard in my chest.

"Yes. We have evidence that the blanks are plotting. They have taken advantage of our weakness. They want to infiltrate and dilute us by weakening our hearts and our morals. You may have heard it yourself; one person at the market says, 'The blanks weren't all bad,' a friend tells you they heard the blanks are a peace-loving people, and a work colleague admits they wonder if the Blank Resettlement Bill wasn't perhaps a bit harsh? And you admire the spirit of your friends: moderate, optimistic, liberal, and open."

He pauses and lets his words settle.

"Drip, drip, drip. The propaganda from the blank spies in our midst (oh yes, they have *spies*) is subtle, but insidious. They have supporters—rebels—within our own community who willingly feed you lies. They let you believe that they are offering you a light to warm yourself by: nice words that make you feel the blanks are no threat and that you are safe. You settle down by the light of their fire: Their words whisper 'peace' and 'ease.' You believe you are finally able to rest. But while you sleep, the rebels will strike and their small, warming flames will become a forest fire that destroys you—destroys *everything*."

He stares at us from the stage, his eyes blazing. And then he *roars*.

"*Wake up! Wake and rise up!*" His shout stuns me. "Our unguardedness has led us into danger. We have been too willing to trust, and the blanks have found a foothold and are ready to take advantage of our guileless acceptance that all is well. But no more."

Looking around I see shocked faces; this is not what we expected to hear. This sounds like a rallying cry: a call to war.

"We will be ready. We will be alert: always watchful, always wary of the snakes within our ranks. We will recover our purity and reclaim history and make it our present. It is time, don't you think?"

Caught up in Mayor Longsight's fervor, we applaud and stamp, and Mayor Longsight signals to someone off the stage, hidden by the black curtain. He waits until we are absolutely silent and bows his head as though he is praying. There is a long, still moment. Then he looks up, right at us. "I have serious news. Here today is the proof that the blanks are rising up. It will come as a shock to many here, for the man to be punished today walked among you; many of you considered him your friend." He draws a deep breath and then bites out the words. "The judgment was made last week that Connor Drew, one of our esteemed flayers, entrusted with our precious dead, is guilty of skin-stealing."

A ripple of shock pulses through the crowd and I shudder. I don't know who Connor Drew is—he's a flayer, so Dad may have—but the idea that anyone would steal skin makes me feel ill. I think of my dad on the flayers' table and how precious his skin is. Without the skin, there is nothing—no story, no way to live on in the hearts and minds of loved ones left behind. Who would dare steal someone's history? And why?

Mayor Longsight signals to one of his aides, and a man is brought onto the stage by two enormous guards. They're obviously here to protect us from this criminal. *Or protect him from us, perhaps?* I think as the crowd hisses ominously. The man has chains around his ankles but his hands are free, his arms held tightly by the men on either side of him. He wears a loincloth like Mayor Longsight's, only this man's is dirty white and looks ragged. His skin is black like Longsight's, only he appears gray with tiredness and defeat.

Following the men onto the platform is the town's storyteller, Mel. She's not much older than I am, but she holds our stories on her skin; she embodies our aims and ideals. If Mel is here, this is even more serious than I first thought.

"You know your history, my friends. You know how the blanks worked to break our spirits. They removed people's marks so that their souls would be forever incomplete. And this man, Connor Drew, may be marked in body, but he is blank in spirit. For he removed skin—of course he did, he is a flayer. But instead of letting it be stitched into a book, he kept it for himself. In stealing one piece, he is guilty of stealing a person's story, of jeopardizing their journey into the next world, of editing what is left for him to be remembered by. He has worked to prevent us from making a judgment on this soul. This is the work of the blanks."

There is a long pause and now no one is cheering; they look frightened. "I can confirm, friends, that Connor Drew's actions were not without motive. He was acting in league with the blanks, aiming to incite a rebellion. He has confessed to having contact with blanks. He is working with them."

Shouts rise through the crowd. *How could he?*

"Here is evidence of their ways; this is just the beginning. We must fight. The blanks are back and are using our own men to steal our skin, our stories, our souls. They will not stop at this. It is not our souls they truly desire, but our destruction. For the blanks hunger and thirst for our land. They won't be happy until they have overtaken our cities, towns, homes, and beds. They desire our land and will stop only when every one of us is without a home and without a hope in our own world."

A woman next to me is weeping. I don't want to cry, not here, so I breathe deeply against the tears and sickness and tell myself to keep my head. There have been rumors for some time that the blanks are on the rise—that they will return and ruin us. I didn't want to believe it—I hadn't believed it, until now.

"You know our history; you've seen the evidence in the museum. When the blanks were among us they maimed and dismembered their victims in order to steal their marks, stories, and souls. They, a weak and lowly people, clawed at our bodies because they wanted to make us like them. They wanted to overcome our strength and righteousness and claim our land: the land that God gave us and Saint died for. We will not allow this, of course. But justice must be done. Connor Drew stands with those evil blank rebels—and he does not stand alone. He is the first of a plague that we must stamp out. Now, my friends, you know that a person can't play God without expecting that God might one day choose to play with him. This man tried to change one human's eternity, and in return he will forfeit his own. He will know what it is to have his future wiped out."

I look around at the silent crowd and feel the cold air drive a shiver through my body. They're going to kill him. They're going to kill him in front of us all—is that what everyone's here to see? I desperately try to remember if I learned about this in school. I don't want to witness this. Someone coughs, and the people in the crowd begin to shift their feet and whisper to one another.

Mayor Longsight is looking at us, his face serene. He's completely in control. I relax a little. I shouldn't worry. I close my eyes and picture his marks, and once again I think of the words we said when he was appointed, I whisper them to myself and feel calmer. *He is good, he is wise, he is the best of us. He is not cruel, he loves us, we will not fear. He does all things for our good.* I tell myself I am not worried. I am not afraid.

"Hold him, please," Mayor Longsight says to the guards. His voice is gentle and courteous.

They force the man to his knees and place his forehead onto a wooden block that has been waiting on the stage. I look at my feet, but hear the man groan and struggle against their strong arms. There is a gasp through the crowd and I can't help but look back up again—Longsight has a slim case in his hands. I watch him open it carefully, and with a flourish, he takes out a knife—short-bladed but gleaming in its readiness. He stands over the criminal, one foot on either side of his body, grasping the prisoner's hair to hold him still and to reveal the bare skin of his neck. Like a lamb to the slaughter. I don't want to watch but I can't look away.

He brings the knife down and a thick lock of the man's hair falls to the ground.

Like a sheep to the shearer.

I'm so relieved I cry out a laughing sob. He'll be OK. He's not going to be killed.

The woman next to me looks at me sharply. "It's no laughing matter—you watch this. Watch this and remember."

The man is weeping. The guards have hold of him still, but he seems punctured—his fight has gone as though he's given himself over to his fate. Longsight raises the knife high and as he does a man dressed completely in black comes to the stage. Two assistants follow with a stool and a table laden with a kit, and then I know what's going to happen. As Longsight wipes his knife and returns it to the case, the man sits and takes a razor from the table. Carefully, he shaves the back of the prisoner's head. Then he removes his black gloves, discards them, and puts on a fresh pair. I see him lift the familiar machine, ready the skin, and then begin to work on the scalp just above the hairline at the back of his head, dipping the needle into a small inkwell on his workstation. The prisoner groans but doesn't move—the guards still holding him help.

There's a commotion in the crowd, and I see a young man shoving his way through, fighting to reach the platform. I see the guards tense, but before he can get close some of those around him reach for him and drag him away. I see his face as they leave—blank with horror, glasses knocked askew—and for a moment I imagine our eyes meet.

The inking continues. It doesn't take as long as some of the tattoos I've seen, but still the buzz of the machine wheedles into my mind like a dull tinnitus. I begin to feel weak as I stand and half watch, half dream while the man in black completes the mark. Then, with a sudden absence of sound, the machine stops, and the inker stands up. He returns the machine to the table and, with a final respectful nod to the mayor, walks away.

Mayor Longsight, who has been standing at the back of the stage while the mark was made, steps forward to the microphone.

"Today, my friends, you have seen justice done. This man will remain in our society—we are generous. His hair will grow and his ink will be hidden. But he has received the mark of the forgotten."

Something pierces the numbness in my brain. *The forgotten?*

"When this criminal dies, this mark will be read, this mark will convict him, and his book will be destroyed in the flames of the fire in the hall of judgment."

How could you live once you've been marked as forgotten? How could you go on, knowing none of it matters, that your life will end at death and oblivion? All I hope is that I will ascend to the ranks of the remembered—that's what we live for. But right here, this man's hope has been blotted out by black ink.

Forgotten.

A dull peal is ringing in my brain—something I'll remember if only I let myself.

"Friends, let this encourage you to live lives worthy of the calling we have received. Live lives to be remembered, friends. Don't let this man's failure be in vain."

A whisper goes through the crowd, ending up as a held-back roar. People are cheering, people are shouting, people are saying over and over, "A crow, a crow. The mark is a crow."

Forgotten. And I remember now. I remember everything.

The man's howl merges with my own and I run home, the bag of onions banging against my thigh and the soil from the potatoes still under my nails.

A crow. A crow. The mark is a crow.

chapter 3

A S I RUN THROUGH THE SQUARE, PAST THE HALL of judgment and the museum, I try to picture my father's book. I try to envisage each page I turned, each moment of his life. I can't help but read people as I dodge past them:

Fourteen, loves music, hates her sister.

Loves his lover, has tricked his wife.

Her dog is more of a friend than any human she's known.

Fifty-six but feels eighty—so many sicknesses have taken her joy.

Past the bakery, keep running. I need to get home, away from the noise, away from the visual cacophony, away from those voices cawing at me.

. . .

I can't get the buzzing of the machine out of my head. A crow. I had forgotten about that day till now. That day . . .

I was little—eight years old maybe. It was late in the afternoon, we were expecting Dad home any minute, and I was playing upstairs when there was a knock at the door, a brief flare of voices, and a few moments later I heard it slam. I wandered downstairs to ask Mom who was there. It was then I discovered I was home alone for the first time. I opened the door and looked down the street—in the distance I saw my mother's red shawl. She was walking quickly, and a man next to her was trotting to keep up. All I knew was that I shouldn't be alone, so I followed my mother, letting the door swing shut behind me. I had nearly caught up when they turned the corner—they were heading to the flayers, where Dad worked. I followed at a distance, all the time meaning to call out, "Mommy! I'm here! You forgot to take me with you!" but my lips wouldn't move, and my voice didn't work.

Outside the battered metal warehouse of the flayers there was a small crowd of people leaning in, looking at something. The group opened to let my Mom in, and an anxious-looking man said, "It was just an accident. It looks worse than it is. A casket fell and cracked him on the head. They were unloading them for us to work on . . ." But Mom moved past him, ignoring his words. As the figures made way I saw my dad sitting on the ground with someone holding a folded pad of fabric to his head. The makeshift bandage was red and his hair looked wet. He blinked his eyes open and when he saw Mom he reached out his hand.

"I'm fine, love. It was only a knock. Don't worry the doctor—I just need to rest up," Dad winced a little as he spoke.

"Oh, Joel," she said. "What have you done?" Mom sounded annoyed rather than scared and I knew Dad must be all right.

"Just an accident. No one's fault. He'll live," the man said again.

I felt then that they might be cross if they saw me, and I scampered home. The door had locked behind me when I left to follow Mom, so I found a window that was half open and climbed into the house through it.

It was dusk when Mom and Dad got back. Julia, my best friend Verity's mom, was with them.

"I'll just sleep down here tonight," Dad said, yawning. So Mom made a bed of cushions and blankets on the floor near the fire because Dad was too tall for the sofa and too heavy to take upstairs. I sat on the stairs and listened to their whispered conversation.

"I didn't know who else to call," Mom murmured. "He's had some painkillers, but I think he could do with some stitches."

"You shouldn't have involved me. If Simon ever found out . . . I don't understand why you didn't just take him straight to the doctor." There was anger in Julia's voice, or maybe it was fear.

"You know I couldn't. Please, Julia."

Julia sighed. "Do you know how risky this is? And I'm no nurse."

"Nobody saw anything. He covered it. Anyway, you stitch women up all the time. Please. There's no one else."

There was a pause, and then:

"Boil some water. Do you have a razor? Joel, this will sting."

No one thought to look for me; they were too preoccupied. I hid in my room until everything was quiet. It must have been the middle of the night when I crept to look at him, to make sure he was OK. I had been so sure he would die. His back was rising and falling, his breath coming out in a quiet snore. His head was bandaged but the dressing had slipped; perhaps Dad had grabbed at it in his sleep because I was able to see what lay beneath. His hair around the injury had been shaved by Julia, and I saw a dark line across the back of his head. I saw the neat stitches holding the skin together and smelled the healing spices mixed with the scents of blood and sweat.

The razor had revealed a hidden secret. Truth laid bare.

Because there it was. Rent in two but joined by the stitches. A mark I'd never seen before.

A picture of a crow.

chapter 4

I LET MYSELF INTO THE HOUSE, DROP THE VEGETABLES on our wooden table, and listen to my own wild, anxious breathing. *That criminal, Connor. My dad. Both marked with a crow. Both forgotten.*

I can't be here. I can't be here when Mom gets back. I pick up my leather bag, put my shawl over my head, and set out for the only place I can think to go.

Verity and I have been best friends for as long as I can remember. I know the story so well: Our mothers met when we were born; we were born on the same day in the same hospital ward. Verity was born healthy and was marked and sent home at the proper time, but I was sick in the hospital and left unmarked for many weeks. Dad had to return to work and Verity's Mom, Julia, kept coming back to visit, to talk and to comfort my mom. She brought fresh fruit and books for Mom to read—little things so she felt less bored and alone. She's a midwife; I suppose it came naturally for her to care for us.

She would bring Verity in too. Something in those days of us being fed and changed and loved side by side created a bond between me and Verity. Julia's fearlessness and Mom's fortitude forged a friendship that was as strong as it was new. Mom always says that Julia was her savior and Verity was mine.

I need a savior right now.

Verity's house is in a nicer part of town than ours. It's only about five minutes' walk but it looks like a different world. It's all so much more spread out—spaces between the houses, which are set back behind hedged-in front gardens so I can't see in easily. Trees line the street, and each neat red-bricked house looks like it belongs in exactly that spot, instead of a hodgepodge of crazy-looking buildings crammed together. Inside, Verity's house is at once calm and cozy. I love it here; sometimes it's easier to be here than at my real home. I can hide.

I knock on the front door and, when I get no answer, let myself in. No one is in the vast, slightly unkempt kitchen, although the fire is lit. I check the sitting room, and when I don't see anyone in there I head up to Verity's room, call out a hello, and go in. She's at her desk, staring out the window that looks onto their garden. Her room is bright pink—a throwback to a time when we were younger and both obsessed with the color.

"Leora!" Her face lights up when she notices me. "Nice timing, I've been procrastinating for *hours*, I need a break." She smiles and stretches with her pencil still in her hand. Her thick, dark hair is roughly tied back and messy from where she's been playing with the strands around her ears while she's been working. She's wearing a striking blue wrap that makes her eyes and deep brown skin look even more lovely than usual. She is the closest thing I've got to a sister. Verity's the one friend who knows me through and through, and loves me even on the days she probably hates me a little bit too. She's my only real friend.

I sit on her large bed and lean against the padded headboard. I try to tell her about the morning, but instead of words spilling out, tears come. I put my hand over my eyes—I'm so tired of crying in front of people, so fed up with the sting as the tears dry on my skin, so weary of the way it makes my lips red and my eyes look swollen. But I can't stop the tears.

Verity has dropped the pencil and comes to sit next to me. She rubs my back. "Oh, Lor. I'm sorry. It will get easier, it will."

That's the problem when your dad dies. Well, there are *lots* of problems when your dad dies, but one of them is that from that day on, whenever you're sad, everyone assumes it's to do with him being dead. And maybe it is, partly. I don't know—my thoughts are going too fast for me to catch one and examine it.

My breath steadies and I try to explain. "It's not Dad. I was in the square and . . . Mayor Longsight was there."

Verity squeals at this but stops when she sees I'm not joining in.

"And there was this man, he . . . they . . . they marked him with a crow . . ." It all comes back to me again: the jeers rising up out of the crowd, that look in the criminal's eyes, like all the life and light had gone out of them. I can't look at Verity or I'll cry again. I draw circles with my finger on the patchwork bedspread.

"You sound like you're telling me about a dream, Lor. Slow down—tell me what's going on."

And so I tell her everything from the beginning. But all the while I'm thinking about my dad, and how he had the same mark, the mark of the crow—the mark that wasn't there when we looked at his book.

Where had it gone?

"But it was right, wasn't it, Verity?" I finish. I can hear the pleading in my voice. "It had to be done. He stole someone's skin. Their afterlife. Mayor Longsight said marking criminals was an old tradition . . ."

Verity goes to her desk and picks up one of her textbooks. She flicks to a page with a chapter called "Marks and Punishment." "Look, Lor—you know this stuff. Actually, I studied it last week." She starts to read.

"*Marks may be used to record an individual's transgressions. Punishment marks must be carried out by an official inker. These marks record crimes and misdemeanors, which will aid the final judgment during the weighing of the soul—*"

"But this wasn't like that," I interrupt. "It wasn't just a new line on his left arm, it was one I've never seen before—a crow. And it meant he was 'forgotten.'"

"I know, I'm getting to that bit." Verity gives me a fake-annoyed glare and goes back to reading.

"*In the most serious cases, the criminal may be marked as a forgotten. Marking a criminal as forgotten was always rare due to the irreversible nature of the action, and has fallen out of common practice in recent years, but there is legal and historical precedent for it.* There you go," she says. "I suppose Mayor Longsight decided this case warranted it."

I can't help smiling at Verity's attempt to solve everything; it's in a book, case closed. "But he said that from now on markings would be more frequent."

She shrugs and closes the book with a thump. I've dried my tears, but I can hear a crack in my voice—it won't take much for me to weep again. "Look at you, Lor. Are you still not sleeping well?" I shake my head. "You're exhausted. Rest—we can talk about it all later. I'll wake you in an hour."

She pushes me gently down onto the soft bed. I try to protest but Verity's bed, with its heavy patchwork quilt that her mom made from pieces of her baby clothes, is too hard to resist. Everything seems better after a sleep, doesn't it?

. . .

I dream I am tiny and I am hidden inside someone's head. Their eyes, their mouth are my windows and door. Someone is trying to get in. I hear a flutter and see a black beak pecking through teeth and lips.

. . .

"Leora?" It's Verity's dad, Simon, standing in the doorway with a tray. "I've brought you something to eat. I bet you missed lunch." He puts the tray on the side table.

Simon's always been kind to me, but ever since Dad died, he's been even kinder. He's tall, with deep brown skin, and his dark hair is starting to match his graying beard. His body is covered in inked-on faces, and when I'm able to see them well enough to read him, I can tell what mood he's in—the faces change for me, depending on how he feels. Today I can't see them, though; he's wearing his work clothes—the pale blue that all the skin doctors in the hospital wear. He's a surgeon and, according to Verity, is researching something very brainy about how skin heals. "Take a bit of time to wake up." He heads toward the bedroom door, then stops. "Does Sophie know you're here? You know she'll worry."

Mom. My heart sinks. She'll have been expecting me home hours ago. I wish I could stay asleep and avoid facing her, but the combination of my strange dream and the smell of toast forces me into alertness.

After I've properly woken up and eaten some toast, I wander down to the kitchen, where Verity is chatting with her dad. Her brother, Seb, isn't back from work yet. He's about five years older than Verity and me, but he was always part of our games as we grew up. He would be the dad when we played "grown-ups," and he was the model when we went through our stage of wanting to be clothing designers. I've never quite known what it is that makes Seb the way he is. Verity calls it a "delay" and his parents say he's "special." His speech isn't always clear and he's struggled to achieve the things Verity and I have managed with ease. I remember once saying I felt sorry for him and Verity smacked me in the arm and said, "Look at him. Is he sorry? Is he any less alive than you and me?" I had shaken my head in shame and shock (Verity had never hit me before). "Well, don't feel sorry for him, then," she'd said, eyes blazing. "He's not sorry and I'm not sorry he is how he is, so don't you dare feel sorry for him."

He's working now—he completed his training as a baker and has been at the local bakery for the last three years. They love him there; he charms all the customers and he works hard. His custard pastries are the best things I have ever eaten.

I love their kitchen. The red tiles on the walls above the dark wooden units make everything seem cheery and warm. It's never exactly messy here, but there are so many things packed onto shelves and hanging from hooks and framed on walls that it has a curated-clutter feel that makes me immediately relax. Verity comes and puts an arm around me and we stand like that for a moment.

"Oh, Dad, Leora saw something today I want to ask about. Did you know anything about a public marking happening in the square today?"

Simon looks up from the pile of papers he had been tidying, his hands suddenly still. "I had heard."

"Mayor Longsight was there and a man got marked as

forgotten." She says it with an excited whisper, as though it's a swear word she's saying out loud for the first time. "The mark was a crow, right, Lor?"

I nod.

"How archaic," Simon says lightly. He turns to the stove and turns on the gas under a pan. It seems the conversation is over. But Verity persists.

"Does it always happen in the square like that? How come I've never seen one?"

Simon sighs, adjusts the burner to low, and turns around, leaning against the smooth slate work surface. He is quiet for a moment, rubbing the side of his face and making his beard look even scruffier than usual.

"When someone's forgotten it's done in public, yes—but it's been such a long time since it last occurred, I couldn't tell you what the usual protocol is. Anyway, shouldn't you know all about this if you want a job in government?"

He winks at Verity, who rolls her eyes. Then she says more quietly, "Have you ever known someone who's a forgotten, Dad?"

Simon stirs the pot, and the comforting smell of chicken stew steams hotly around the room. For a long time I think he won't answer. Then, quietly—all the time watching the bubbling pan as he stirs—he says, "Yes, I did once. It very nearly broke my heart, my love." He looks up and to my astonishment I see his eyes are bright. *Could he be talking about Dad?* "Let's not talk about this anymore, girls. Some things are too much. Now then, Leora, are you staying for dinner?"

I am tempted to say yes and then just stay in this lovely house for good, but I know I can't.

"Thanks, but I should be getting home. Mom'll be wondering where I've gotten to."

"OK, well give my love to Sophie; tell her we need to arrange another night out soon. Julia and I will check our shifts." I nod and say goodbye, feeling glad to know Mom has people looking out for her.

Verity comes to the door with me. "Are you going to be OK?"

"Yeah, I'll be fine." I smile and try to look normal, but I expect it makes me look slightly deranged.

"All right. Well, should I come over tomorrow? We could study a bit together?"

"That'd be nice—I am so behind it's not even funny. And Verity—sorry for getting so upset earlier. I don't know why it bothered me so much." She gives me a hug and I head out into the streets to go home.

chapter 5

MOM IS EATING ALREADY WHEN I GET BACK. THIS is a bad sign; she's pretty fanatical about us eating together every night—even more so since Dad died. It's good for relationships or digestion or something, I can never remember. When I walk in, she carries on as though she hasn't noticed me. This is her not incredibly subtle way of letting me know I'm in trouble. I'd prefer shouting, but she is always so poised, so careful. Even her emotions seem neat.

On the walk home I decided I wouldn't confront Mom about Dad and his mark. Not yet. I don't have the words. And part of me wants to see if she'll tell me the truth about Dad herself.

"Sorry I'm late," I venture as I hang my things up. "I went over to Verity's and we lost track of time."

Mom puts down her fork and takes a sip of water. "You know I worry, love." I'm not sure she *was* worried—just cross with me, I expect. I try to look my most penitent, but I don't think it's working. "If you had just left a note . . ."

"I know, I'm sorry." I put my hand on her shoulder, make her look at me. "It won't happen again. I promise." When I turned fourteen Mom told me I had earned greater freedom. From then on, as long as I told her where I was, who I was with, what I was doing, when I would be back, and what I was wearing (in case I got lost and she had to tell the police), I could stay out until the streetlamps were lit. Some freedom. I know it's because she cares, and I know it's all more intense now because of Dad, but I wish she would just trust me.

She sighs and wipes her mouth on a napkin. Sometimes I feel like she's resigned herself to be disappointed in me, as though she'd prefer to notice my mistakes rather than have to make the effort to see when I get things right. She brushes my hair to one side in a way that I hate, but I let it go.

"There are sausages in the oven—they should still be warm." Mom goes back to eating and I guess I'm forgiven for now. Maybe I'm being unkind. I grab a tea towel and remove the tray with the leftover sausages; I almost burn myself as I put a couple on a plate with my fingers. There are mashed potatoes in one of the pans on the side and I help myself. She doesn't pay much attention when I sit down at the table; she's reading a book now that she's finished her food.

I know what to do. I'm going to test her.

There's some paper on the sideboard and I bring a piece with me to the table. With my fork in my left hand as I eat, I begin a rough sketch.

"Do you *have* to always draw at the table, love?" She's joking, kind of. It used to be a standing joke—she always reads and I always draw and Dad would always tell us off for being unsociable. But it sounds a little hollow tonight.

"I've got to keep practicing, Mom—exams soon, remember?" She's watching now and I make my strokes clearer, shading a feathered wing. She lowers her book, and I know I've got her full attention.

"There was a marking in town today," I say, keeping my eyes on my drawing and shoveling a dripping forkful of potatoes into my mouth.

"Oh yes, I heard." Her voice is calm, maybe a little higher than usual, but nothing noticeable. "It caused quite a stir—it was all anyone spoke about at readings today. I've never seen one of those. I didn't even know they still took place." Her fingers flick through the pages of her book, but when I glance up she's looking right at me. "Was it well attended?"

"It was busy." I turn my paper around, so that I can work more closely on the beak. I know she's still watching. "The man got a mark like this." I slide my drawing across the wooden table and she brings it closer. Does she flinch just a little? "It means he's a *forgotten*. Scary, right?" *Come on, Mom, just tell me.* She spends time examining my picture, avoiding my gaze. Maybe I haven't done it right; the memory of Dad's mark remains vivid in my mind, but it was hidden by bloody stitches.

"You'll make an excellent inker, my little light," she says, passing the paper back to me. "But I hope you never have to make a mark like that." I make myself carry on drawing, adding texture to the feathers, willing her to say more. "I'll come with you next time, if you like. Who was it?" she asks. "Anyone you recognized?" She gets up and takes her plate to the sink.

"No. I'd never heard of him. But his crime was terrible. He stole someone's skin." I watch her back as she puts the plates into the sink and for a moment I think she goes still.

I look again at the bird I've drawn. The crow looks at me with its dead eye and I screw the piece of paper into a tight ball and push back my chair. As I stand I see what Mom has been reading. The book of our fables lies open on the table; she's been reading about the White Witch. While Mom's attention is on the dishes, I take the book upstairs with me and reread the familiar tale. Dad used to read this book to me all the time, way after I protested that I was getting too old for stories.

chapter 6

The Sisters

There was once a girl who was as good as she was beautiful. And she was very beautiful. She had golden hair and ruby-red lips. Her voice was like a thousand angels laughing, and her eyes sparkled like the stars in the heavens. People from the town would visit her home in the woods just to catch a glimpse of her lovely face. Her fame spread far and wide and her name, Moriah, was known throughout the land.

Moriah had a twin sister. Now, the sister didn't have golden hair or ruby-red lips, her voice wasn't like a thousand angels laughing, and her eyes didn't sparkle like the stars in the heavens. If you asked about her in the town, people would frown and say, "Oh yes. The sister . . ." but she left such little impression that no one could really remember her, except for a vague sense of unease. All they knew was she was not like the girl who was as good as she was beautiful, and they called the sister the ghost-girl, because no one could remember her name.

Now the sisters had a father and he was a woodcutter. He had cut the wood that built their house. He cut the wood that built his wife's coffin when she died, and he cut the wood that made the bed in which he slept and would soon die.

The father wasn't only a woodcutter, though. He had been given two magical gifts at birth. The first gift promised that whatever he wished for on his deathbed would be granted, and the second gift was the power to tell tales that captivated the listener. He wove tales more beautiful than any tapestry. He told stories that made men weep and women fall in love. He told stories that broke hearts and mended souls. People would come to the woodcutter's home to see his beautiful daughter, but they would stay for the stories.

Each day he would tell a new story, and each day the ghostly daughter would write them down in her book. But there came a time when the stories got shorter and the storyteller's voice got quieter. Until one day, the stories stopped and the woodcutter took to his bed.

The woodcutter had lived a good life. He had been a kind husband and a fine father. But he had one regret: of all the stories he had told, he had never told his own. As he lay in bed, consumed by silence, he rued the days he had told stories of imps and kings, of fairies and fawns. His life was worth nothing if his story went to the grave with him. But his voice could not carry his tale and his life didn't hold enough minutes.

On the evening of his death, the woodcutter's daughters sat with their father.

"Oh, Father," they said, "if only you would live." But the woodcutter shook his head and the daughters cried hot tears.

"Oh, Father," said the daughters, "if you are to die—do you have voice enough to tell us your dying wish?" For they knew that his dying wish would be granted and they hoped he would choose it wisely.

They gave him some water and he coughed and looked closely at their faces. He had saved just a few words for this moment. He knew what his dying wish would be and he knew that it would come true.

"My dying wish," he gasped, "is that your stories will be remembered. I wish that the stories of your lives will be part of you, that your stories go with you wherever you go and that you two girls are known forever. That is my dying wish." And with one final rasping breath, the woodcutter died.

The daughters cried bitterly and their father was soon buried and mourned and longed for. But before much time passed, he was forgotten, and his name was rarely spoken, just as he knew would happen. His story had never been told.

One day, soon after the woodcutter died, a prince was walking in the woods. He happened upon the sisters' cottage and knocked on the door—enchanted by its prettiness. When Moriah, the twin who was as good as she was beautiful, opened the door, the prince fell immediately in love. *The next day, he took Moriah to his palace to be his wife, and she was the talk of all the kingdom. The morning after they had married, the girl woke and smiled shyly at her new husband. He held her hand and gasped when he saw that it was painted. On her hand was a picture of their wedding day. She washed and washed her hand, but the picture never came off. Moriah told the prince of her father's dying wish—and they agreed delightedly this must be what he had wanted. Soon the girl and the prince grew used to the image and smiled at it as they remembered their happy day.*

With each new and special moment in her life, Moriah discovered a new and special mark upon her lovely skin. Every moment was recorded and there for all to see (if they only knew where to look). And it seemed that as the woodcutter's prophecy came true, so prosperity was coming to the land. At first, the people were afraid to see their new ruler covered in pictures like ink. They feared that she was a sorceress who had bewitched their prince. But when the prince told the people of the woodcutter's dying wish, and when they saw the harmony that the princess brought to the land, they were satisfied. For with their new princess the people enjoyed peace unlike any that had come before. The harvests flourished and the kingdom grew in wealth and power. This woodcutter's daughter was soon the toast of the land, for surely she had brought them good fortune when she became their princess.

When the young princess discovered she was with child, she asked her husband if he would allow her to visit her sister, whom she hadn't seen since the wedding day.

"I wonder what tales her skin will tell," Moriah said to her prince, for she knew her father's wish had been for them both. The prince gave her horses and guards, and she went on her way, back to the cottage built by the wood of the trees her father felled.

When the princess reached her old home, she saw the cottage was overgrown with ivy, and the garden had been taken over by thorns and weeds. Crows roosted in the trees around the cottage and cawed sharply as Moriah approached. She knocked on the door and was shocked when her sister opened it. It seemed that the years apart had made her plainer and increasingly ghostly. The sister had grown thin, and ever more unsightly. Her hair was as wild as the thornbushes growing outside, and her eyes as dark as the stormy sky.

But the sisters embraced and chattered and recounted tales from the years they had been apart. The princess lit a fire in the grate, and, as the cottage warmed up and the fire flickered to life, she removed her cloak. The sister responded with a gasp when she saw the golden-haired princess's illustrated skin. Moriah showed her sister each mark and told each story. She sighed when she realized she was the only sister with marks.

"I had thought you would be marked too. After all, Father's dying wish was for us both. How curious." And Moriah frowned.

"I lead a quiet life. I have no riches, no husband, no splendor. Perhaps my skin is blank because my life is too," the ghostly sister said quietly.

The princess stayed until dusk, and then rode through the night, back to the palace. She returned perplexed and anxious about her blank sister. But soon her mind was distracted by the joy of feeling the first movements of her baby, and she forgot all about her sister for whom their father's dying wish had not come true.

As the day of the baby's birth drew nearer, the prince and princess's joy was marred by news coming from one corner of the kingdom. While the rest of the land flourished and the people rejoiced, there was a small pocket where it seemed that the princess's good fortune could not penetrate. They looked on their maps and, with sorrow, Moriah saw that it was her hometown that refused to thrive.

Messengers came telling tales of failed crops, sick livestock, barren women, and fear. There was a curse upon the town.

When the royal baby was born, the prince and princess discovered the curse's cause.

Family, friends, and notable nobility gathered to celebrate the birth of a royal baby girl. The guests cooed over the baby and admired Moriah's new mark, which had appeared the moment the baby was born. They gasped and clapped when they were shown the baby's own birth mark; she had been born with her name imprinted in her skin. The blessing of the father's dying wish had been handed down to the princess's own daughter.

But they had forgotten someone. Late in the day, before the sun was due to set, the palace became dark. Wind whistled through the great hall, making candles flicker and snuff out. The guests shivered and clung to one another, hardly able to see in the dusky gloom. They all heard the door open and felt the icy air that whipped through the hall. They breathed in the smell of moss and fog and mold and ivy.

The remnants of the wine on their lips tasted bitter and made them think of blood. And they saw a ghostly figure winding her way through the crowd, stroking fearful faces with her skeletal fingers, laughing at their frozen impotence.

For Moriah had not invited her sister to the party; and yet, here she was. She brought her gift to the crib where the baby was sleeping; her gift was the promise of early death, of misery and frantic worry, of fighting with fate and losing every time. For she told her sister that her baby would die before she became an adult.

And then, like frost thaws after winter, the sister disappeared, leaving just a black crow feather in the baby's crib.

All that could be heard over Moriah's screams were the frantic shouts of the prince.

"Seize her! Seize the witch."

Days passed, then weeks and months, and no sign of the sister was found. But stories came trickling through the kingdom, until they flooded the palace with their horror. The sister had been poisoning the land for many years; she cursed the cows and their milk curdled, she stole secrets and broke families, she scared children and told them lies about their parents that made them feel unsafe in their beds at night. Her creeping, insidious ways had taken hold in that corner of the kingdom and the verdict was clear: Moriah's blank and ghostly sister was, without doubt, a witch. This was why their father's wish had not taken effect on her skin or in her heart; she had already given herself over to dark and more powerful magic.

And so there was a royal decree. The town that had been ravaged by the witch's curse would be cut off from the rest of the land. Walls were built and a feeling of safety reigned within the fortress. The blank woman—the White Witch—was banished, and, although no one ever saw her after the curse at the baby's celebration, there were always rumors of ghosts in the woodcutter's forest.

And once again the kingdom flourished. The land was blessed and the people were happy. The prince and his beautiful princess ruled with wisdom and justice.

Princess Moriah lived a long and happy life. You can read all about it from her skin. And ever since then, to maintain the peace that came from her rule, the people across the kingdom have written their stories on their skin. For, just like the woodcutter, they know their lives are worth nothing if their stories go with them to the grave.

chapter 7

I SIT ON MY BED WITH THE OLD STORY WHISPERING in my ears. My room is nothing like Verity's. I was never allowed to indulge my passion for pink, so the walls are white and impersonal. I used to be so jealous of Verity, but now I like it. I open the tall chest of drawers and get my sketchbook from where it's hidden underneath my tops. Everyone does this— thinks about their future ink. We don't get any say in our official marks, of course, the standard ones that everyone gets: our birth mark with our name, a new age dot each year, our family tree on our back and marks to record which immunizations we've had. We have lines of different lengths and colors to record the things we've achieved on our right forearm. Our left arm is reserved for our failures. A thin orange line is for someone who has failed to repay a debt, a red line for a thief, and a thick black line is for a killer, but I've never seen one of those. So far my left arm is still empty, but we talk endlessly about what our chosen marks will be. The first ones that we choose will explain who we really are.

I could have had a mark done on my sixteenth birthday if I'd wanted, but I've held back. I want to show people who I really am—show them that I'm not just this quiet girl who gets good grades and tries to be nice to her mom. But now I wonder if I'll ever make up my mind. I want it to be perfect. I keep waiting for the ideal design to come to mind; something beautiful, timeless, and exactly "me."

As I sit at my desk, I end up drawing Verity and me. Verity is laughing and her hair is looking wild; somehow I've messed up my eyebrows so I just look angry, but I quite like it anyway. After a while I stop drawing. A moth flits around my desk lamp. It's not big enough to bother me, but it makes the light seem eerie as it projects clumsy shadows, and the scuffling sound reminds me of tearing paper and flapping feathers. But I don't turn the light off. I don't like the dark anymore. Over the last month, thanks to Dad's last words to me (*Watch out for the blanks, Leora*), some of my childhood fears have returned. The sounds that used to lull me to sleep now make my heart race, and my mind creates new monsters from the old fears.

Long before I was born, before the Blank Resettlement Bill, blanks used to live alongside us. I can't even imagine what that must have been like—a whole set of people who chose not to be marked. It began as one or two who decided not to add to their birth mark or official ink and then it became a rebellion; they refused to get their children inked and chose fines and jail rather than submit to the laws of the land. People used to have to walk past blank, unreadable people every day—my mom told me her mother remembered it. No one could understand why they chose to reject salvation; why they would live a life that left them damned.

But then people discovered the truth. That they had secrets so terrible they wouldn't dare to wear them. It started off with little things: the seams of your clothes adjusted by the blank seamstress would burst open, revealing their shoddy workmanship and your marked flesh. Your post would arrive with the telltale marks of tampering and you knew not to trust the blank postmistress any longer. The blank baker sold you stale bread, the blank teacher at school taught your children to lie, the blank doctor gave medicine that seemed to make your child sicker. They claimed not to need marks or skin books for their souls to be cleansed. They called themselves righteous. But their actions revealed the real state of their souls. For, in a carefully orchestrated uprising, they showed their true selves: houses burned, bodies maimed, skin ripped from the dead, life ripped from the living. And so, after terrible violence, the marked were forced to fight back. The blanks were no match for the marked, and when the battles ceased they were expelled, sent far away, beyond the wall, to live in communities where they could no longer hurt us. For a while everything was all right.

So long had passed that we forgot to be afraid. There were rumors, of course. Every child at school had a story about their dad or cousin or somebody who had seen a blank roaming around the town at night.

"He was just like a ghost," they would say. "His skin almost glowed and he was creeping around the Ewings' house, trying to find a window to crawl through."

At playtime at school it all seemed like a great joke, but at night I would look at my curtains and wonder if the sound I could hear from the window was just the wind.

"You know how sometimes a kid doesn't come back to school after the weekend and you don't hear nothing about it? That's when you know. That's when a blank has got 'em."

We would squeal with delighted horror, pretending it was all just fun, but at night when I hid under my blanket and fought sleep, it all seemed different. I wouldn't dream of letting my hands out from under the bedclothes; I would curl my legs up to my chest so no blank could grab my feet. And that kid's words would haunt me.

"The blanks come at night and they steal souls. All that is left in the morning is a feather, and then you know they've got you."

And then when I was ten my dog, Amity, went missing. It wasn't like her. We searched everywhere—we went out looking every day for weeks and weeks. I made posters and we asked anyone we saw if they had seen our golden friend. A month later I was in the woods near school and I slipped down a muddy bank. In among the leaves I saw it—Amity's collar. There was no other sign of her, but her red leather collar was surrounded by glossy feathers. Dad told me not to be silly, that she must have gotten into a fight, but I just know they took her. I still miss her.

Now, with the wind blowing branches against my window and the darkness black outside, it's all too easy to think about those stories. But I tell myself to stop being foolish; I should have grown out of these fears. But I can't forget Mayor Longsight's warnings; the threat is real. I catch the moth in my hands, feeling it fluttering against my palms for a second before it is still. Easing the window open with my elbow, I open my hands and let the moth out. Instead of flying away it falls like a stone. Its temporary captivity killed it before it could be freed. I rub my hands on my pants. It's late so I change into my nightclothes, climb into bed, and close my eyes.

I think of Dad, his soul suspended in limbo while he waits for it to be weighed and judged.

I think of Connor, the man who was marked, and the way his eyes looked before the needle struck.

I think of the White Witch and Mayor Longsight's solemn words of warning.

I think of the fire of judgment, burning all night and all day, forever and ever.

My lamp stays lit. Eventually I fall asleep.

I dream that I am in a hospital bed. I have a needle in my arm with a tube attached. I look at the bag slowly filling with dark liquid and wonder why they're taking my blood. As I watch my arm, I see my tattoos slowly unraveling. Each mark, word, and image is being unwritten before my eyes.

It's not my blood they're taking but my ink. I look down at my bare skin. I am naked. I am lost. I rip the needle from my arm.

I wake up breathless with fear. Clambering out of bed, I take off my nightclothes and stand in front of the mirror to make sure my marks are all there. I turn and try to make out each name on the tree that grows up my back. I am struck by the emptiness. I have lived sixteen years, but what does my skin have to show for it? If I died tonight, my book would look the same as any other person's my age. Except for the names being different and a few other small changes, the story's the same.

My life is worth more than my marks show, surely? I have more to tell than this. My skin tells the tale the government has chosen for me. I have a sudden yearning to fill every inch so that nothing is lost: the beauty I've seen, my friends' names—well, Verity's at least, my first love. First love. The thought almost makes me laugh out loud. I won't have any romance to ink on my skin. Who would want me?

Of course none of the boys at school or on the apprentice-ship were worth me worrying about—there's been the odd one that has made me blush or somehow gotten me thinking about how my hair looks or whether I'm too clever or too quiet. But no one has ever turned my head, not really. And I know for a fact I've never turned anyone else's. I've got to be the only sixteen-year-old on earth who has never kissed anyone.

I look at the stretch marks across my hips and the paleness of my skin. I get tired of the people who tell me how refined it is to be pale, how lucky I am. I'm not the right kind of pale—there's no alabaster beauty about me; I'm more of a dull gray. I'm not the right kind of anything. My breasts are too small for me to be curvy; my butt is too big for me to be slim. My face is too quirky to be pretty and too plain to be striking. My hair is too straight to be curly and too wavy to be straight and no matter how many times I say I'll grow it long I always get bored and chop it short again. I know for a fact that no one has ever chosen to dye their hair the color mine is: No one asks for mousy brown. I do quite like my blue eyes, but whatever it takes to be beautiful, I certainly don't have it.

I notice a new stretch mark and try to rub it away. I see the purple lines clawing their way down my breast and feel ashamed. Surely it's not fair to have stretch marks on my practically nonexistent boobs? Where is the justice in that?

My body lets me down, betrays the real me to everyone watching—the me who is not the right kind of anything. It doesn't matter, though. I'll soon cover this skin with new shades of black and gray; I'll become someone new. Through blood and pain and ink I can be remade.

I have more to tell than this.

With a sigh I see that it's light already; Verity will be here soon to help me study. I dress in brown pants that are cuffed short to show my favorite soft leather boots. My top is a turquoise shift that Verity passed on to me; it's plain apart from the buttons at the neck and it's long enough to cover my bum. One of the perks of having a friend taller than me. I wrap my wide orange belt around my waist twice, tying it tightly in front. I like to cover up; I like the feeling of being unreadable. Maybe if people can't see how bare my skin is they'll make up a better story than the truth.

I head downstairs but pause in the doorway when I hear voices: Verity and Mom talking. I must have slept later than I realized. From where I'm standing, I can see them sitting at the kitchen table. From where I'm standing, a few steps up, I can see the scuffed wooden work tops that have been marked by years of Dad and me chopping things without bothering to use a board (Mom would tell us both off, like Dad was a kid she had to look after). I peer through the gleaming pots that hang from a rafter and smile at Mom, who pours an extra cup of tea when she sees me come down. I greet my ancestors by name and light a candle on the table beneath their bookshelf. I wish we had Dad's, but he grew up in Riverton and didn't have any skin books to bring with him when he moved here. He never really spoke about his family.

When I get closer I see that Mom is examining Verity's right arm. Mom can't resist reading people—she loves it. Her idea of a perfect afternoon is sitting outside watching people as they walk past and sneaking a peek into their secrets. Not that Verity would ever have anything seedy in her marks—she's about as perfect as they get.

"How's the studying going?" Mom releases Verity's arm and takes a sip of tea.

"All right, I think," Verity says, easing her sleeve down a little, "but I keep having crazy dreams that the exams are on everything I've forgotten to study!" I laugh at Verity—she's going to be fine. Mom moves the teapot to pour another cup and I see the picture I drew last night is still out on the table. Mom's flattened the screwed-up paper and must have been looking at it. I wonder if she showed it to Verity.

"Come on, Vetty. I need you to help me—my brain's stopped working!" Verity puts her bag over her shoulder, and we pick up our cups of tea and head to my room.

These exams matter. They cover all the main subjects we've done in school, plus extra tests based on our chosen specialty: Mine is tattooing. And the exams make all the difference in the world; they decide our futures. If I don't do well, I'll get assigned to some boring job and will be pretty much stuck in it forever. They let us choose our specialties in our final year, but there's no guarantee that we'll qualify to work in our chosen profession; you've got to be good enough. If I end up sitting at a desk in an office I think my soul will shrivel up and die. I've longed to be an inker ever since I was small, when Dad first taught me to draw, and the apprenticeship I did last year has only made me more certain. I love the feel of the pen beneath my hand. I love making marks. I love the history behind each one and the way that each can be interpreted in more than one way.

I've never actually tattooed anyone—you aren't allowed to when you're just on the school elective course. I've learned to clean and sterilize, I've practiced marks on paper and pigskin.

I've discovered that I have an obsession for detail, and I've learned that inking is all I really want to do.

Verity's hoping to go into government work—admin and policies and stuff like that. The sitting-at-a-desk thing doesn't hold the same fear of soul-shriveling for Verity. Her work experience has mainly been spent at the government building. Verity has to be able to remember laws and statutes. Her grades need to be amazing. She really wants to be part of the Funerary and Soul-Weighing team: the department that is entrusted with the books of the recently deceased. She wants to be part of the process of preparing the dead for judgment by studying their books and recommending the worthy for remembrance. It's one of the most important departments there is, and the most shrouded in secrecy. I watch my friend setting out her books and chattering away, and try to imagine her sitting behind a big desk, making decisions about people's fates.

Things are changing, and fast.

Verity and I spend what's left of the morning working—Verity at my rickety desk, going through her notes and books, and me sprawled on the floor adding drawings to my portfolio and picking bits of dried paint from the carpet. I've got a lot to do before my work is complete.

It feels strange to be struggling. I've never needed to study especially hard before; it always came so easily. But then Dad got ill. Thinking about the future would always mean having to think about Dad—about him getting sicker, about him not being here, about having to live without him. The future without Dad had too many awful gaps, too much missing. But now the future's here and life has sort of expanded to fill the gap. I don't want to have to carry on without my dad, but I have to. I can't just stop.

I realize I've been staring into space, and that Verity is watching me.

"Are you OK, Lor? Dad was worried about you yesterday." She rocks back on the chair and catches herself before she tips too far. "Actually, so was I. That marking really upset you, didn't it?"

The image of the man—Connor—being marked flashes into my mind, along with the sound of the machine injecting him with the ink.

"I've been trying not to think about it, to be honest," I say, swallowing. "How can he go on, knowing that he's forgotten?"

"I don't know, Lor—but remember, he did a terrible thing."

I nod. I know she's trying to comfort me.

"Seb said he saw the end of it on his break," Verity goes on. "Mel the storyteller was there and she did a telling of the Saint's fable—it was meant to remind everyone of the value of our marks and how flaying should be treated with honor."

I shrug, wearily. Perhaps if I'd been there, that would have been some comfort, but compared to the starkness of the deed, a story seems less than adequate.

"Do you think your dad knew him, if he was a flayer?" Verity asks. I swallow and shake my head.

"I don't think so. I really don't like imagining that someone like him could have worked with Dad," I murmur. "Dad took the job so seriously; he'd be furious if he knew someone could be so unscrupulous. So *evil*." I sigh shakily.

"Oh, Leora. You miss him terribly, don't you?"

I nod, and the predictable tears flood my eyes. "I hate having to wait for the weighing of the soul, and I hate his book being kept at the museum—I wish it was all done and he was home with us."

"It must be awful not having him with you, Lor. But remember the books of your ancestors. They can be a comfort. They're taking care of you."

Verity's right—my ancestors watch over me all the time, they make things go the way they should, they guide and help us. I ought to be able to trust them. Some days I don't feel their care and it's easy to forget them. But I guess that's faith, isn't it?

Verity is looking at me, so I smile and say, "Speaking of our ancestors, it's our turn to do the speaking of the names tonight."

Verity groans. She hates the speaking of the names ritual—it's all a bit too "smells and bells" for her taste. I'm pretty sure she only signed up to keep me company. "My favorite," she mutters bitterly.

"Meet you outside the hall and we can go in together?"

I try hard after that. I push all the dark thoughts to the back of my mind and I focus on the work in front of me. We spend the rest of the day working and quizzing each other. There are so many times when I nearly tell her about Dad and his mark, but it just never seems to be the right moment. I'll wait until the time is right. But when I hug Verity before she leaves for home, guilt twists inside me; we shouldn't keep secrets.

chapter 8

NO ONE IS TRULY GONE AND FORGOTTEN UNTIL their name is no longer spoken. That's why we greet our ancestors each morning and that's why we have the speaking of the names ritual. It happens every day; people in the community volunteer their time and are assigned a session. Mine comes around about once a month. It's our responsibility to ensure that not one of the town's worthy ancestors is forgotten. Some people don't have any family still living, and without us, it may be that no one would say their name. They must be remembered—it's our duty to their life and memory.

It's Mom's turn tonight too; she always comes with Verity

and me. After supper, we get changed. We're encouraged to wear oranges, yellows, and reds when we attend a speaking; they evoke the fire of judgment. I wear an old saffron-colored dress of Mom's that is just the right color but a little too big (*"Room to grow, Leora"*) and skims the floor; Mom wraps a heavy gold cloak over her daytime clothes. We look like two flames. Mom prepares a flask of hot lemon and honey to take with us—it's good to have something to drink during an official speaking ritual in case your voice gets tired. We walk through fallen leaves toward the square where the hall of remembrance is. I link my arm with Mom's, partly because I'm cold, and partly because I need to know she's with me. She gives me a little smile, but when she sighs and squeezes my arm I wonder if she's as composed as she appears. Mom wasn't exactly warm before Dad died, but she wasn't quite so tightly wound. Dad would always help her lighten up, loosen up. I want to be able to forget all the mess, just for tonight. This is my first speaking since Dad died and I'm worried my voice will give away my broken heart. I wonder how she feels.

Verity is waiting for us outside the hall of remembrance. To start with I don't see her; she melts into the shadows with her dark skin, black hair, and gray shawl. The windows of the hall glint with the light from the fire and make the rest of the building seem somber and looming. Verity steps into the street light and gives a tiny wave when she sees us coming, and we walk together to the small door at the side of the building. The speaking of the names happens in a smaller room off the main hall called the room of remembrance. It's always so hot, though, you can't forget that you're near the constantly raging fire. We enter through a heavy wooden door, and once we're inside, tall, thin slits of windows make it feel like we're hidden away. Thoughts of the cold outside are overtaken by the misty incense and warm, wood-clad walls. I love the way the sounds sink into the room. When we read the names it's as though we give the room a life of its own. The walls hold the memories the mind no longer sees.

There are a few listeners sitting on the wooden blocks, which serve as seating or tables or whatever they're needed for. They're usually set up in rows, but people are allowed to move them wherever they like. It always helps to have listeners—they keep me focused on the importance and beauty of what I'm doing and help me to read each name with love. Maybe it's the name they came to hear. The speaking ritual is open to anyone from the community who wants to attend. The speakers couldn't possibly get through all the names in the book of the dead in one go—but as the days, weeks, months, and years pass, each name gets its chance to be spoken once again—words carried on breath, breath that revives the dead for a moment longer.

I can feel my dry eyes each time I blink. I just hope that I stay awake for the duration of the evening. Yawns are frowned upon in readings; the occasion is a solemn one. Mom leads the way to the front of the room and Verity and I follow. My dress gets caught under my feet when I go up the steps of the dais and I stumble a little. Mom flashes me a warning look and Verity stifles a giggle. We light new white candles from the ones that have been burning all day—it's important that the light doesn't go out.

We say the opening words of the speaking ritual and begin to read the names:

Our ancestors, wise and beloved. We remember you. Those whose thoughts have brought justice and peace, whose words have brought knowledge and mercy, and whose deeds have brought security and wealth. We honor you. We remember you. Breathe again as we speak your names; show us your wisdom and guide our community in the way we should go.

> James Peace
> Isaac Adofu
> Henry Chalice
> Hope Mainu
> Rangan Singh
> Jane Hendle

After every fifty names, the speaker says, "We remember you," and another speaker stands to read the next fifty. We get through a thousand names this way.

But not my father's. Not yet.

. . .

That night I dream.

I dream that someone is standing in the room of remembrance, saying my name, and I wonder why they are reading it when I am alive and well. Then, in my dream, the reader gets a pen and crosses my name out; she looks up and right at me and slams the book of the dead shut.

chapter 9

THE NEXT TWO WEEKS CARRY ON IN MUCH THE same way. I sleep, study, run errands, and study with Verity. Mom wakes me on the first day of the exam week and I'm groggy—unused to waking before nine o'clock.

The week passes in perfect exam silence. I find I'm soothed by it and enjoy knowing where I'm going and what I'm doing each day. The tutor asks hard and searching questions when I present my portfolio of work—quizzing me about my "feminine" style and wondering out loud whether men will want to be marked by a girl. I say something neat about how important it is to have a range of inkers and personalities, but not for the first time I find myself biting down hard on my tongue to stop myself saying something rude. Women inkers are unusual, certainly, but as Dad always said, attitudes won't change unless we do something about it.

I'm still not sleeping well, so by the end of the week I'm tired and my thoughts seem to sink before they can be used—I find myself staring into space toward the end of my final exam, which is history. I look around the high-ceilinged hall where I've sat through so many assemblies and lectures, and my mind wanders. If Dad were alive he'd be picking me up after and we'd be doing something to mark the occasion; he knew how to make things feel significant and special. But instead after this I'll go home and wait for Mom. Maybe I'll cook tonight. Without Dad we both seem to have lost our ability to celebrate.

I force myself back to my paper and the final question. I read it through once, then twice, and stop. I look around to see if anyone else looks puzzled, but they all have their heads down, and their pens are moving rapidly across their papers.

> Give three examples of how Saintstone would be
> different if the Blank Resettlement Bill had not
> come into effect.

This is not a question I have studied for. It's not a question we've ever discussed in class; it feels slightly illicit even imagining what life would be like with blanks living here alongside us. I tap my pen against my mouth and try to figure out how things would be.

1. *If we still lived with blanks, our way of life would be under threat. The marked would be upholding the aims of truth, justice, and candor, while the blanks' thoughts and actions would be hidden. We would be vulnerable because of this. The blanks were committed to violence against the marked, so it's logical to assume that this persecution would only have increased; the blanks were killers at heart. Not only would our culture and faith be in jeopardy, but our lives would be at risk too.*

That makes sense. I can't imagine living alongside people I could never really know.

2. *Society would be divided. It would be hard for such diverse groups to live together without conflict. The blanks might take advantage of the marked people's openness, while hiding their own violent secrets. We need unity in our faith and society in order to maintain our tradition and honor our ancestors. Without transparency, integrity is impossible.*

Before the resettlement, Saintstone was all factions and fights and fear. The blanks made the most of our vulnerability.

3. *Statistics show us that crime has greatly reduced since the resettlement; therefore it is logical to suggest that if blanks still lived in Saintstone, we would not be experiencing the peace and safety that we currently enjoy. Violence is almost*

unheard-of, and other crimes that diminish society, like

robbery, bribery, and vandalism, are effectively prevented

using the policy of marking criminals.

I can't see how the examiner could find fault with that one.

The proctor tells us time is up. I close my exam paper and put down my pen. That's it. My future is ready to be marked.

Just like me, then.

Verity waits for me as we leave the exam hall. It takes me a while to find my bag at the back of the room, and I get in a tangle with my shawl. She's breathless with enthusiasm about the test.

"Really, they couldn't have been better questions!"

"What, even the one about blanks?" I ask, still feeling bewildered by the unexpected question.

She frowns, her eyebrows furrowing, and shakes her head. "What? I don't—" she begins, but then she sees the time and her eyes widen. "I'm going to be late. You're sure you won't come out with us?" Verity's parents are taking her and Seb out for ice cream; she invited me earlier but I don't feel like it. I think Mom might be upset if I do something familyish without her involved.

"I should get home; Mom will want to hear how it went."

I watch as Verity walks away through the crowd of excited students to meet her parents. She waves at a couple of people and hitches the strap of her bag up where it's slipped off her shoulder. She always makes life look so easy. I feel a pang of sadness, a sense that everything is ending and changing. I can't believe I won't get to see her every day at school once our results come in.

I close my eyes and whisper a prayer to my ancestors: *"Please let our lives stay firmly intertwined. Please."* The leaves on a tree nearby rustle and two fall to the ground. It's silly, it's nothing, but I choose to take them as a sign; they can be a talisman, even if it just means something to me. I pick up the leaves and put them in my pocket before I tuck my dad's pendant into my top, wrap my shawl tighter around my shoulders, and head for home.

chapter 10

WALKING HOME I KEEP THINKING ABOUT THAT last exam question. What would life be like if they still lived among us? I imagine them walking along this very street, empty, terrifyingly unknowable, and I shudder.

When you're a child, everything is just a story. People dress things up: fables instead of fact, fairy tales instead of history. But then you grow up.

I remember so clearly the day I heard the truth about the blanks. That the stories, which we had believed for so long were just folklore made up to scare naughty children, were true.

. . .

None of us will ever forget that green door in the museum.

I'm not sure I even noticed it until I went through for the first time.

We all knew the stories. The tale of the ghostly, cursed White Witch and her beautiful sister, Moriah, and the very different paths they took—one blank, the other marked. The sister who was evil and the sister who was good. We had heard it before so many times. We had played it at recess, and I remember fighting with Verity about which of us would get to be the beautiful, good one this time. I used to dream about living in the forest, waiting for a prince to come and find me. We knew about blanks, and how the White Witch was the first of their kind, but we spoke of them as one might speak of fairies or goblins. They didn't seem real.

Then one day, when we were nine or ten, we were told we were going on a class trip to the museum. The mood on the way there was odd—walking through the rain, there was an almost electric feeling in the air. Our teacher was quiet and told us not to tell the younger kids about what we would see there that day.

Verity and I held hands on the whispered walk to the museum.

I remember it so clearly. I remember that we wiped our feet and hung up our coats on little pegs in the cloakroom. I remember that the stone floor got wet anyway and that the chill from outside swept in with us. I remember that Verity and I kept on holding hands even after coats were off and our feet were dry, even though we were inside and we should have felt safe.

And then we were led to the green door—the door we'd walked past so many times without wondering what lay within. The guard stepped aside and smiled as we walked past her into the dimly lit space.

Truth laid bare. So bare that I could see every inch of his empty skin. The unknown, unnamed man. Palms open, facing up. An elbow, still rough-looking, pressed against the glass. An unmoving chest, skin blued slightly from the liquid. His private parts made public; I couldn't help but look. Eyes closed, mouth slightly open, ready to breathe, ready to speak, ready to scream. A person preserved, not as a book, but as an exhibit: a warning, a trophy.

Blank.

We stood and looked, close enough to track the swirls of his fingerprints, near enough to count the hairs on his legs, intimate enough to feel that we had walked in on him having a bath. Only this was a tank, and he drifted beneath the surface.

I was close enough to see everything, except I saw nothing. No ink, no words, no pictures, no marks. His body was silent. Mute. He was kept as a cautionary tale, a blank who had been captured and preserved to warn us. Our teacher told us that only someone with something to hide would keep their story inside them. I imagined his secrets like worms under his skin, eating him from within. In my mind, this body was a jar full of decay, a box full of shame that had to be kept locked.

Panic flooded through me and I looked down at my hand and counted my age marks. I looked at Verity and my other classmates. I read them, relieved. I knew their stories. Nothing was hidden. Truth laid bare.

The rest of the exhibits in that tiny space were brutal and left me weary. Glass-covered display cases reflected the light and told us the terrible truth. Small white cards with handwritten explanations hung next to pictures: written testimony, even notes written by the blanks themselves that showed their plans to hurt us. Some boys called out, "Come and look at this!" sounding excited. Verity and I followed their voices to a well-lit exhibit at the back of the room, and I read the card.

This knife was used by Tobias Clement. With it he removed the hands of his victims.

The knife looked rusty. "Blood," whispered the boy next to me delightedly. The handle was worn, as though it had been held fondly by warm hands. It reminded me of the knife in our kitchen that my parents used to cut meat and vegetables.

Clement was not the only blank to dismember innocent members of our community in order to steal their marks and silence their souls, but he was perhaps the most prolific. Like all blanks he worked with conscienceless malice. Men, women, and children all died at his merciless hands. He was finally captured and put to death two years before the Resettlement Bill came into effect.

We all knew why they did it. It would be clever if it wasn't so horrifying. If you don't have all your deeds marked on your skin and saved in your skin book—if one piece is lost—then they say your deeds will stay on your soul, weighing it down, forfeiting your place in eternity. It's the worst thing that any of us could imagine.

My eyes scanned across the display, past a heap of black feathers, to a crumpled pile of fabric next to the knife. The other kids had grown bored and moved on, so I stepped along to see what this next item was. Standing closer, I saw that it wasn't fabric. It looked like old sacking or worn leather, but now that I was right in front of it, I saw it was skin. A tiny, severed hand had been preserved. I counted the age marks. One, two, three . . . four.

I murmured my shock to Verity, and she furrowed her brow and nodded. *So, this is the world we live in,* we realized. It was bigger and more frightening than before. I closed my eyes and planned my future marks; longing to be grown up—desperate for armor to clothe myself in, piece by piece.

We got back to school and wrote about our day in our topic books. Our teacher warned us not to tell the younger pupils. We didn't play games about the White Witch anymore. And we didn't have story time anymore either; it was called history instead.

chapter 11

THE DAY OF THE EXAM RESULTS DAWNS BRIGHT and chilly. I'm too nervous about my results to eat lunch, so I spend extra time getting ready. I choose my favorite wrap-around dress. I try on a shawl that has purple, gray, and orange threads. I wrap it so that my hands can be free and fasten it with the leafy brooch Mom and Dad gave me for my last birthday. The pendant Dad gave me is tucked away under my dress; I hope it will bring me good fortune. I twist my short hair away from my eyes and clip it back, clean my face, and apply the tiniest bit of oil to my skin—enough to show my marks at their best, but not so much that I will look like I've gone to too much effort.

My hands shake a little as I get my bag. My fingers are slippery with sweat and the oil that wouldn't completely wash away.

Mom gave me a hug and a little pep talk before she left this morning. It felt like seeing the old Mom again, the one whose cool levelheadedness was balanced out by Dad's warmth and playfulness. She used to smile; she used to love pretending to be annoyed by Dad's teasing until she would burst out laughing. I feel like part of her went when Dad did, and I'd never admit it out loud, but I wonder if it was the part of her I loved.

"I know how hard you've worked, Leora, my little light. Whatever happens today, I am so proud of you. Your ancestors will have been working it all out behind the scenes—don't you worry." She brushed her hand over our ancestors' books and blew me a kiss before heading out the door. "Make sure you don't go out celebrating before you've told me, OK? I'll be back by five."

As I thrust my keys into my bag, I find a card. It reads, *Your dad would be so proud of you. You shine with his light, my lovely Leora.* I gulp back tears.

"Well, off I go," I say to my ancestors, who are huddled together in their books. "Wish me luck and go before me. I remember you—I hope I'll honor you with good results." I blow a kiss, feeling a little silly, and then set my bag across my shoulder and lock the door behind me as I leave. My shawl blows in the wind and I worry that my hair will be unkempt by the time I get there. Not much I can do now, though. Not much I can do about anything.

We're all given mentors when we complete our exams, and they're the ones who give us our results. Verity's mentor is in the government building. To my astonishment, I have been assigned our town's storyteller, Mel. I've no idea why I've been given someone so important—surely she has better things to do than to bother with me? She is famous, as famous as Mayor Longsight. She has no surname; storytellers embody our community's tales, not their own. I've seen her at big events but never up close. As storyteller, she keeps all our community's fables and tales on her skin and is entrusted with preserving all those precious stories. She works from a room in the lower level of the museum. I know Verity's mentor is in the government building, but I don't see her in the square when I arrive for my results.

When I reach the museum, the gates are open, bolted in place so they don't clang shut in the wind. I look at the black iron bars and imagine the museum as a benevolent prison for the artifacts it contains. This is their sentence—examined and scrutinized in their glass jails. Each book and object with his or her story to tell. I take a deep breath before I go in. This was our place—mine and Dad's.

I walk up the worn stone steps, tread over the grate near the entrance, and push one of the big doors open. The cold wind fights with the warm air as I walk in and ease the door shut. My hair has blown into my face in spite of the clips and I search my pockets for a handkerchief so I can stop sniffing. Everyone goes to different venues for their results: wherever their new mentor has asked them to come. My results meeting is happening in one of the basement rooms; it'll probably be cold down there but I can feel sweat prickling under my arms. I unpin my brooch and take my shawl off.

The woman at the reception desk, Beatrice, knows me well. She's worked here for as long as I can remember. She smiles. "Big day, hey, Leora?" I can't help but grin too. "I can't believe you're getting your results; I remember when your dad would bring you in here, carrying you in that blue sling. It feels like that was only a few months ago." She must notice my smile fade because she changes the subject, checking the book in front of her. "Sorry, Leora, you don't need me distracting you. Mel will be ready for you soon."

I tuck my shawl into my bag and sit nervously in reception, the minutes crawling by. Just when I think I'll take a moment to go to the bathroom to calm myself and check my hair, my name is called. A young man with short, neat hair and a studious-looking face gestures for me to follow him behind the welcome desk. We walk through a corridor and down a tight flight of steps into the dank basement, where the offices and storerooms are. The man knocks on one of the doors, nods at me, and walks away when a deep voice from inside says, "Come in!"

Mel is seated at a table, wearing her official storytellers' apparel: the breastplate and skirt of our traditional garments. Hers are golden. Her legs are hidden by the table as she sits down, but I can just see glimpses of stories on her ankles as she crosses them. I think I spot the depiction of "The Lovers," hands entwined. That was Dad's favorite. I've only heard about the illustration of "The Sisters" on her back; it's meant to echo the trees on our backs. Moriah stands like the tree; she is spring and summer all in one day—a life in full bloom. The White Witch is below, upside down, like a reflection, like roots buried deep. She is the decay of autumn, the death of winter. I'd love to see the mark in real life. The stories, ones we all know, cover her. She was chosen when she was just a child to preserve our fables. She has no family to remember or be remembered by; instead she lives with the honor of being an open book, telling our community's stories. We mustn't forget them. Even though we have them printed on paper in books in almost every house, it's the skin that matters—her skin. That's what lasts, and as each storyteller takes on each tale, embracing the pain, spilling blood as they are inked on their body, they take on the soul of our community and preserve our history. Mel's study is small and feels more welcoming than it seemed from the outside. There are illustrations on the walls—similar in style to the marks she has on her body. On the wall behind her is a wooden engraving with the words from Saintstone's creed:

The stories are our past. Through our past we shall live our present.

I notice a pile of floor cushions in rich colors at the base of a bookcase that is overflowing with books piled on top of one another. An open book rests on one of the cushions, and it's easy to imagine Mel curled up there reading. A tall lamp with a yellowish glass shade gives the light a golden tone.

As she sits, her round stomach rests in folds and her chest is pressed more firmly against the leather breast piece. She is given only the best food, and plenty of it, so that her skin is soft and her bountiful body has ample space for all her marks. Her uniform is designed to show her marks clearly at all times. I wonder if the leather digs in, but I guess she's used to it.

She smiles, and her brown eyes flash with a sense of humor that lightens the nerves I'm feeling. "Leora?" she asks. "Take a seat."

We chat politely for a minute—she offers me condolences for Dad. I feel small in Mel's presence—as though I'm a child trying to fit in with a grown-up. She can't be more than ten years older than me, but Mel has the calm of someone who knows who she is, knows her purpose. She lives for our society and it's clear that she loves it. Her voice is deep and strong; her storyteller training has given it richness. Even when she's only talking to me it sounds as though each word has been warmed in her mouth to make it easier to receive. She looks younger now that I see her close up, and her freckles make me imagine her as a girl. Her red hair is pulled away from her face and the curls flow down her back.

"Go on then, how do you think you've done?" Mel grins impishly.

I stare at her. If I say I think I've done well, will I sound boastful? If I tell her how distracted I was after Dad's illness, will it sound like I'm trying to make excuses for bad results?

"Um, I have no idea." My voice quivers. "Have I passed?"

Mel makes a show of slowly flipping through the papers on the desk. Finally, she looks up.

"More than passed." She smiles broadly and passes a page listing my results across the table. "You've done so well, Leora—exceptional marks in everything. It looks like you've got your dream: You're going to be an inker! If that's what you still want . . ."

My hands are on my hot cheeks; I'm so relieved I think I might cry. Mel steps around the desk and places a hand on my shoulder.

"Were you really in any doubt, Leora?" she says as she lets go of my shoulder, "I didn't imagine you would be so nervous."

"I—I just missed so much work. I wasn't sure I'd done enough to catch up after—"

"You've had a lot to cope with. But things are going to change now—and you can forget about all those subjects you've never cared about and just do the things you enjoy." She gives me a little wink when I looked shocked; I'm used to adults telling me how important everything is. "You've done what you needed to do. You can get on and enjoy training now." Mel sits back in her chair and I resettle myself, letting my shoulders relax a little.

"There is just one thing we should discuss." My heart sinks as Mel pulls out a sheet from the papers in front of her. "The examiner has made an additional recommendation—an alternative to a career in inking. You're the first person I've mentored, but as far as I know, that's quite unusual."

"I don't want to be a reader," I blurt out, and Mel laughs. Her lightness and calm are comforting. I'm relieved she isn't offended.

"No, it's not that." She looks down at the paper and frowns a little. "This is interesting. They've said you've got all the skills that would suit flaying. They would fast-track you—you wouldn't need to do an apprenticeship."

My brow furrows. "A flayer? Like my dad?" Mel nods and passes me the sheet of paper, which I read out loud.

"*The candidate shows impressive dexterity, care for detail, and admirable tolerance for blood. Her obvious skills as a reader, while useful in inking, would also be a great asset to a flayer, which is a trade that is in great need of new recruits.*"

"I think you've got a choice, Leora." She leans forward. "Do you want to stick needles in the living or scalpels in the dead?"

chapter 12

I STARE AT HER FOR A LONG MOMENT. SEEING MY confusion, she puts a warm hand on my arm. "Let me tell you a story, Leora. It's one you'll know; in fact, I told it at a public marking recently, but perhaps it will help you make up your mind."

Mel stands and shows me the picture of Saint on her calf. I've seen his statue so many times in the square. I nod and she clears her throat, ready to begin.

. . .

The Saint

There was once a man in the kingdom of the marked who did nothing but good. He loved the poor and cared for the sick. He lived simply, gave generously, and spread a message of kindness wherever he went. His skin told a tale of unblemished righteousness; the people called him Saint.

One day Saint wandered right to the boundary of the kingdom. He came to a wall that was lichen-covered and forbidding. Saint called on God for guidance and soon found a section that was crumbling and lower than the rest. Testing the broken brickwork gingerly, Saint scaled the wall and came down into a new territory, away from the town he knew and into a rugged and empty-looking land. He was looking for new needs to meet, new souls to save, so on he walked. He walked through oppressive forest and eventually came upon a town that throbbed with darkness and heaved bleak trepidation onto Saint's heart as his feet stepped through the city gates. Saint was afraid but he told his timid mind to hush—if ever there was a place that needed him, this was it—fear or no fear.

For a while Saint thought the land was abandoned—perhaps God had already judged this place and destroyed the evil within it. He entered a lonely-looking square with a well, but no bucket to lower and fetch water. He sat by the well, unsheltered from the beating sun, and with every breath his mouth became drier. His cracked lips stung, and each time he swallowed he felt the tightness of his parched throat and the deep longing for something to ease his desperate need. For hours he sat and waited for something, someone to help him. Just at the moment he thought he could wait no longer and prayed for his thirst to be sated by death, a woman came past, a crow perched on her shoulder and a bucket hanging from her bag by its handle.

"Help me, please," begged Saint, his voice cracking with dry desperation. "Bring me water or I will die." The woman looked at Saint, taking in his marked body, glancing at her own bare skin, and she smiled.

"It will cost you." Saint fell at her feet and promised her all his worldly goods in exchange for a drink. Slowly the woman shook her head. She told Saint her terms, and if only he had tears to cry, he would have wept, but he simply nodded and watched as the woman swung her bucket on its rope and brought up clear, gleaming water for Saint to drink.

His parched throat was revived and he thanked the woman with all the voice he had. She looked at him with disdain and told him to follow her, for Saint had promised his soul to the woman. The crow cocked its head and clicked its beak. Anyone listening would think it was laughing.

The blank and ghostly woman was, of course, the White Witch. She ruled the town with her dark power. Each person Saint saw was empty in body and soul. Unmarked, unloved, unknowable. How he longed to share his knowledge with them. How desperately he wished to heal their wounds and lead them into righteousness. But the Witch worked him long hours, scrubbing floors, cleaning latrines, feeding the animals, and he barely had enough energy to live his own life, let alone bring life to others.

One day, after years of faithful service, Saint was sent into the forest to get food. He was sent with a child from the town who would help him carry his goods back. To pass the time, Saint told the child stories that day, and the child listened with shining eyes and parted lips. Soon the child brought more and more helpers on their daily errands. The children were entranced by Saint's tales and they begged him to tell them more and more again and again. Saint treated them kindly; he didn't make them walk farther than their small legs could bear and he showed them which herbs would ease their sickness and which foods would bring them strength. Before long, Saint had a troupe of young followers all charmed by his kindness and wisdom.

But, one day, the youngest child in the group told his father of all the adventures Saint took them on, and the man knew that soon the children would love Saint more than their own parents. The child recounted the tales Saint had told them and the man saw that Saint was no longer their slave but was, in fact, taking the children captive. Because, for as long as the White Witch had ruled, stories had been forbidden. Saint was hauled before the Witch, who passed judgment and called out his sentence: death by flaying.

Saint was tied up and paraded before the townsfolk, who stripped him and jeered at his marked skin and his kindly soul. The blank masses roared as the Witch came at him with her knife. She sliced into his beautiful skin and peeled it off, inch, by inch, by bloody inch. All the while, her crow pecked and she taunted, and told him to turn from his goodly ways and submit to her. She mocked him as she ripped his story from his sinews. But with each tug, with each cut,

Saint sighed in agonized ecstasy. She could take his skin, but she couldn't take his life.

"My soul is free!" he cried as his skin gave way. "At last, at last, my soul is free!"

Legend has it that is how Saint returned to his own land: muscles and sinews, bones and tendons on display. Draped around him like a kingly robe was his flayed skin no longer encumbering that pure soul. Never was there a man as good as Saint. From that day, women and men have set their souls free by imitating the Saint, taking off their worldly clothing, their skin-stories, at their death so they may live on in the next world. And they will never stop telling stories or the tale of the Saint.

"So you see," Mel says quietly, "both roles are essential. The inker marks the skin and unburdens the soul, but the flayer is the one who frees it from its prison. You will honor our society with whichever trade you choose. But choose wisely."

chapter 13

I PASS THE STATUE OF SAINT AS I LEAVE THE MUSEUM, my mind buzzing with thoughts. I think I've made the right decision. But I suppose I'll also always wonder how things might have been different. Mel seemed quiet after I told her my choice. Is she disappointed? Would Dad have been?

I rub my arm where my new mark will go. There'll be no turning back soon. Ink to show that I am an inker. It's what I've always wanted. It still is.

. . .

I go to see Verity and, of course, she's done brilliantly in all subjects. She's all set to start at the government on Monday. She has to begin working in the archives, getting to know the systems like the other trainees, but her mentor has assured her that a career in funerary preparation is in the cards.

"An inker! You did it, Leora. And I can't believe Mel is your mentor—you are so lucky!" We talk excitedly and then I notice the time and jump up.

"I've got to get back! Mom'll kill me if she finds out I saw you first—act surprised if she tells you. Well done, Vetty— I'm so happy for you."

I dash home and have just enough time to catch my breath before Mom gets back.

"So?" she says as she sets her shawl and bag down. "How was it? I am dying to know!"

I tell her the news and she squeezes me into a tight hug. I can hear her laughing and she says, "Oh, Leora—an inker! You'll be wonderful. I couldn't be more thrilled." I don't tell her about the choice Mel gave me. It's my secret and I want to keep it close.

. . .

Verity and I go to the government inker together the day after our results. We each hand over our certificate—it's the most official document I've ever seen, all crests and signatures and fancy penmanship. Then we are sent to different rooms to receive our marks.

I don't think the pain ever gets easier to bear. The ink bites its way into my wrist. This is a larger mark than our small age spots. My mark will show a crossed pen and a sword with a pool of ink beneath it. The inkers' mark. It will be beautiful when it's healed, but for now all I can feel is the pain. I breathe deeply and try to let my mind take me somewhere else.

I attempt to engage my inker in conversation. I ask how many people he's marked today. I thought he might open up because I'm going to be an inker too, but he just kind of grunted when he read my notes. He seems bored. For a second panic overshadows the pain; I don't want to be bored. But then, my days won't be spent like his. Mel told me that my training will be at a studio, and not the government inkers'. I'll be able to work on people's chosen marks, not just have to churn out the same official marks day after day. Right then I thank my ancestors that my training will be at a studio and not at the government inkers'.

When we've both finished, Verity and I admire each other's marks through the film that protects them. Her inker has done a good job—the lines are fine and clear. Her mark is a wheel with a set of scales beneath it. Our wrists are red and sore, but soon enough they'll be something we're proud to show, something that people's eyes will flick to automatically to see who we are and what it is that we do.

chapter 14

"I'M GOING TO FREEZE," I TELL VERITY WHEN SHE opens the door to let me in.

The end of exams party the day after we get our marks is practically compulsory. Everyone is invited and everyone goes—even me. I'm dreading it a bit; it sounds just like school, only probably with alcohol. We're not really allowed to drink yet but there's bound to be someone who has convinced their parents to buy some booze. Plus, from the conversations I heard at school, lots of other people are hoping their parents won't notice a missing bottle of something. I'd rather stay at home; I've never been that close to anyone else at school, except Verity. But

Verity—who manages to be friends with everyone—has made me promise I'll go. It's almost worth it just to stop her saying "rite of passage" every three minutes.

Verity and I are walking to the party together. Everyone will be wearing traditional celebratory clothing and I'd like to have a serious chat with whoever thought bare legs, bare stomachs, and bare arms was a good idea. The pleated skirt and the chest piece are both made from leather—a less fancy version of what Mel wears every day. I don't know how she does it.

Verity looks at me with undisguised dismay. "I don't know how you think you'll manage to freeze when you're wrapped in all that nonsense." She tugs at the layers I've covered myself up in. "You look like you're about ninety." She shakes her head and steps to the side so I can come in.

"I wish I was ninety—then I could just stay inside and be warm." Verity makes an exasperated face at me and takes my hand, once she's found it under all the layers.

"Come on, grandma, you're not getting out of this one."

Julia's in the kitchen and she laughs at us both as we traipse upstairs.

Verity has been planning how she's going to look tonight for weeks. She is wearing her thick, dark hair loose; it has been curled, and she pins the front back with little golden clips that look like buds and that shine and glint. She looks like she's wearing a crown. Her brown skin gleams. It's like she was born to wear our traditional dress.

"You know we're going to be outside all night, don't you?" I grumble as Verity unwraps my shawl.

"We're not dressing for a woodland hike, Lor—this is a party. No sensible footwear, no giant shawls, no holey cardigans!" I grudgingly take my warm, comfortable camouflage off and Verity puts my stuff in a pile on her bed. I shift my breastplate to make sure my stretch mark can't be seen; it's more pronounced than ever. Verity sits me on her chair and pulls my hair into little twists, clipping it back. She makes it look easy. She lends me jewelry and we rub our skin with oil and shimmering powder, taking care not to catch our sore wrists with their marks.

When we're both ready, Verity turns me to look in the mirror. I open my mouth ready to complain, but I close it again when I see that I actually look good. Not *Verity* good (that's never going to happen), but good nonetheless. My bare arms and shoulders show how few marks I have, but the golden dust has made my skin look less pasty. Verity doesn't have any chosen marks either, but she is beautiful enough already; she doesn't need any adornment to look enticing.

"You look amazing," Seb tells me when we go downstairs. He's in pajamas already, his straight brown hair mussed a little. He goes to bed so early now that he has to be up to bake.

I give him a hug and whisper into his ear, "I wish you could come too. It would be more fun." He laughs and backs off, shaking his head.

"One leaving party was enough." He smiles. He is so like Simon; he's lovely. Julia is in her work clothes, about to leave. She looks tired and her hair seems a shade grayer than since I last saw her. Her blue eyes gleam, though, and she holds our hands and looks like she might cry.

"Would you two just stop growing, please?" Verity has been taller than Julia for a couple of years. "You're both gorgeous." Verity rolls her eyes but I can tell she's pleased. Julia puts an arm around Simon, who kisses the top of her head. They both look so proud of Verity, I feel a pang of envy.

We head out with promises to Simon that we will be good and that Verity will be back on time. Julia's already left for her shift on the maternity ward. On the way there, Verity stumbles in her heels and I feel a little triumphant that I am wearing my "sensible footwear." Nothing of Verity's would have fit. I may freeze, but I won't twist my ankle. Anyway, I like my boots.

The party is happening in the little patch of woodland near the school, and as we get closer to the site we can hear music and shouting and screechy singing. The comforting fragrance of smoke wafts our way as we walk into the woods. Verity "oohs" at the lanterns hanging from trees and I'm glad to see a brazier in the middle of a clearing. There are old classmates sitting on blankets around it, some toasting marshmallows, some chucking on bits of whatever they find on the ground and watching them burn. It's fairly busy already, I notice with relief; we can just sort of blend in. So far everyone is excessively friendly; Verity and

I have already been hugged by about ten people that we hardly spoke to at school. It must be the mixture of alcohol and freedom from school and exams.

A guy from my inking classes gives me and Verity bottles and shouts, "Cheers." It's Karl—one of those good-looking, over-confident types who intimidate me. He's blond and tall, and I suppose some people must think he's charming, because lots of the girls at school seemed to have crushes on him. I don't see it myself. At the start of the course he realized how easily I blush, and after that he made it his mission to embarrass me as often as possible. Now all it takes is for him to be near me and I tense up. He always claimed he was only doing the inking training as a backup; he was sure his dad would have a job for him in the family business. He'd never tell anyone what the business actually was. Something shady, probably. I'm too shy to tell him I don't want to drink, so I take the bottle, but put it straight down on the table with the rest of the drinks when he looks away, content that he doesn't seem to be trying to single me out tonight. We walk across to the brazier (well, I walk, Verity staggers—heels and forests don't mix), where Verity sees a boy she knows from her politics classes. He and his friends make space for us on their blanket. I'm not sure how to sit without showing my underwear to the world, so I kneel, feeling totally awkward. I half listen to Verity and her friend chatting and have a look around, taking it all in. This is what I'm like at parties; on the rare occasions that I go, I'm happiest if I can be quiet and just watch people, soak it up.

Most people seem to have taken tonight as their chance to show off their marks. They're all checking out one another's new trade marks on their wrists and squealing or hugging or bumping fists. Our school uniform hid most of our marks and, of course, it's only in the final year that students are old enough to choose their own ink. The guys' outfits are made of soft leather too. They all have bare chests, but at least they get to wear pants. Some of them have made up for their lack of marks by using mud as war paint on their chests. They holler and wrestle, showing off to anyone who will look.

I naturally switch into reading mode, watching the tales that people's previously hidden tattoos tell. I notice one girl, whose blonde hair reaches her collarbone and whose smile is wide and relaxed, has already gone for a large mark on the back of her thigh. A snake curls over her skin. As I watch, its tongue flicks, and I see that it's a mark inspired by her boyfriend. In fact, it looks as though it might have been chosen by him. I can sense the way the snake's scaly body jars with the softness of her soul and the way it dominates her, taking up too much space on her leg. I feel relief as I read that she's not with this guy anymore, but am then filled with sadness that he has left such a mark on her.

What would it be like to be a snake—to be able to shed your skin and begin again?

Some people, like Mom and Dad, choose a theme for their marks—a kind of framework for all their future marks to fit inside. That's often people's approach. All Mom's marks are flowers. Not bouquets; she's more like a living herbarium. Each bloom is inked on her like a botanical specimen, neat, ordered and annotated. Just like her, the flowers are beautiful, restrained, discreet. When you first see her you are overwhelmed by the detail that adorns her—you can almost smell their scent. But look closely, really read her, and you will see that each flower has a meaning. Some are buds preserved at the moment they are ready to burst open. Some are blooms so ripe you just want to touch them. And some have the brown curled edges of a pressed flower past its prime. She's hard for me to read, though; whether that's because I'm too close, or because she's so good at being closed off, I don't know.

Dad's marks all spoke of the ocean. He visited the coast once when he was a child; we've still got some shells and pebbles he gathered that day. He was all waves of blue and green, all fish and gulls and mermaids and seahorses.

Apart from the crow.

I shake away that thought. Looking around the party now, I can tell that lots of my peers have chosen their first marks in a less methodical fashion. In class, my inking tutor would talk about people like them in sneering tones; people who chose their marks without thought. He said they would regret their decisions. He said their very tastelessness would be marks against them forever. Maybe he's right, but all I can think right now, looking at all them laughing and chattering in the firelight, is that at least they've done *something*—at least they've gone and gotten a mark, put a line on their skin. At least they weren't afraid.

Verity sees another friend and tells me she's going to say hello. She slips off her shoes and strolls over, leaving her beer on the ground next to me. The other guys on the blanket leave too. I smile and wave, then go back to watching the fire, hypnotized by its flames. I imagine my body covered in flames and ash and inhale the smoke as it drifts from the brazier. Perhaps fire could be my theme. But fire isn't really "me"; I'm not sultry enough. I could never smolder.

There's a movement to my left and a group of boys sit down on the rug. They've been drinking; I can tell from their slurred voices. One of them knocks over a bottle and I quickly move Verity's shoes out of the way. Suddenly one of the boys turns to me and I realize it's Karl.

He smells of beer, and from the way he blinks a bit too slowly as his eyes pass over me, I can tell he's had quite a lot. I dodge from his hand and fix my eyes on the fire again, hoping he will forget I'm here. A yawn takes me over and I shiver. How early is too early to leave a party like this?

"Whoa, don't fall asleep, Laura!" Karl shakes my shoulder as if trying to wake me up. I give him a tight smile and shift a few inches away from him.

"My name's Leora," I say coolly, smoothing down my skirt.

"Yeah, I know. But I can tell it annoys you when I call you Laura. You go all red." I scowl but feel myself blushing. "See! You're doing it now!"

I shrug. "I'm sitting right next to the fire, Karl. Don't be too pleased with yourself."

But Karl is staring at my inker's mark, his bleary eyes suddenly focused. "You passed too, then?"

I nod, just barely.

"Me too." He holds out his wrist and I can see his own inker's mark there.

I raise my eyebrows. "I thought you were going to work with your dad?" He runs a hand through his hair, looking thoughtful, then leans forward and speaks quietly. His breath smells of beer.

"Change of plan, Laura. Dad wants me to have a trade." His disappointment is plain.

"You'll be really good, though," I say, trying to reassure him. "I'm sure it'll be for the best." In spite of coming across as a bit of a fool, he was always one of the most talented in the course.

He doesn't seem to know how to react to me being nice to him, and he goes quiet for a moment. Then he blurts out, "I never knew they let girls do inking. But for ages I thought you were a boy."

I stare at him, not sure how to respond.

"No, not that you *look* like a bloke or anything," Karl is saying. "It's just I never expected to see a girl taking inking class, so I assumed . . ."

"You assumed I was a man because I wanted to be an inker? Thanks, Karl, you've made my night." I move to stand up but he grabs my hand.

"No, don't go. Listen, I'm just teasing. You don't look like a man. Actually, you look really pretty tonight." I roll my eyes and reach over to pick up Verity's shoes; when I look back Karl's face is close to mine and I realize with a shock that he's going to try and kiss me.

"Urgh, Karl, get off!" I put both hands on his chest and shove him away, hard. His eyes open wide as though he's just woken up, and I see anger flash across his face. A couple of his friends start to laugh at him.

I stand up, brush the dirt from my knees, and walk quickly toward the trees. As I leave I hear Karl saying, "What a freak, as if I'd kiss her." But his friends are still jeering.

I find Verity chatting with Rahul, a boy she's liked for ages. He's totally her type—neat hair and tidy clothes that belie a wicked sense of humor. I hand over her shoes and whisper in her ear that I'm going home. She says she'll leave with me but I can tell she wants to stay, so I give her a wink and hope she has better luck than me.

I probably shouldn't walk back on my own, but I have the distinct feeling that I've left any real threat behind at the party. Karl. What an idiot. Still, at least now that school is finished I'll never have to see him again.

chapter 15

MY TRAINING STARTS ON MONDAY. I SPEND A lazy Sunday going through the information pack, laying out my new uniform (steel-gray tunic and pants, thrilling), looking up where to go (a little studio in the center of town, which is pretty new but already very well-thought-of—the owner, Obel Whitworth, is semi-famous), and flicking through my old textbooks. I attempt to draw a few marks in my sketchbook, but everything looks stupid and childish. I'm too nervous about tomorrow.

. . .

I wake up with that sinking feeling that is halfway between nerves and excitement. Like deep down, I'm excited, but the excitement is really, *really* deep below the nerves I'm experiencing. My mind is full of questions—what will Obel be like? What if I make a mistake? Will I be awful? Will I be the only girl? What if I need to pee and there are only men's toilets? But then whispering in the background of my noisy mind I can hear a tiny voice asking, *What if it's wonderful? What if I love it? What if I'm meant for this?*

Mom's prepared breakfast: fresh fruit, yogurt, and what smells like freshly baked bread. She must have gone out early to buy it specially. She cuts it and tiny shards of crisp crust scatter on the board. This would usually be my perfect breakfast but I'm too nervous to eat.

"You look nice, love," says Mom as she brushes creases from my uniform and reties my sash.

"Mom, I'm wearing gray from head to foot. I don't look nice, I look like a mouse." Mom pulls me in for a hug and kisses my hair.

"You're no mouse. Eat some breakfast and then we'll light the candles and ask the family to take care of you today." She takes a bite of toast and, while she's still chewing, says, "I remember my first day, love. It's scary—but believe me, by the end of the week you'll feel like you've been there forever. I'm sure you'll be great. You were born to do this." It feels like she's working hard to be gentle with me, almost like she's trying to channel Dad and say what he would have said to me if he were here. It's sweet of her. "I remember my mentor's advice: Don't say you 'just want to make a difference,' and try to remember people's names. Remember that and you'll be fine."

I smiled. "Do you think you'll let me mark you, then?"

Mom's eyes widen and she coughs on a crumb that's gone the wrong way. "Ask me again when you're fully trained, love." She grins back and we both get the giggles. It's only then I realize she might be nervous too. It matters to her that I'm happy; it matters to her that I do my best and flourish.

Mom and I leave the house at the same time—she's doing a reading for a client who lives on the edge of town, and the studio where I'll be working is in the town center. We hug goodbye at the end of the street, and then I walk on alone. I breathe in the warm smell of bread from the bakery and dodge the florist who is bringing bucketfuls of blooms out to display in front of the shop. I walk through crisp leaves on the ground and relish the feeling of the warm sun on my face. The wind is chilly, though, and I hug my arms around myself while I walk. I can almost hear Dad's voice saying, "These are my favorite kind of days—bright with a bite in the air." I smile and then feel the choke of sadness. *Not now, Leora,* I tell myself. *You can't show up at your new job looking tearstained.* And, as I walk past the museum, I have a comforting thought: I can go and see his book after work. You're allowed to visit. I'll be able to tell him about my day, and he'll give me strength.

Feeling brighter and braver, I lift my chin and walk on. I pass other people walking to work; some are starting their training today, just like me. Each wears a different color to represent their role, but I'm the only one wearing gray. Inkers are few and far between.

I find the little side alley where the inking studio is and turn down it. As I get closer, though, I see another figure dressed in gray: another apprentice, it must be. And as I walk closer, my heart sinks.

Karl. Of all the apprenticeships, he would have to be on mine.

What would Verity tell me to do? I think. Verity would say I should ignore him: *He's nothing, Lor—he's ignorant, childish, and dull—you'll look back and wonder why you let someone so insignificant have any impact on your life.* Which, of course, is fine for her to say.

Karl doesn't look pleased to see me either. He had been leaning against the wall but now stands to face me. He's broad, and although his blond hair has been pushed back, a few strands fall in front of his blue eyes. He suits the gray uniform and, typically, shows no sign of nerves.

"You aren't serious?" he says. "This is a joke, right? No one told me I'd have to share my training."

I shrug. Saying nothing, I keep my arms crossed over my chest and stand with my back against the wall to wait. I don't get too close. The alley is quiet; I look down at my shoes and try not to do anything to attract his scorn. This is not how today was meant to go.

Just then the sound of a bolt being pulled and the door being unlocked makes us both stand up straight. The door opens and the most beautifully marked man I've ever seen stands in the entrance.

"Karl? Leora? You had better come this way."

Inside, everything is either wooden or gray. Wooden tables, pale gray walls, steel seats. The man who has ushered us in stands in glorious contrast to the surroundings. I'm no good at guessing ages—but he's younger than Mom, midthirties, probably. His head is shaved and his bare arms are strong and pale. There's something about him that feels off, unusual, but I can't put my finger on it—something aside from the colors and the beauty of his skin and his undeniable presence. I can't quite work it out. I realize I'm gaping at him when he says, "You OK there, girl?" I flush and nod, embarrassed to be caught staring.

"Right, you two. Aprons on. My name is Obel. You may have heard my name and you'll definitely have seen my marks. You're training with the best and I expect exceptional things from you. Please remember that." His words are arrogant but spoken so matter-of-factly it comes across simply as confidence. "And remember this too: I don't care about *you*, I care about *me*. If you don't meet my expectations I will drop you without a second thought. Everything you do is a reflection on me, so—do well. Understood?" Karl and I both murmur our agreement and I'm a little bit pleased that Karl seems as awestruck as I am.

"Now—tell me," says Obel, "what made you choose inking? You first." He nods toward me. Fabulous.

"Um. I've always liked drawing and I . . ." I'm so awed by this man's presence that my mind goes blank. I blurt out, "I wanted to do something that will make a difference to people."

No. I used the "I want to make a difference" line. What is wrong with me?

"Right, that's nice. But that doesn't really tell me anything. So I'll ask again. Why inking?"

I take a deep breath and focus. "I can read people and I don't mind blood." I'm so nervous now that I speak without thinking and I see him hold back a smile. "I've always been fascinated by people's marks—what they mean and why they've chosen them. I'm not squeamish. Inking seemed to fit." I shrug and realize I could have been saying exactly the same thing as a trainee flayer.

He laughs at that and suddenly he seems a little less stern. "You can read people? Are you sure about that, Leora?" His voice is teasing but there's a seriousness in his eyes.

And that's when I see it. I notice what it is that seems different about him. *I can't read him.* His marks are all there—they tell the world his age, his hometown, list his perfect qualifications. But apart from the surface meaning, his marks are silent. I can't read anything deeper. Puzzled, my eyes meet his and just for a second his eyebrows dip, as though he's asking a question or he's concerned.

"I can usually read people—yes," I manage to say before his attention slides from me to Karl. Karl is looking at me and smirking.

"What about you, boy—why inking? And please don't tell me you want to make a difference." I blush at this and notice Karl standing a bit taller.

"Inking is what I've always wanted to do." *Liar*, I think. "I've done my own work already." Karl pulls up the leg of his pants and shows a mark depicting a dragon. It's pretty good. Damn it.

"You did that?" Obel asks, eyebrows raised. Karl grins proudly and nods.

"You idiot. You come here with an illegal mark and expect me to be impressed? Don't let anyone see that, *ever*—OK? Not until I've made it look less like a child did it. I can't have people thinking that this is the sort of work associated with my studio." Karl covers his leg, flushing. I guess he never expected to be here, illicit marks on show, having to answer to an expert inker, and I can't help but feel a little bit pleased that Obel has taken him down a peg.

Obel sighs and looks at the two of us without any pleasure. "Well. You might as well come this way," he says, and we follow him through to the studio.

It's sleek and bright, with white walls. A metal reception desk helps to divide the space so that customers can't just walk in and watch someone being marked. The floor is tiled with black stone and I notice a large folding screen with wheels at its base that has been painted with traditional marks. Behind the screen is the black leather chair. My heart thrills—this is the place I'm going to make my first mark. The fear I'd felt earlier dissipates and I embrace the excitement that takes its place. This is where I belong, I just know it.

Obel shows us around. He explains that today our job is just to listen and watch, so that's what we do: pay attention and, as the clients begin to come in, run to get the equipment Obel asks for.

The first person who comes in is a man, probably late twenties. He's hoping to have a mark to celebrate a promotion, and he wants it done in his lunch break, in a couple of hours' time.

"I'm happy to do it, but I won't mark you today." Obel says in a firm but respectful tone. "We have a consultation first, and then the inking in a week."

The man frowns. "The last inker I saw always let me have work done right away, when it was convenient to me."

Obel dips his head in understanding. "I'm very happy to agree to a time that works for you, sir, but I won't mark anyone without going through a thorough consultation and at least a week's reflection period." The man's jaw clenches and I wonder if he'll get up and leave. Obel carries on, talking calmly and quietly. "If you regret your mark or rush into something that isn't entirely right, I will have failed in my job. I want you to love the ink you get here. I want you to be proud of the marks your family will treasure after you die."

Obel's confidence seems to placate the man, and his annoyance fades. He talks with Obel about his ideas and by the time he returns to work he seems to be as much under Obel's spell as I am.

As the morning goes on, I begin to anticipate the instruments he will request as each client comes into the studio. Karl and I listen closely to the questions he asks each person as they describe the new mark they want. He doesn't just accept their decisions; he interrogates them.

"Have you seen this mark on anyone before? What did it make you think of? Do any of your family's books bear the mark you're considering? Where would you like the mark placed? What size? Will this be part of a larger piece? What do you want people to feel when they see your mark? What's your temperament? Are you fiery or calm? Are you a loner, or do you need to be surrounded by people? What do you like about your job? What do you hate?"

He asks the questions, then sits back and listens. That's when I watch him. Sometimes he is totally still—as though not wanting to interrupt or sway their answers by doing anything more than breathing. With other clients he is animated and conversation flows easily. But the moment the needle is dipped and loaded with ink and he switches on the machine he is silent. It is as though he is in the ink and the ink is in him. He seems almost to become the person he is marking, his soul mixing with the blood and the ink. I see Karl watching too, his gaze almost hungry. We're both impressed.

At the end of the day Obel calls me and Karl to where he's working.

"Just so you know, I'm planning to grow this business. At the end of your training I will have an opening for a new inker to join me in the studio. Prove to me you're worth it and I might just choose one of you."

Karl and I look at each other. The stakes have just been raised—and I know we both intend to win.

I leave the studio at the end of the day feeling dazed. This morning and all its anxiety feels like it was days ago. I grin as I walk into town, the excitement still buzzing through me. I want that job, I decide. Trust my luck to be competing against Karl, though. I bet he doesn't even really want the job; he just wants to win. Karl may be irritating, and he may only be here because his dad is making him do it, but I have to admit he has some skill.

And then I remember my plan to stop by the museum and see Dad's book, and my grin stretches broader. I can't wait.

chapter 16

THE AIR IN THE STREETS IS PLEASANTLY COOL after the heat of the studio. It's lovely to notice the breeze on my face and to feel my nervous energy ebb away. OK, Karl was an unwelcome surprise, but I survived my first day and I didn't make a fool of myself. *Let's see how tomorrow goes, shall we?* says the little voice in my head, but I shrug it off.

The route to the museum is busy with people and voices. Shoppers walk by me laden with bags full of things they've bought at the market. I can't bring myself to match their speed—for the first time in months I'm feeling a hint of contentment; I've had an unexpectedly good first day at work and I'm going to see my dad in a few minutes' time. I let myself smile. I'm not exactly happy, I'm not ready to be, but it's like I can smell the fragrance of happiness just around the corner—it's not far away from me now.

Above the wide doors at the museum's entrance is the inscription TRUTH LAID BARE. It makes me shiver with anticipation and a little nervousness. Oh, I can't wait to see him! My soft boots don't make much sound on the tiled floor—but it's enough for Beatrice at the reception desk to glance up at me. She smiles broadly; she's been working here since I was tiny. When he died she sent us flowers.

"Hi, Leora! Was this your first day?" I nod and smile.

"I'm at an inker's down the road," I tell her, grinning. "I thought I'd come and tell Dad all about it." She nods, her eyes warm with sympathy, and she gestures toward the library section of the museum.

I walk through the atrium, feeling the winter sun shining on me from the rooftop window that seems so high it must make birds dizzy. Glancing at the displays as I pass through, I push open the glass doors to the library. The high stacks of books shield the room from sunlight, and it always seems dingy and unwelcoming to me. The smell of old books makes me think of winter and Dad lighting twisted sheets of paper to start the fire. Verity sometimes comes here to study; she finds the quiet helps her concentrate and she likes choosing a desk and staying all day. I don't know why, but it makes me feel out of place and on show. Taking a deep breath in, I close my eyes. I'm not here to study; I'm here for Dad.

The librarian at the desk isn't someone I know but she's attentive and smiley, and when I tell her why I'm here she just opens a drawer, gets out a form, and shows me how to fill it in. Then she sends my book request down the chute to the floor below where the archives are kept, and where those whose books have recently been completed are held.

While I wait, I look out through the doors back into the atrium. All the other floors in the building look down into this one, like it's a stage. I can see some of the temporary exhibits from where I stand—they change them quite often. Right now all our most respected leaders' books are there, and the largest display case holds a replica of Mayor Longsight's marks. I glance around the library to see if anyone I recognize is here today. There's just a boy reading quietly at a desk in the corner.

I sigh, wondering how long I'll have to wait. Suddenly I'm desperate to see Dad's book and don't want to wait a second more, but it seems to be taking forever.

I must have been here for about ten minutes when I hear a chair scrape. I look up and see the boy walking from his study table toward the library reception. He stands a little way from me, and puts a book on the desk. He looks a bit older than me and I feel like I recognize him from somewhere—maybe he was at my school in the year above or something. He's *gorgeous*, though; I would remember him from school, surely. He has warm, black skin and intelligent eyes behind gold-rimmed glasses.

While he waits for the librarian to come to him, he puts a notebook in his leather satchel, fastens it, and passes his hand over his tight curls, knocks his glasses slightly, and adjusts them. Oh no. He's seen me looking. He's going to think I was *looking,* and I wasn't. Well, maybe I was looking a bit, but I don't want him to know that. I begin to study the wooden surface of the reception desk. Oh to be effortless. Oh to be like Verity— just once.

"Excuse me," he says to the librarian, and his voice is nice: kind of husky and deep. "I'm looking for volume two—do you have it?"

She glances at the slip of paper he shows her. "Are you OK to wait while I check?" she asks him. "I can't promise anything."

The boy agrees, and when she's gone, he looks over at me and smiles. It's an open, conspiratorial kind of grin and it takes me by surprise. I smile back and try not to giggle.

Just as I shift my weight for the thousandth time an assistant walks in and passes a slip of paper to the librarian, who looks up, startled. She puts down the file she's looking through, takes the note, reads it, looks at me, and folds the piece of paper in half.

"The book you requested can't be accessed at this time." She speaks quietly, her eyebrows furrowed.

"What?"

She hands me the piece of paper and turns back to her work, giving me privacy as I read. I stare at the paper but the words blur before my eyes. *Unavailable. Confiscated until further notice.*

"Wait—I'm sure there's a mistake." My heart is thumping hard, suddenly, all my excitement at seeing Dad turning to fear. "He—his book is here—it's just waiting for the weighing ceremony."

The librarian looks at me and sighs, but stays silent. Her eyes look anxious, as though she hasn't dealt with this situation before.

"Maybe they looked in the wrong place or searched for the wrong name?" I ask with a hint of desperation in my voice. It must be a mistake. It must be.

The librarian gets up and comes around the desk, obviously worried I'm going to make a scene. "There is no mistake. If you look at your paperwork you'll see." She touches the piece of paper in my hand cautiously, as though it might burn her. "Your father's book is unavailable. It's been confiscated." She points her finger at the words and they begin to shake and wobble as tears come to my eyes.

"If it's been confiscated, then I want to know why!" My voice is louder than I intend and I see the librarian bristle. "Please, you have to help me. *Please*—I need you to get my dad."

The librarian looks past me nervously and I see her mouthing something to someone in the distance. Just then I feel a hand on my arm and realize it's the boy, who has been watching the whole thing. I jerk back indignantly but he pulls me toward him, his grip surprisingly firm.

"This won't help. You don't want to get in trouble here," he whispers in my ear. He nods to a guard heading our way and I let the boy guide me out of the museum, still holding the piece of paper in one hand, with sudden tears dripping down to my chin.

"What are you doing?" I hiss, trying to pull my arm away.

"Keep moving. We can't talk now. Come on." He takes his hand from my arm and heads down the stone steps. I hesitate a moment, then follow, feeling dazed. I don't want to leave Dad. I have too many questions to just walk away. But despite his quiet manner, the boy has authority. I feel the cold wind chill my damp skin. I go quickly down the steps to catch up with the boy. He starts walking and I follow; as I do he turns his head and gives me a little half smile that I think is sympathetic.

When I turn and look behind me I see the guards standing at the top of the museum steps, watching us.

We walk in silence for a few minutes, leaving the square and heading to dingier streets of offices, shops, and businesses. I feel the first drops of icy rain and begin to shiver. "Let's go in here." He grabs my hand suddenly, and we duck through a low door. It's a coffeehouse I've never been in before. The packed room is warm and glowing with lights and there's a pleasant warm fug of coffee and conversation. The boy says a few words to the man working at the register and, still holding my hand, guides me toward a booth in the corner of the room. The walls muffle the sounds of people talking and laughing and it feels safe.

I realize I'm clinging to his hand quite tightly. I drop it and try to hide my embarrassment by busily unwrapping my shawl and arranging it *just so* before I sit down. It's only then that I look at the boy and the strangeness of the situation fully hits me. An hour ago I had been waiting to see my father's book. Now I'm sitting in a place I've never been, with a total stranger.

"Hello," he says, a grin starting. "I'm Oscar." He dries the rain from his glasses on his shirt. He has dimples when he smiles. "You probably think I'm very strange. I don't normally kidnap girls at the museum—I promise." He dips his head to look at me and says, "Are you all right?" I run my fingers across the edge of the table and feel the aged grain of the wood. "I'm OK. No, actually I'm *not* OK, but *this* is OK, I mean, it's OK that we're here."

Internally, I roll my eyes at myself. "I'm Leora." I reach my hand out to him and he shakes it and smiles.

Coffee is brought to our table in earthenware mugs that look handmade. I take a too-hot sip while I try to think of something to say.

"So what happened in there?" Oscar asks. "They wouldn't let you see someone?"

I look at him. I don't like talking about myself at the best of times. But the circumstances of our meeting are stranger than he is and I find myself feeling like I can trust him. Am I an idiot? Am I just being blinded by a pretty face and a cup of coffee? Perhaps. I'm too tired and too wired to know. But I know I want to talk.

"My dad. He . . . he died." I swallow.

"I'm sorry to hear that," says Oscar, replacing his glasses, pushing them up the bridge of his nose while he leans forward to listen.

"Anyway, his book is being held at the museum until they're ready for his weighing of the soul ceremony, just like everyone's always is. But—well, you must have heard—the librarian gave me this." I produce the crumpled slip of paper and hand it to Oscar, who looks at it in silence before sliding it back across the table. "It says his book's been confiscated and I . . . don't know what to do. What does that even mean?" I dig my nail into the table and score a line along the grain while I talk. I can hear the bewilderment in my voice. I sound like a child.

The boy is looking at me thoughtfully. "They confiscate books if something . . . controversial has come up during their audit. Something that needs to be taken into account at the ceremony." He inclines his head, still leaning toward me. "Do you have any idea what that would be? What they could've found?"

Of course I know. My mind flashes back to the moment I first saw the crow on his scalp. The mark of the forgotten.

Instead I say, "No, I . . . I can't think of anything." My voice sounds stiff and awkward even to me. "Can they really just take his book away like that?"

"Well. *They* can do what they like, can't they?" Then, before I can ask what he means, he goes on quickly, his voice quiet. "Tell me, was your father a good man, Leora?" The coffee machine hisses.

"He was. He was the best man I've known."

He was. He was. But why was he marked?

"Then all will be well. We can trust justice." The words sound dry and spiked in his throat. He gestures to my clothes and with an amused smile asks, "Are you really an inker?"

The change of subject takes me by surprise and I laugh and say, "Well, yes. But I've only been there a day! What do you do?"

"I'm a bookbinder—second year of training. I was trying to study when I saw you in the museum. I bet I'll never get hold of that second volume."

I mumble an amused "sorry" and tell him about discovering I'm training alongside someone who hates me.

"Isn't it still quite unusual for a girl to be an inker?"

"I was the only one in my course. Maybe people are put off by the stereotype that most inkers seem to be all biceps." I hold out my arm, thinnish and pale. "I'm bucking the trend."

Oscar laughs, and the skin around his eyes creases in a way that makes me want to make him laugh more so I can see it happen again. The amusement stays on his lips even when his laughter ends. But I'm suddenly completely out of conversation. I can't think of a single thing to say. It's crazy that I'm still here. I straighten up a little in my chair and try to work out how to leave without being rude.

"It's really kind of you to have come to my rescue, Oscar. Do you really think those guards would have kicked me out?" I ask as I take a more drinkable sip of coffee.

He shrugs. "Maybe," he says quietly.

"Well. I won't take any more of your time; I feel much better. I should be getting back to my mom."

Oscar drains the rest of his coffee and smiles. "Well, this has been nice. Chatting and stuff." He slides his mug away to the edge of the table. "If I can help with anything—with your dad—you only have to ask." His tone is light but he looks at me from the corner of his eye, as though daring me to take the bait.

"Oh," I say doubtfully. "It's a kind offer." He has no idea what he'd be getting into if he tried to help; not that I have much idea either. "I'm not sure what use bookbinding is for the trouble I'm in." Oscar raises an eyebrow but doesn't stop me when I get up.

I can see out of the window that it's still raining, so I pull my shawl over my head and turn to say goodbye, when I see something that makes me stop. Oscar is reaching for his satchel and as he bends down his shirt rides up and I glimpse a portion of his family tree. His marks are smoky against his black skin. And suddenly I read him.

A name has been removed and there is a bird pecking at the base of his tree.

A cuckoo. I know what that means.

In a flash I know where I've seen Oscar before. He was at the square that day of the marking. The boy with the glasses reaching out for the marked man.

As Oscar straightens up he notices me staring. I look him in the eyes.

"Tell me. Was your father a good man, Oscar?"

chapter 17

MY MIND IS NOT ON THE STREETS AS I HURRY home. I can't fathom what's just happened. There are too many questions in my mind. I could ask Mom if she knows what's going on with Dad's book—but where do I begin? Can I even trust her? My mind keeps turning back to Oscar: his silence as we left the coffeehouse, his jaw tight as he scribbled something on a piece of paper and thrust it into my hand before hurrying away, head down against the wind. The note's in my pocket, but I'm too scared to look at it.

"Leora!" Mom is sitting at the table, and as I come in she sweeps me into a hug and squeezes me tightly. "They kept you late! How did it go, my love? I've been dying to know!" I stare at her, disoriented. The studio and Obel and Karl all feel like days ago, so much has happened since. It takes a moment for my mind to shift from the strange events of this afternoon. I force myself to smile.

"It was brilliant, Mom. Much better than I thought it would be." I breathe in the familiar scents of home and allow my tight shoulders to relax. Mom pushes me away gently and turns to grab an oven glove and take a tray of scones out of the oven. I should have guessed she would bake something nice on my first day. She looks at me expectantly, wanting me to go on talking.

And so I tell her about Obel, and how he's as impressive as people say he is. I don't mention Karl. I tell her about some of the customers I saw Obel working with and how his own marks are beautiful but nothing in comparison to the work he does on others. I leave out the part about not being able to read him— she would make it into a big *thing* and freak out that he wasn't "normal"—and then I can't keep it in, and I say, "And I went to the museum to see Dad."

Mom fumbles and drops one of the hot scones she is putting on the cooling rack. She picks it up with an oven-gloved hand, brushes it off, and puts it with the rest. Her face is entirely still.

"Where is he, Mom?" I watch her. She knows something, I can tell; she's always been a horrible liar. "Mom? When were you going to tell me?"

"Tell you what?" She's trying to sound calm, but I can hear the edge of defensiveness in her voice.

"Do you know where his book is? Do you know why they've taken him away?" Mom gets two plates out, resolutely looking anywhere but at me. "You're not the only one who loved him, Mom. Please."

Mom drops the baking tray onto the work top and turns to face me, frowning as she shakes off the oven glove and puts it on the side.

"That's not fair, Leora—"

"It's not fair that you know stuff about Dad that you're not telling me." My voice is wobbling. Mom's refusal to admit what she knows is just making me more angry. "I'm scared, Mom. What does all this mean for his weighing of the soul ceremony?"

"Sweetheart," she says as she comes and tries to hug me, which irritates me, "you're getting worked up." I shake her off. "Look." She takes my face in her hands. "I should have warned you—I did get a letter. I didn't realize you were so keen to visit him. They're withholding his book before his ceremony. But sweetheart, this is . . . it's a technicality; it happens sometimes. Something they have to investigate, but nothing to worry about."

I can't tell anymore if she believes this or if she's lying to me. "No, Mom. I know something's wrong." She opens her mouth to speak. "Don't. There are things you've been keeping from me. I know there's stuff about Dad you don't want me to know."

"You make it sound like there's some big secret," she says dismissively, as though I'm a schoolgirl asking silly questions, and my frustration rises.

"He was marked, wasn't he? With the crow." I whisper it and I watch her face. It is completely unreadable. She won't let me in. I will get no answers from her tonight.

"I don't know what you're talking about, Leora." Her voice strives for authority, but it sounds whisper-thin.

I drop my plate with the scone back onto the table. "I'm not hungry," I say as I pick up my shawl. "Don't wait up."

I leave the house with Mom calling after me, *"Leora, come on! Don't be so silly."*

I have never disobeyed her before.

I walk without giving much thought to where I am going.

I like it when the streets are empty. I like walking past houses and imagining who lives there. During the day, when people are out and about, their lives shout at you from their marks—there's no avoiding people's life stories and no room for guessing at who they are and what their lives consist of. But when everyone is hidden behind walls and doors and curtained windows I can picture the bits of their lives the tattoos cannot show. I imagine what conversations they're having before they brush their teeth, what they're reading, what made them cry today.

We were all so close before he got ill. We all had our roles in our little family. Mom was the calm, sensible one. Dad was always telling stories. He loved the fables and old tales—the White Witch, Saint. I would listen with eyes like saucers. And if they got too scary, Mom would stop him, saying he'd give me nightmares. Then he'd end up telling us some silly story about the trouble he used to get into when he was a boy and Mom and

I would laugh until our cheeks went pink; Mom shaking her head, disapproving a bit, knowing Dad was teasing her, and me amazed at the idea that a grown-up had ever been naughty. And I bounced between the two of them—usually quiet and docile, but occasionally, just occasionally, flaring into rebellion.

I don't know how long I walk for—hours maybe—but I stay out till I'm sure Mom will have gone to bed. When I arrive back at my house, I stop for a moment outside, looking up at it. If I don't go in, I can still pretend that everyone is still in there, that Dad isn't just a book to be read. That he's not missing.

That Mom is just Mom, and not a liar in Mom's clothing.

. . .

When I get downstairs in the morning, there's a chicken defrosting on a plate and a note on the table from Mom: *Gone to work early, have a good day. Please put dinner on when you get back.* She's avoiding me.

And I know that I have no choice but to take out the scrap of paper Oscar gave me. I check my pocket and unfold it.

What makes a good man? You can trust me, Leora.

If you want to talk, meet me Friday 6:00 p.m. At the square.

Beneath the words is a tiny scrawled picture of a crow.

chapter 18

I STARE AT OSCAR'S NOTE FOR SO LONG THAT I'M IN danger of making myself late for work. I gulp down some tea and take a cold scone with me to eat on the way. There was more rain last night and the leaves on the ground are mushy and fragrant.

I get to the studio just on time. Karl's waiting and he opens his mouth to say something—something rude, probably—but then Obel appears at the door and he can't. It doesn't stop him from looking at me like dirt. I glare at the back of his head as I follow him in. Now that we're both stuck with each other, I don't know why he can't just get on with it.

Obel lets us in and gets right to the point.

"Different tasks for you both today. Karl, I want you to work on perfecting your drawing skills. The mark you made on your leg shows some natural talent—but that's only going to take you so far. It needs refining. I need you to be making lines that are faultless. Go through this book"—Obel slides a textbook of tattoo styles across the table—"and try to imitate the marks. But don't just copy—I want you to feel the emotions of each mark—OK?"

"Erm, right." Karl looks baffled but picks up the book, a dip pen and ink, and sets to work. As he passes me he whispers, "Hear that? 'Natural talent.'"

"Leora, you're with me again." Obel nods his head toward the studio and I follow him into the light space, Karl glaring as I go. The man of sympathy and feeling I saw yesterday when he spoke to his clients seems to disappear when Obel speaks to me and Karl. I still can't read him—I feel like he is behind glass in the museum—beautiful but dead.

Obel has a lot of clients. Some are coming to be marked, others to talk about the ideas they have for future markings. I smile when one man comes in with his tiny white dog and asks whether Obel will ink his "best friend" on his buttock in place of a marriage mark. "Well, I'm never going to get married, am I?" I am struck by the fact that each customer comes to the inkers alone.

When there's a brief lull and I'm sorting out the instruments for the next customer, I decide to ask Obel about it.

"Everyone comes to see you on their own. Why? My best friend and I have always planned to get our first chosen marks together. Is that not allowed?"

Obel is wiping down a surface and he takes his time before answering. "Some studios don't mind either way, but I like to see people alone. I need to know they're choosing their mark for themselves and not being swayed by anyone else. Some people are very suggestible. They like to be told what to think. But their mark must be their own; their story is too important. I won't allow someone's story to be influenced by anyone else." He moves a chair into position for the next customer.

"You don't think that you influence them?" I ask, worried he will think I'm asking too many questions.

He pauses and seems to consider what I've said.

"Part of my job is to act as a mirror for each of my clients. I try to lose the sense of being their inker and aim to become simply another part of them. I reflect their passions and fears. I become their safe place. You'd be surprised how many people tell me things they've never told their closest friend." He gives me a thoughtful look. "This is part of the job that can't be taught, Leora. The part that takes you from someone with a bit of talent to a real inker."

Over the course of the day we see a man who wants to mark the occasion of his son's birth without letting his wife know that he has a mistress. We see an elderly woman who wants to record a memory she has of the first time she kissed a man. "My mind is going, you see, and there are some things you don't want to forget."

I get a delivery of flowers, with a card from Mel that reads *Hope you're settling in well. You have chosen one of our noblest professions.* And underneath she's drawn a picture of Saint. At the end of the day, after Karl has gone, I am tidying up a few pieces and arranging my flowers in a jug when a woman walks in. Obel looks up as she enters. She's slight and dark, and there's something in her eyes that makes me pause.

"We're closed," he says, but he says it kindly.

"I know. I just . . . do you have time to see me?" she asks, and hands a piece of paper to Obel. He looks at it and then flips the sign on the door to CLOSED.

"Please. Come and sit down," he says courteously, pushing the piece of paper she had passed him into his back pocket. I hesitate, unsure whether I should stay or leave, and catch Obel looking at me thoughtfully. Then he seems to make a decision and says, "This is Leora, she's training with me—are you happy for her to be with us?"

The woman looks at me with eyes shining and red from too many tears. She pauses a moment and then seems to make up her mind. "Yes, that's fine."

As Obel speaks to the woman, I hear the sadness of her soul. She tells us she has lost her newborn baby and wants a leaf at the base of her family tree to mark his life.

Obel is quiet and nods at her request, apparently willing to break his own rule and mark her right away. She sits on a stool and I help her lift her top and she leans on her forearms against the chair, ready for the ink to begin. As she settles herself down I see her crumpled stomach with angry purple stretch marks. I look at her back and see that her family tree already has two fallen leaves resting at the base of the trunk—brown and skeletal compared to the rich green of the rest of the family represented on her tree. I touch her shoulder and there is an almost electric connection between us. I sense the heaviness of breasts that are full, yet with no baby to feed. I feel the emptiness, the grief, the rage, the guilt, the brokenness that says, *I can't do it again,* and the yearning that whispers, *But I must, I must.* The woman looks up and I realize my eyes are full of tears.

"I'm sorry." I'm ashamed by the strength of my emotions and am desperately afraid that I will have increased her pain—or that she'll think I pity her. Obel has been watching us in silence and now takes me to one side, out of earshot of the woman waiting.

"It's clear to me that this is your job, Leora. You must make the mark."

I catch his eye to see if he means it. "But I can't," I whisper. "I've never done this before."

"The connection is enough." He holds out the tub of gloves, insistent. "—*if* you're a true inker. You might as well find out sooner rather than later, hey?"

I take the machine with shaking hands and Obel gives me an almost imperceptible nod of encouragement.

The woman nods too, smiling gently at me.

I carefully set up my workstation, cleaning everything and laying out all that I will need. I pick up a pen. A leaf—a leaf for his short life. I barely think as I draw guidelines on her skin, as I collect the ink and prepare another machine and lay it on my workstation. Only as I pick up the machine to start work do I falter; it feels heavy in my hand and I am afraid of hurting her. I am afraid of dishonoring her longed-for baby by marking her badly.

But as I press my foot down on the pad and the machine switches on I am lulled into a trance. I hear only the buzz and I feel only the emotions of the woman whose back I am branding. The lines come easily; the colors show me where to blend, where to hold back. I forget everything apart from the skin under my hand. I am not creating the image; it is pouring out of me.

As the sound of the machine fades I am brought back to life. I wipe away the ink that spills over the image and lift a mirror so the woman can see what I've done.

She gasps. And even I am surprised. I haven't done a brown leaf to match the other lost children; this one shines red and gold. Even in its demise it shows beauty and hope for a new season to come.

"It's perfect. Oh. It's just how I think of him. I can't thank you enough." The tears are coming now. She lets me cover the mark, dresses, and wipes her eyes on a cream-colored handker-chief. Then suddenly the words tumble out of her as if a dam has broken. "Thank you so much again, both of you. I was so unsure about coming, my husband thinks I should just forget—I know I'm supposed to forget them when they die before they're marked, but I can't do it. He was only two days old. And I know we mustn't—" She blots tears from her cheeks. "But I was meant to see you. And you saw me, you saw right into me. Thank you." As she speaks, I see Obel's jaw tense—his eyes shine with feeling and understanding.

She pays Obel and leaves, wrapping her cloak around herself. I'm so overwhelmed I can hardly speak.

"Obel, that felt amazing. What happened? It was as if she was leading my hands—it's like . . . it wasn't *me* who did that." I laugh with relief and pleasure and Obel smiles widely at me.

"I knew it, girl. You're born to mark." His face is suddenly serious. "Leora, there's no need to tell anyone about customers we see out of hours, all right? Consider it inker-inked confidentiality."

I just look at him and nod, but when I empty the trash can before I leave I see the piece of paper she'd given Obel. I flatten it out and smooth the creases. On it is a picture of a feather.

A feather—the sign of the blanks. But she seemed so normal, and so broken. And then, with a horrible rush of adrenaline, it clicks. If her baby was two days old, he couldn't have had his birth mark. Babies who die before they're marked are officially considered blank. I don't know what to do—my first mark, and Obel let me break the law, made me do it.

I've just made a mark of remembrance for a baby that should be forgotten.

chapter 19

THE HOUSE IS STILL EMPTY WHEN I GET BACK. I open my notebook and draw the mark I made today. On paper it looks like a passable attempt at a drawing of a leaf, but on the woman's back it looked ... alive. I am torn between my pride and excitement at this milestone and my total terror that someone will find out. I close my eyes and try to remember how it felt to become so in tune with someone that their feelings become your feelings. I can't help but smile. I hold her face in my mind and wish her happiness.

I put the chicken in the oven and peel and chop the vegetables. When I check the clock, it's not as late as I had thought. I'm desperate to share my news with someone and Mom won't be back for a while yet. I scribble a note to her, promising to be home in time to finish cooking, and then I grab my bag and head out to Verity's.

She's still out at her training when I arrive, but Julia is home and we sit chatting at the kitchen table while I wait for Verity. I can't stop thinking about the woman I marked, and I end up asking Julia about her work at the hospital. She's a midwife—she always oversees the babies getting their birth marks. It must be an amazing moment, to be there when someone is named and marked for the first time. I say as much to Julia and she looks thoughtful, tucking her wiry, chin-length, gray-brown hair behind her ear.

"You're right—it can be amazing. I've never been able to relax, though—there's so much at stake . . ." I am about to ask her more when Verity clatters in, dumps her bag on the table, and gives me a hug as she stands behind my chair.

"You're here! My inker friend—you have no idea how cool the people at work think I am for knowing a female inker—you've done me all kinds of good! It doesn't feel like we've only been there two days, does it? Oof, I'm exhausted!" I smile at Verity's mass of words. Julia attempts to hang Verity's bag up but the hooks are so full of coats and shawls and bags that it just falls on the floor. Julia sighs, leaving it where it is, and gives Verity a kiss on the cheek.

"You two can catch up, I'm going to try to get some sleep—my shift was busy. Listen out for Seb, he should get home soon."

We decide to stay at the kitchen table rather than go up to Verity's room—we're less likely to disturb Julia if we're down here. Verity looks through some tins in one of the cupboards and emerges with cake. She uses the lid of the tin as a plate and slices the cake, and we eat, letting the crumbs scatter on the table.

"Is it going all right, then?" says Verity, her mouth full of cake.

"I actually really love it, Vetty. The guy training me is a bit serious and hard to work out but I think he sees potential in me. Oh! You'll never guess who I'm training with, though." Verity's eyes widen in a question—her mouth is still too full for her to speak properly. I pause for dramatic effect. "Karl Novak." Verity splutters and sprays cake out her mouth. "He makes me shudder," I say.

Verity swallows what's left of the food in her mouth. I'd told her all about the party and Karl lunging for me and she knows enough about him to understand why that made my skin crawl. She shakes her head and exhales loudly. "Well, that's *impressively* bad luck—only you, Leora. Maybe he won't last?"

"He seems pretty committed," I tell her with a grim smile. "And he's actually being fine. I'll survive." The cake is really good—it's gingery and sticky, one of Seb's finest, and I'm eyeing a second piece. "Anyway, tell me about working at the government. Just look at how professional you are!" She's wearing a slim-fitted, blue linen dress with a wide leather belt that shows her waist beautifully. She has a huge sash with the government crest on it. Of course, she would get the flattering uniform. Verity smiles, gets up, and twirls.

"It's an all right uniform, actually, isn't it?" She sits down. "And yours is, um, very *gray*?"

We both laugh.

"I've been given a good project to work on already—it's quite interesting."

I raise an eyebrow—I can't really imagine anything at the administration being described as interesting.

"No, really it is!" Verity grins. "Honestly! I might even get to meet Mayor Longsight tomorrow!" She squeals and pretends to swoon, making me laugh. "He's coming in for a briefing."

"Wow, that's amazing." I can't help feeling a little envious; it makes my news about making my first mark feel feeble.

"Apparently he's bringing in all sorts of new reforms, really radical—people are buzzing with what he plans to do. It affects the whole country, not just us. I'm not in on it all, but there's a definite . . . *feeling* about the place." She shrugs but her eyes are shining. "People are excited, that's it."

"I remember at the marking . . ." I clear my throat, which is suddenly dry. "He's serious about the blanks, isn't he? They're really a threat?"

Verity nods, eyes wide. "It's real, Lor—more than we ever realized. To be honest, I'm a bit scared. But we're doing everything it takes to strengthen our position. I'm sure Mayor Longsight has it all in hand." She grins shyly. "Actually, what I'm working on is all part of that." I raise an eyebrow. She leans in. "Until they decide I'm ready to start at the Funerary and Soul-Weighing Department, I'm creating complete lists of everyone's marks."

"Um, exciting, Vetty." I smirk. "It doesn't exactly sound like top secret work. I hate to break it to you, but I don't think you're a spy just yet." She flashes me an annoyed look and I reach for a second piece of cake. "Anyway, I thought inkers had to report all the marks they make to the government. I've seen the paperwork. So that list must already exist?"

"Well, yeah, but let's just say that inkers aren't renowned for their admin skills." She looks at me pointedly and smiles wickedly. I roll my eyes, but she's right; I'm far more absentminded than her. "The record-keeping has been pretty atrocious up until now, and it's been allowed to become very slack under previous governments—but all that's changing. They need to know exactly who has been marked and when, and what their marks mean. We're going to modernize and become totally slick." Verity presses her thumb on the cake crumbs in front of her and pops them into her mouth. She looks thoughtful. "I think they had stopped believing it mattered so much—knowing who was marked, with what, where, and stuff—but Mayor Longsight wants that to change. He knows that for his reforms to work, everything and everyone needs to be recorded. Nothing can hide under the radar anymore. We're going to"—she makes a serious face as though reciting from memory—"*return to the roots of our tradition and remember that marking isn't just for self-expression—it's about remembrance and proving we are worthy.*" She laughs at her impression.

The image of the marked man at the square flashes into my mind and I remember Mayor Longsight's promise that we would be seeing more public markings. I remember the conviction in his voice, the sense I had, amidst my terror, that he would always make things right.

"So that's why he's going back to public markings, then?" I ask. I keep my voice casual but my heart is beating fast. I can't get the image of the man in the square and his broken, defeated face out of my mind. And I can't stop thinking about Dad. Why was he marked? What had he done?

Verity nods. "Yes. That was the first. Like I said, the threat from the blanks is increasing—has been for years, because the old regime wasn't tough enough. We're cracking down on any treachery. Mayor Longsight has a big job to do—to root out all that dissent. First of all, he's making sure that anyone who is in support of the blanks is made an example of. The government is investigating potential rebels. They have information that rebel cells are helping the blanks—even wanting them to be able to move freely among us—and now Mayor Longsight is putting a stop to it. There will be more people marked as forgotten, if my guess is correct. It's no longer just an ancient tradition; it's becoming a reality."

I watch Verity, her eyes sparkling with excitement, and inside I just feel hollow. Cracking down. More people marked as forgotten. Investigating potential rebels.

Does this have anything to do with why Dad's book is missing?

"Who would support the blanks, though? After all they've done—why?" *Could Dad have had something to do with these rebel cells?* I shake myself—he wouldn't. Joel Flint, model family man, loving father, wise husband, pillar of the community—there was no way. Suddenly I am desperate to confide in my best friend—and not just about Dad's mark but about his book being confiscated, and Oscar taking me to the café, and how Mom won't tell me anything.

"Verity—" I begin.

We both look up as Julia comes into the kitchen. "Couldn't sleep," she says with a sigh, slumping down on the bench beside us. She seems so slight next to Verity now. I remember when I thought she was the most *grown up* grown-up I knew, apart from Mom, of course. She looks at the cake and absently cuts a slice. Now is not the time for confessions. Then I notice the time and get up to go home; if I don't leave right now I'll be late. I think of the chicken in the oven and the silent dinner Mom and I will have.

"Do you have to go?" Verity asks. I nod and go to give her a hug. "Sorry, we've hardly talked about you—I've just been rambling on. Let's meet up this weekend and catch-up, OK?"

"Sounds perfect, Vetty. Give Seb a hug from me."

She's giving me an odd look so I reassure her with a smile that feels plastered on, and head home, waving and beaming till I get out the door, when my face slumps. Digging my hands deep into my pockets I feel the leaves I picked up that last day of exams. So much has happened since then; Verity is still the same, happy-go-lucky and sure of herself, and I'm a different person. I clench my fists and they close around something else—something that is at once hard and soft.

I pull the object out and stand under a streetlamp to see what it is.

A gleaming black feather.

The sign of the blanks.

I hold it only for a moment before the wind catches it and blows it from my hand. I look around me, half expecting to see a blank right there behind me. I run home feeling like I'm six again and the blanks are chasing me, ready to steal my soul.

chapter 20

MOM IS BACK WHEN I GET HOME. SHE IS SITTING at the table, drinking a cup of tea, reading one of our ancestors' books. Her face is calm and peaceful and I can't imagine what is going on underneath—nothing? Or everything?

Trying to catch my breath, I hang my coat up and take off my shawl. There's part of me that wants to pretend everything's fine and just tell her about my day—it'd be nice to share it all with someone who will be excited too.

But I know she's keeping so much from me.

"How did day two go?" she asks, giving me a small, expectant smile. It's her attempt at a truce.

I pause. "I'm going to tell you, because it was so exciting, but don't think it means you're forgiven." I scowl. "In fact, I'll make a deal with you. I'll tell you *my* stuff at dinner and then you can tell me *yours*." Mom rolls her eyes and smiles as though I'm just an amusing kid; I glare at her and she has the decency to look sorry.

"So. Me first," I say, when I've nearly finished eating. Mom puts her knife and fork down and looks at me expectantly. I can't stop my smile. "Today was amazing. I did my first mark!" Mom gasps and claps her hands to her face. I feel a warm glow of pride, which turns to shame when I remember what I've done. It may be my first mark, but it was also my first crime. *What was Obel thinking?* I try to keep my face calm. Mom can't know. "I'm exhausted, Mom. I never realized how much of their soul an inker leaves in each tattoo. I know it sounds weird, but it felt almost spiritual."

"Oh, Leora, that is amazing!" Her eyes look a bit wet. I hope she's not going to cry. "And it *is* exhausting. That's why marks are alive—can be read as living things—because of the energy poured into them. The life."

I'd never thought of that.

"So, what was the mark of?" Mom asks. She's just interested, but I change the subject.

"I can tell what you're doing," I say, and Mom raises her eyebrows. "You think that if you get me talking about all this, I'll forget about your side of the bargain."

"I don't remember actually agreeing to anything, Leora," she says as she pushes her plate away and goes back to the book.

"Don't, Mom." Suddenly the cozy evening falls away and all my calm evaporates. "I *know*, OK?" She sits back in her chair and looks at me in apparent confusion. "I know about Dad; I know that he had the mark—the crow. I remember seeing it when I was little. That time he hurt his head—remember?" She closes her eyes and I know she does. "And I think—I think that's why his book's been confiscated." I let my breath out in a sigh. I'm relieved to be able to admit what I know, but it's scary talking about it.

Mom sets the book to one side. She takes a deep breath and looks at me. "Do you trust me, Leora?" she asks.

My eyes fill with tears. This is one question I don't know how to answer. "I want to," I say, and my voice sounds small. "I always *have* trusted you. But now I don't know what to think. Show me I can. Tell me what's going on." I blink back the tears. I won't cry; even though my cheeks are hot and my nose is running, I refuse to cry. I'll show her I'm not a child.

"There are things that I promised your father I would never tell anyone—not even you." Her eyes implore me to listen, to believe her. "I can't betray him, love. I'm sorry."

I gulp back my anger. "But Dad is *dead*. He's not here. Those promises don't count any more."

Mom shakes her head and I see her eyes shining with tears too. I go round to her side of the table, trying to make her look at me: to really listen. I kneel next to her. "All these secrets, they're not helping Dad. He's going to be destroyed—somebody knows he was marked as forgotten, and unless we do something he will be." Mom puts a hand on my shoulder. "Why?" I whisper it.

This is the question I have dreaded asking. "Why was he marked?"

She moves to hold my hand and sits straighter in her chair. I'm looking up at her, so hopeful. But then: "I can't tell you, Leora."

I pull away in anger and she grips my arm. "Leora—please. Look at me. I want you to think back. Think back to the man you knew." I try not to close my eyes. I try not to remember. "You may hear rumors. You may hear gossip and whispers. But all that matters is that he is remembered for what he was: truly good. That . . . that mark didn't belong on his skin. He didn't deserve it." I try to interrupt but she holds up her hand. "And so it is gone. We have a friend who did all that was needed. We've known this was coming, Leora. We've saved money and planned everything. Your father *won't* be forgotten. You mustn't tell a soul, but you have nothing to worry about. I promise."

I stare at her. "What did you do?" I whisper. "You and this friend—what did you do?" She stands up from the table and takes her mug to wash it in the sink, leaving me kneeling on the floor looking after her.

"Mom!" I cry, and at the sound of my voice, she drops her mug in the sink and I hear it break. She turns to me with tears on her face and icy frustration in her voice.

"Leora. This is the only time I'll say this—so listen carefully. Do you remember seeing your father's book?" Slowly I nod. "We sat and looked through it together, didn't we? And did you see the mark?" I shake my head, mutely. She's right. We looked at every page, and there was no crow to blot those perfect pages.

"Well then—you should stop worrying. That book is all anyone will see. A good life. No one will know any different." She wipes a hand across her face and I see how tired she is. "I will not speak of this again, do you understand? And you must not either. Don't tell a soul, not even Verity. I mean it."

Mom leaves the room silently, a cold draft in her wake, and I'm left to pick the shards of broken ceramic from the soapy water. She's never spoken to me like that.

I grab a dirty plate and plunge it into the sink, distracted by my thoughts. I feel for the dish brush under the water and catch the back of my hand on a chunk of broken mug I hadn't seen under the suds. The bubbles turn pink as blood wafts through the water. I draw my hand out and see I've sliced deeply across the skin—as though my age marks were a "cut here" dotted line. The skin is already looking bruised around the cut and it's bleeding profusely—dripping down my wet wrist toward my elbow. I swallow as the pain begins to blossom and I call out: "Mom—I need you."

. . .

That night I dream I'm being flayed.

My skin is being sliced. Only instead of my marks being preserved, each one is being divided by the knife in two or three or four. Every bit of my meaning and my memory is being shattered and scattered. I am a puzzle that will never be pieced together.

chapter 21

I'M FAIRLY USELESS AT THE STUDIO THE NEXT DAY.
My hand doesn't hurt so much, but the bandage I need to wear
means I can't do a lot. Obel tuts at me when he sees me trying
to draw—badly—with my left hand. I can't quite meet his eye,
not after yesterday. He's been clever, I realize now; he must have
known that getting me to mark that woman was his best way of
making sure I'd keep his secret. If I tell anyone about the marks
he does out of hours, he can report me for inking a mark of
remembrance for a blank.

I spend most of the next day thinking about Oscar and worrying endlessly about his note. By the time Friday arrives, the

day he wants to meet, I've talked myself into and out of going a hundred times. I don't know anything about him, other than that he's the son of a convicted criminal. That's reason enough not to meet. *But he could help me*, I argue with myself. *My dad was a marked man too.*

In the end I decide I'm curious, and that's enough of a reason to go.

My thoughts help to break up the monotony of the day, spent helping to tidy shelves and organize things, greeting new clients and doing my best to avoid Karl. He's being extra mean to me today—messing up things I've cleaned up, jostling me to make me stumble and appear clumsy. It wouldn't surprise me if he was the one who put the feather in my pocket, just to freak me out; he's childish and vindictive enough. That's probably all it is—a prank—Karl trying to knock my focus on training, trying to put me off competing for the permanent job here. I don't want to think about how much it frightened me.

As if to punish me for my clumsiness, Obel lets Karl do lots of studio time. Karl is gloating and I'm nervous that he might be better than me. I've seen some of the drawings he's done and I have to admit he's good.

As I hang up my apron at the end of the day, Obel opens the door, but stops me before I leave. He's hardly spoken to me since I made the mark. "What were you today?"

I look at him in confusion. "I don't know what you mean," I say.

He looks at my hand and his lips grow thin. "You were nothing. An inker is *nothing* without his hands."

"Or *her* hands," I remind him.

"OK, or *her* hands. Be more careful, Leora—that's all."

I mumble an apology. Obel gives me a quick smile.

"See you Monday, girl."

I pull on my shawl and pause as I leave the door, taking a deep breath to harden my resolve. I can't help feeling that this meeting with Oscar will mean something—that I might find something out—and a large part of me doesn't want to. The part that wants to believe Mom when she says everything will be OK. But the curious part wins and I set off.

I check the town hall clock as I walk—it's almost six o'clock. I arrive at the square with a few minutes to spare and wait outside the gloomy government building. I shelter under a tree, listening to its remaining leaves rustling in the cold breeze. The statue of Saint watches over us; the sun makes the bronze of his sinewy features gleam. He looks like the human body pictures in our science textbooks; all you see is the muscles and tendons taut and defined over bones. With his flayed skin held like a robe around him, and despite the vulnerable flesh on display, he is poised and strong. The statue represents his tale perfectly—immortalized in the moment that should have been his undoing, at the hands of the White Witch. Being flayed couldn't kill him; it only set him free.

The little sections of grass are leaf-covered and patchy with mud now; it'll be spring before they're used for lunch break picnics again. I read some of the people as they walk past to pass the time. One woman stops near me to rearrange her shopping bags. I see her wrinkled hands as they weigh and repack the bags. Her age marks melt into movements that speak loudly of her life: a happy one. Until recently. I see the last few years are sodden with sadness and drenched with lonely tears. Without seeing more I can only guess at the reasons for her misery—maybe a death, maybe a different kind of loss, maybe a quarrel that never got resolved. I look at my own bandaged hand and wonder what my marks will say when I'm old. I'm so afraid of the sadness I've felt since Dad got ill. I'm so scared of it lasting forever. Is that it for me now? Will all my years be tainted by his absence?

Just as I'm dwelling on my cheerful thoughts I feel a hand on my shoulder. I turn around and see Oscar. He wears his bag strap across his chest and has rammed his hands back in his pockets. His glasses are slightly awry on his nose, and his curls are rumpled.

"You came," he says with an interested look on his face.

"You seem surprised!" I can't help but smile. It all seems so silly, as though we're playing at being grown-ups. Or spies. "I didn't feel like I had much choice." At that he lets out a laugh.

"Yeah, sorry about that—it was probably a bit more mysterious than it needed to be." He shuffles his feet in the fallen leaves and looks around. "So, do you feel like a walk?"

I nod, and we set off at a slow pace, kicking the leaves as we go.

We walk in silence away from the government building. At least, we don't *say* anything—my mind is anything but silent. Before we've walked ten steps my brain has already tried to decide what his tattoos mean (I see one that looks like tree bark climbing his neck), and suddenly the thought pops into my mind—does he have a girlfriend? I toss that thought out quickly.

He glances at me. "Same café as last time OK?"

I hesitate. "Actually, I have somewhere else in mind."

"Sure." His expression is mildly curious.

"Come on, then." He follows as I set off walking toward the museum. It's just across the square and it's still open. A curator I don't recognize murmurs, "We shut at seven," as we walk past the welcome desk. I smile and nod. Plenty of time.

"The museum—really? You don't mind coming back?" Oscar whispers as he takes off his hat and folds it into his bag.

"I can't stay away forever," I whisper back. "Besides, there's something I want to show you."

There are two staircases on either side of the entrance foyer that curl their way up to the same floor. I used to make Dad wait for ages until I chose which side to go up.

I start up the steps and Oscar follows. I know exactly where I want to go. Dad used to bring me to the museum on Saturday mornings while Mom slept in. We would try to see a different part each time, but we always ended up in the same place. Our place.

There are inscriptions in the stone walls as we climb the stairs, framed pictures, a worn brass handrail. The steps are worn too—just on one side, as though everyone throughout history has chosen the quickest route up and down. I always walk up on the other, neglected side of the steps.

Our steps echo as we climb the stairs—a little song of ascent.

When we reach the first floor we pause. If we carried on up the next flight of steps, we would reach the floor with the skin books—the ones that belong to people who don't have family to care for them anymore. They stay here, in the museum, so that the community can honor and remember them even when they have no loved ones to greet them each day.

Instead we walk through the arched entrance off the first staircase to the floor dedicated to our history. The rooms filled with our fables.

Everything about this place reminds me of Dad. It's like he's here, as though if I just turn the corner he'll be bending over a display, saying, "Leora, come here—look at this one." He loved this place so much. He loved all these stories.

"Right." Oscar looks around at the glass cases housing so many pages and relics: the artifacts of our past. Some cases have books of fables open so we can read our town's tales; others have beautiful artwork and handmade figurines telling our history: the stories that tell us how our community began and the way its beginnings continue to shape it. "So why are we here? Fancied a bedtime story?" He wanders to a case and looks in. "I don't think I've properly been here since I was a kid." The lights shine on the exhibits, and because there is no daylight coming from the atrium, it leaves the rest of the space in shadow, the displays glowing like ghosts.

"Are they just stories?" I ask curiously. "I mean, this is our history, our faith."

In the gloom I see his eyebrows furrow.

"I suppose that's what we've been told," he says, leaning against one of the glass cases. "*The stories are our past. Through our past we shall live our present.*" It's a quote from the town's creed, which we all had to learn at school.

"You say that like it's a bad thing." I look around to see if there's anyone nearby who might hear us. There's only one other person browsing, and he's on the other side of the room. I don't know why I'm nervous—we're just talking, and that's no crime. Is it? "You don't really choose whether to believe history."

I'm grateful for the half light that hides my blush. I'm not used to arguing. I'm not used to needing to.

"So you think all this actually happened?" There's an odd little smile playing about his mouth. He gestures at the displays and I look around at the pictures of Saint and the White Witch and all the other players in our community's story. I take in the old texts opened at the pages where their stories have sat for years. I think of Mel with the tales drawn on her skin and the statue of Saint and all that I learned at school.

"Of course it did." I am defiant, feeling brave in the low light, not able to see his reaction. "I mean—some of them sound like stories because they're so old. Some of them have made-up parts—because that was how people thought of things back then. But the truth is in there. It's like . . ." I close my eyes and think of how my dad used to explain them to me. "It's like a flower: the pretty part with all the petals are the bits that are made up, and the root is the truth. The stuff that really happened." There's something about not being able to see his face perfectly that makes me feel I could whisper secrets and it would almost be like talking to myself. "Everyone knows that."

"Maybe." He sighs quietly and turns to the exhibit of the White Witch, leaning to look more closely at the glass case. "This one always scared me when I was little. When I still believed in fairy stories." He rests his hand on the glass, over the illustration of the White Witch and her chilling, ghostly face.

I move to stand next to him and point out one of the smaller illustrations. Beautiful Moriah is shown discovering her marks for the first time, while her new husband looks on in delighted astonishment. Meanwhile, the White Witch stares out, her skin blank and terrible. The pages of these old books remind me of the stained glass in the hall of judgment. "Actually, this is my favorite story." My hand is next to his and the glass is starting to fog from the heat of my skin.

"Why's it your favorite?" He turns, and his face seems very close to mine. "I wouldn't have thought witches were your thing."

"How would you know what my kind of thing is?" I realize how prickly I sound. "Anyway, I just love the story. It's comforting." He has strolled on a ways but now he turns and looks back at me.

"How is it comforting?" he asks quietly.

I follow him. "Well—Moriah's marks appearing as her father told her they would—his dying wish coming true. And the White Witch being banished. I love that the good sister wins." He stops suddenly and I almost walk into him as he turns to look at me. He's so close I can feel the heat from his body, and I breathe him in. There's a warmth in my lungs that makes me nervous, but it's a kind of nervous I don't mind. He doesn't move, so I take a step back.

"How the good sister wins," he repeats slowly, musingly.

He walks on, farther away from the little light there is, and I think I hear him sigh.

"Anyway, my dad used to bring me here. It reminds me of him." I feel a little defensive. It's like sharing a book you've loved only to have that person say they thought it was silly.

"When did he die?" he asks, still standing with his back to me.

"Almost three months ago. Sometimes it feels like yesterday—"

"—and sometimes it feels like years have passed," he finishes. I nod and blink back tears.

"You know. Who have you lost?" There's silence and I feel awkward. "I'm sorry—I just assumed."

I sigh and sit down with my back against the display case. The other visitor has left and we've got the space to ourselves now. The carpet is rough and I let my finger trace the ugly pattern. I keep my bandaged hand on my lap and feel it throbbing with my frustrated heartbeat. The silence drags until Oscar sits down next to me.

"My mom. She died when I was eleven. She got sick." He brushes invisible fluff from his knees. "I'm sorry about your dad."

"I'm sorry about your mom," I reply quietly.

We sit quietly and minutes pass. Or maybe seconds. I can't tell.

"What did you do to your hand?" Oscar asks.

"A dish-washing accident." I giggle.

"Ah, it's a dangerous business—I'd avoid it if I were you." I can hear the smile in his voice.

"I saw you. At the marking," I tell him, and my fingers pause from their tracing.

"Oh?" He is unnervingly still. I should shut up. I should stop but I can't now.

"It was your dad, wasn't it?" There. I've said it.

He sighs and straightens his legs. He rests his head against the display cabinet as he looks toward the ceiling. "I wondered whether you had seen me. I saw you there, at the back—I recognized you. Dad had pointed you out to me once in the street."

I frown at this. Pointed me out? Why would his father have known who I was?

"But yes—that was my father. Marked in the town square. Forgotten now. He's still in prison; they haven't let him go free yet, even after what they've done to him." His hand slams down on the floor. "And, now, that's it." He pauses and starts drawing with his finger on the floor between us too, his hand scarily close to mine. "But you'd know something about that, wouldn't you, Leora?" His little finger brushes mine and I freeze.

"What do you mean? What are you talking about?"

"Your dad."

"Whatever you think you know—" I swallow down my fear, but I can feel my breath and my chest shaking. I stagger upright.

"Leora, it's all right," he says calmly as he gets to his feet. "I don't *know* anything—I'm just putting two and two together. Why else would your dad's book be confiscated? Why else would you be so afraid? Just tell me, just say it—he was a forgotten too."

I drop my head into my hands. I've said nothing and yet I've said too much. In the darkness behind my hands I hear Oscar whisper: "I'm sorry. I'm so sorry."

With my face still hidden by my hands I tell him the story of seeing my father's mark when I was a little girl. I leave nothing out—telling it for the first time feels cathartic. Dangerous too.

"Mom's right, though," I finish, emerging with my face flushed. "There was nothing there when we saw his book. It must have been removed somehow." Am I imagining it, or does Oscar's face flinch when I say that? "But if they haven't found the mark, then why would his book be confiscated?" I finish and look up at Oscar. "Mom says it will all be OK, but how can it be?" A tear spills out onto my cheek and before I can wipe it away, Oscar brushes my cheek with the cuff of his jacket. I take some deep breaths and thankfully he gives me a moment to recover.

"Leora . . ." Oscar is looking at the ugly carpet now, as though he's trying to find the right words. "There's something I have to tell you."

I sniff hard. "What?"

He is still looking at the floor and suddenly I feel my neck prickle. I'm so stupid. Why didn't I see it before?

"Just say it, Oscar," I say roughly.

He looks at me then. "My dad—well, you know what he was punished for. For stealing someone's skin." He passes a hand over his eyes. I am right. I know the words he's about to say before he says them, and my heart nearly stops in horror. "The skin he stole—it was your father's."

chapter 22

"TELL ME A STORY, DADDY," I WOULD BEG. "TELL ME the one about you and Mommy."

Mom would protest, "Oh, not again, Leora. You've heard it so many times."

But Dad's eyes would sparkle and, with a grin, he would begin. "You've heard of love at first sight? You've heard of a prince that falls in love with the beautiful maiden the moment he sees her? You've heard the fairy tales and the happily ever afters?"

I would nod, eyes wide.

"Well, that's not our story." And Mom would try to hide her smile.

. . .

They met when Dad moved to Saintstone. Back then, readers were more respected; it wasn't just bereft children asking Mom to find out family secrets from their dead relative's skin book or possessive lovers asking her to read infidelity on their partner's skin. She had a contract with the government that meant she would read any newcomers to the town and ensure they were suitable for employment. She would make recommendations for their work placements and vouch for their trustworthiness.

The story goes that she arrived for Dad's reading in the government building and that he was there, waiting nervously in a bare room, ready to be examined. The way Mom tells it, it was just a routine appointment; she saw all she needed to see, recommended him for flaying, and that was that. But Dad's version is different.

Dad would say that Mom came in, all frowns and paperwork. She didn't look at his face, just at his skin, and all the time Dad was trying to talk to her. Mom, ever the professional, ignored him and kept reading, making notes as she did so. She made him turn around so she could read his back, and the next thing Dad knew, she was weeping with laughter, completely helpless, tears running down her face as she covered her mouth and laughed and laughed and laughed. Eventually someone knocked on the door to see if Mom was all right, took one look at Dad and ran off, only to return a moment later with some underpants for him to wear, scolding him: *"You're not supposed to take* everything *off!*" Eventually, once Dad was a little more clothed, Mom calmed down enough to continue the assessment, letting out the odd giggle and apologizing for her impropriety.

When Dad told the rest of the story Mom would nod and smile; they had become friends that day and had fallen in love soon after, and although Mom's parents disapproved of the match, they married a year later.

It was only when I got older that I really thought about the story and, well, no one wants to think about their parents naked. Utterly mortified, I never asked for the story after that. Now I would do anything to hear it, just to listen to his voice again.

When I wake the next morning, I wonder if it was all some strange anxiety dream. I wish it had been.

I go down to the kitchen early, shivering in my nightclothes. Mom is up already, or maybe she never slept. Of course, she knew it all. When I told her about Connor Drew last night, she cried. For the first time since this all happened I feel like I've seen a wave of uncertainty, a little chink in her resolve.

Now, this morning, she comes to me and clings to me and I break her grip on my hand as gently as I can and reach to get a mug.

"I'm happy you know the truth, Leora." Her eyes follow me anxiously. "Did this boy—Oscar?—did he say anything else? Connor hasn't . . . hasn't let anything slip has he?"

"I've told you all I know, Mom. Connor's still under arrest because he won't talk; he hasn't told them where he kept his work and so far nobody has found it. It's not good, Mom, but for now, I think Dad is still safe. They might know, but they can't prove anything."

I pour water into my mug, spilling a little on the wooden work surface.

"They would have told me." Mom speaks quietly, more to reassure herself than to share with me. "Yes, I'm sure they would have said if there was trouble." I mop up the spilled water with a cloth. Mom is still murmuring her anxious thoughts, so I hug her, damp cloth still in one hand.

"Mom," I say gently, "who are *they*?" The idea that there are more people out there, people like Connor, makes me feel uneasy. I can't forget what Mayor Longsight said about Connor working to help the blanks. But she just shakes her head.

"Listen, it's going to be OK," I say. I'm the calm one now. One of us has to be. "Whatever happens, whatever it takes, I will make sure Dad is safe." Mom nods into my neck.

"Thank you, sweetheart," she sighs. "God, I should never have involved you in all this." She lets go of me and wipes her eyes. Clearing her throat and blinking, she looks at me sternly. "We have nothing to worry about. We'll do what we've always done: heads down; be normal, helpful citizens." She breathes deeply to collect herself and eventually smiles. "I'm sorry, darling. It really will be all right."

I nod. But she can't pretend to me; her fear was the most real thing I've seen from her in weeks.

. . .

The next few weeks at the studio are quiet. I can't believe my first month is nearly over. I'm still waiting for my hand to be healed enough to work on customers, so I spend most of my time in the back, out of the way of the ink and needles. This lesson in frustration is confirming to me how much I want this life—how much I want to be free to mark and to create and to feel that amazing connection again. Plus, I am having to watch Karl steal my opportunities to work and practice. Every time Obel calls him into the studio to help him, Karl takes the chance to walk past me and knock my elbow as I draw. Or he'll make a joke about my being too lazy to work when he knows how desperate I am to be able to. At this rate he's certain to get the job. I wish I knew whether it was him who planted that feather in my pocket. I could just come out and ask him but it's not like he'd tell me the truth anyway. Mel sends me little cards with words of encouragement, little quotes from fables. They're at once heartening and confusing. Just fairy stories, Oscar said.

Obel has given me work to do: I'm to make a study of classic marks and tattoos that have gone out of favor in recent years. Obel says that knowing the history and tradition is crucial to being a great inker; the meaning behind the marks is everything. We all learn what the common marks mean in school: We know that a thin red line on someone's left arm means they've stolen something. A thick red line means it's more serious and they committed a violent theft. We know that a leaf at the base of a tree means someone died. But an inker has to know more than that. They have to know that calendula signifies grief and a foxglove is for protection. I enjoy the task; all these old marks and their tales remind me of story time with Dad, or wandering through the museum.

Oscar's voice rings in my ears—*When I still believed in fairy stories.* I push it away.

Today, Friday, while Karl is busy in the studio, Obel wanders in to check on me. I have been playing with Dad's wooden leaf, which hangs around my neck, and now I tuck it back into my tunic. I don't know why, but I don't want him to see.

As instructed, I've been making notes and copying some of the marks that most appeal to me. He takes up the pages I've been working on and flicks through them. "Interesting. Tell me about this," he says, putting one of the pieces of paper I've been working on next to me on the desk. "Why did you draw this one?"

It's a scruffily drawn sketch of the White Witch from the fable, a copy of an unusual drawing I found in one of the old books that had caught my eye. I shift in my seat, feeling embarrassed.

"I know, it's not very good. I had just never seen her drawn like this before. Usually she's portrayed as a terrifying creature, but there is something so beautiful about this image." I look from the picture to Obel's curious face and shyly admit, "I liked it."

He gives a little nod and sets down the rest of my notes. "I like it too, actually. Have you ever seen anyone with this mark?"

I get the feeling that he's not just chatting—that there's a meaning behind his words, an intent. He's watching me. Trying to catch me out, somehow. I look closely at the sketch and rub my finger over the pencil lines. I try to think—have I ever seen her on anyone's skin? Why would anyone want to mark themselves with the terrible White Witch? I look up to Obel, who is still looking at me intently.

"I've not seen it before, no. Have you?"

He suddenly smiles broadly at me and it's as though some secret has been passed between us. "That'd be telling, wouldn't it, girl?" he says with a wry chuckle. "I'll be back in a minute. I've got a book I think you might like."

He goes to his storeroom and is out of sight for a moment. He returns with a book that looks antique. He lays its heft gently on the wooden desk and I gasp. It's an old book of fairy tales. But not just *any* book of fairy tales. I recognize the cover plate illustration from the museum. "Is this the *Encyclopedia of Tales*?" I ask, astonished, and I reach out to touch it with shaking hands. Obel sits on a chair next to mine and nods at me, his eyes sparkling with excitement.

"You've seen it before?" he asks as he gently opens the cover.

I can't resist leaning forward for a closer look.

"No—at least, not in real life." I reach out to touch the thick parchment with its embossed text. "They mention it in a display in the museum but I thought it was lost. I didn't think there were any copies left."

Obel pulls the book nearer to us and carefully turns the pages. He touches it like it's a frail friend. It feels like a book of spells: titles in careful calligraphic script, painstakingly perfect penmanship, each page hand-painted. The colors are faded, an autumnal version of their first shades. As each page turns, a waft of musty, tobacco-stained scent fills my nostrils. I never understood Verity's obsession with the smell of old books, but now I am intoxicated. Obel is as bewitched as I am. I reach out to feel a page—to touch the paper-leaf fragility of this amazing book that I thought no longer existed.

"Why would you show me this? Why would you let *me* look at something so precious?"

He stops for a moment, while he looks at me thoughtfully. "I don't know. I think I knew you would love it too." He carries on turning the pages, avoiding my gaze. I look at the marks on his arms and wish they would stop being mute—I want them to tell me something about this man who makes me feel so uneasy, and yet so understood. He catches me looking and I glance away quickly.

"Here," he says, opening the book at the page he's been searching for, "here she is."

I lean in for a closer look and she's right there. The White Witch. It's just like the picture I sketched from, but larger, and so much more detailed. I'm struck by the peculiarity of seeing a completely naked woman. There is nothing at all on her. Not a stitch of clothing and not a drop of ink. She is completely blank. The image makes me tremble—the inhumanness of her, the unreadableness. She is the Queen of Lies and the Keeper of Secrets. And yet, here, she is also enchanting and strikingly beautiful. High cheekbones, which in the smaller picture made her look cruel, here just make her appear fragile, and yet her stance is so bold. She doesn't look like she's trying to hide anything, even though I know she holds deception beneath that perfect skin. The whole picture, on this scale, feels dissident. I feel strangely uneasy. Someone so terrible—so utterly blank—should not be so beautiful.

"Draw her again, Leora," Obel says as he leaves the room. "Draw her from the original."

I pick up my pencil and a new piece of paper, and, with a nameless fear in my heart, begin to copy her empty form. Her hair swirls like roses, like ocean waves. Her small breasts are almost hidden by her flowing locks. She reminds me of the mermaids on Dad's skin and she is no less beguiling. It's only when I've been drawing for ten minutes or more that I see it. As I shade the cut of her jaw and the slant of her nose, as I draw the arch of her eyebrow and the gentle, but proud, smile, I see it.

She's me. I am her. I am the exact image of the White Witch.

I look up and Obel is watching me. Our eyes meet and I stand up, dropping my pencil. I slam the book shut, not caring any longer about its age or its value.

"I . . . I've forgotten—my mother needed me back early. Is that—"

He nods without speaking.

I shove my papers in my bag, pick up my pencil from the hard stone floor, and stumble out of the room. I shut the door behind me and leave, grateful for the fresh, cold air to revive my frightened mind.

I walk mindlessly for a while, letting my flushed cheeks cool and allowing my shaking hands to go still in my pockets. When I come to, I find myself at the museum again, looking up at the imposing metal doors. I let my legs take me up the cool steps. I make my way up into mine and Dad's place. The place of stories.

It used to be my safe place.

I try to recapture the memories of me and Dad looking at each glass case, whispering, laughing, pointing, and reading. I try to conjure up that feeling of warmth, of curiosity that comes when you feel safe. I pause when I reach the case dedicated to the White Witch.

I read the short description on the thick card next to her picture. THE WHITE WITCH. DEVIANT SISTER OF MORIAH; ENEMY OF SAINT. I remember how Dad used to linger here; how he used to always make me stand and look.

"What did you want me to see?" I whisper to Dad. And there she is. Looking back at me with my own eyes.

As I walk home I think of her fable. The story of that White Witch who is, apparently, so like me. Shivering in the weak winter sun, I tighten my shawl around my head, unravel the bandage around my hand and throw it in a bin. I look at my hand, at the mark that will become a scar, at the paleness of my skin, and all I see is *her* skin—her terrifying blank beauty. And I run.

chapter 23

I WAKE TOO EARLY THE NEXT MORNING. THE SUN IS just barely shining on the remnants of the night's dew and I wonder if we'll be due a frost soon—it's cold enough, surely. I catch a glimpse of my empty skin in the mirror and hurriedly pull on my dressing gown. I can't stay like this; the need to think of a first mark feels more urgent than ever. But I still can't decide. Every time I think of something that appeals I overanalyze it and can't commit. What if I end up without marks—as pure and blank as the White Witch, whose cold eyes I share? I shudder.

I wrap myself in a blanket and flop onto the faded red sofa near the front door. The springs gave up their springiness ages ago and the cushions sag, but it's still the most comfortable sofa in the world. Maybe I should light a fire, but it would involve going outside to the yard to get wood and I can't quite face getting colder in order to get warm again.

Closing my eyes, I doze for a while, until I'm almost warm enough to take my dressing gown off. I heave myself out of the sagging sofa and decide to treat myself to some hot chocolate. Maybe I'll make a cup for Mom, like Dad used to do when she had her Saturday sleep-ins. She's still in bed now, luxuriating in her morning off. Some things haven't changed.

I make it just as Dad used to. First I pour milk into two mugs to make certain we've got enough, and then I empty them into the pan. I let the milk heat gently on the stove while I chop some dark chocolate into small chunks. I'm using my favorite kitchen knife and only feel a hint of pain in my bad hand as the blade thuds through the chocolate. As tiny bubbles fizz at the edge of the pan, I drop the chocolate into the milk. Fragments stick to my fingers and melt. I rub my hands together and smell my palms, inhaling the warm, spicy aroma. I stir the chocolate gently so it doesn't stick to the bottom of the pan, and grate orange rind over the swirling milk. The liquid begins to look murky, as morsels of melting chocolate rise to the surface. I stir more quickly now, letting foam form as I whisk. Before it boils—*just* before those first bubbles of air gasp to the surface—I pour the hot chocolate into the two mugs. Flecks of orange rind float on the milky foam and I carry the mugs carefully up to Mom's bedroom.

She's propped up on a large cushion, and her book is in her hand—but she isn't looking at it. She is staring straight ahead and her face is desperately worried.

As I walk in, she smiles and raises herself to sit.

"Hello, love, how long have you been up?" She sees the hot chocolate and grins. "What a treat! I haven't had hot chocolate brought to me in bed since—" She catches herself, winces, then takes a cup of steaming hot chocolate from me, and I put mine on her bedside table while I settle myself next to her under the covers.

"Not too long. It's freezing, so I thought I'd make something warm." I reach to get my hot chocolate and lift it gently, careful not to spill a drop on Mom's bedclothes. I am still for a while, enjoying the fragrant blend of the citrusy chocolate and the scent of Mom's perfume mixed in with the warm smell of sleep.

Mom wriggles a bit to bring her covers up higher on her chest and takes a sip of her drink. "Are things all right between us, love?" Her voice is cautious and quiet and she's looking at the wall straight ahead. "All I ever want to do is keep you safe. You know that, don't you?"

"I know, Mom." I edge a little closer to her and quickly slurp a bit of hot chocolate when I see it almost swill over the edge of the mug. "And I know you think you need to protect me, but I'm fine. I'm not a child anymore."

"Oh, but you are," Mom says, nudging me in the ribs. "You're my child forever, even when you're eighty." Mom moves her cup to her other hand and puts her arm around me. "My child for-ever," she says again, so quietly I can hardly catch it.

We snuggle together in silence for a while and I feel safe and sleepy. Mom's breath shudders and I realize she's crying. I put my drink down and cuddle against her chest.

Her tears drip onto my hair and she whispers, "You're a good girl, Leora."

We stay like that until our drinks have gone cold and I'm on the verge of sleep. Mom stirs me with a tight squeeze, and clears her throat.

"Well, I can't stay in my nightclothes all day. I'd better get going." She gives my head a kiss and strokes my hair where her tears dripped.

I right myself and stretch while I give a drowsy nod.

"You know I love you, don't you?"

I smile and open a sleepy eye. "You're my mom—you don't get a choice!" She shakes her head at me while she smiles and swats my head.

"Do you want me to heat up your hot chocolate again? I'm going to do mine." I pass her my mug and snuggle down in her warm bed while she goes and refreshes our drinks.

I wake up to find my cold chocolate on the bedside table. How long have I been asleep? Reluctantly I throw off the covers and carry my drink downstairs. There is a pot of coffee steaming on the table, and Mom is on the sofa reading a book. I tip my drink away and pour coffee into a clean mug. I hold it in both hands and take a sip. It's hot enough to wake me up a little, and I murmur a sleepy hello to Mom.

My eyes rest on the plain-looking shelves of our ancestors. Colors from their marks peep out at me. It's been a long time since I've properly looked at their books. You'd think we'd do it all the time, but really they're like a favorite novel—once you've read it you know the story, but you still need to know it's nearby just in case you need to read it again. They're all Mom's family, though. Because Dad didn't grow up here, we don't have any of his ancestors. Their absence always seems to throw the shelf off balance.

I place my cup on the table and reach up to get a book at random off the shelf. I ask my ancestors' permission and pray a blessing on their memory and honor. I lay the book softly on the table. Mom looks up and smiles for a second before she's drawn back to the words in her hands. I look at the cover. It's Bill Tomlinson—Mom's father, my grandfather. He was a tanner, and he died before I was born. I've sometimes wondered whether he was desperate to get away from my grandma's nagging. The way Mom talks about her, she sounds like she was a nightmare. She doesn't talk about either of her parents much, though.

I turn the pages and his marks come to life. I see his childhood—his brothers who loved him and teased him, his sister who died. I see his work and his career progressing with each new age mark. I see the marriage mark and am stunned by its intricate beauty. There's no doubt—he wasn't trying to get away from Grandma—they adored each other. She died soon after him; maybe her heart was too broken. I wonder what it must be like to find the love of your life, to love and be loved so completely—and then I realize I am gazing at what was my granddad's backside, and I turn the page in a hurry.

And here it is—always the most splendid set of marks— Granddad's family tree. His parents are here, his brothers and the lost sister—her name was Sophie. My mom must have been named after her. I can read the closeness that was between Granddad and his little sister. I can read the sorrow and loss too.

Then there's Mom's name—with space left next to her. Maybe they'd hoped to have more children. Dad's name is next—a little lower than Mom's. I love seeing those letters and I feel the warmth of happy memories flicker in my mind. But then I look more closely, and I am transported, as though I am seeing through Granddad's eyes. All I can see is blackness around Dad's name. There's a heaviness in my heart. There is no love, no joy, no affection here. I feel an alien sense of rage and revulsion that can only come from my grandfather.

I look away in shock. It is absolutely clear that Granddad hated my father. No; he *despised* him. The sourness of the emotion taints the whole tree and I'm left feeling sick.

All the warmth has left my skin and I reach a shaking hand toward my cup of coffee. I bring it to my lips but manage to miss my mouth, spilling scalding liquid onto the book. I leap up, grab a cloth, and soak up the spill. Thankfully skin books are resilient and the ink won't smudge, but I'm afraid that I might have damaged some of the preservative, and that his book will warp and degrade. Mom shoots a look at me and gasps as she sees what I've done. She springs out of the sofa and sees the page I've been reading.

"What do you think you're doing?" she hisses, wrenching it away. "You stupid, *stupid* girl."

chapter 24

M OM RECOVERS QUICKLY. SHE APOLOGIZES AND
dabs at the book, which I've already cleaned. Her steely
composure is back in place. There are more secrets here,
though: secrets around Granddad and why he hated my father.
I can't bear it; it feels like walking through sand, all unsteady on
my feet. I need something solid. I grab my coat, shawl, and bag
and head to Verity's.

It's started to rain and the drops are so painfully cold it feels
like hail. My hair and face are covered by my shawl and I walk
quickly. Only my eyes peep out, and my fast breath warms my

cheeks. My head is dipped down, and I pass people without looking up, without acknowledging or reading them.

My mind is heavy with the excess of confusing thoughts. Oscar, Obel, Mom, Dad—lies and uncertainty surround each of them. *At least there's still Verity*, I think to myself gratefully as I reach her house. The door is answered quickly by Seb. He greets me with his ever-present smile and invites me in.

I love reading Seb—I can see the real story.

There was an awful time a few years ago when he came home pale and tearstained. A group of boys had surrounded him, laughing at his arms so bare of qualifications and achievement marks. They had threatened to mark him with a compass and had called him a stupid blank.

But I can see the heart beneath Seb's skin. I can see how he adores his sister and would fiercely protect her should the need ever arise. I can see that he's more worthy of honor than most. And there are marks there now—not many, but there are his baker's qualification and the times he's won star employee.

"How's life as an inker?" Seb asks as he hangs my coat up.

"It's fun, Seb. I'm really enjoying it," I say, smiling as I lay my wet shawl over the back of a chair to dry it out a bit. "How about you? How's the bakery?"

Seb moves the chair a little closer to the roaring fire so my shawl will dry more quickly. "It's all right—I got employee of the month last week. They gave me a bottle of wine."

"Employee of the month? Again?" I smile and give Seb a hug. "That's brilliant! So where's this wine, then?"

"I'm not sharing," Seb quips, and I laugh just as Verity comes down to the kitchen.

"Ah! I thought I heard you!" Verity gives me a hug. For a moment she looks tired and a little distracted, but the next she brightens and seems herself again. She's wearing a scruffy knitted sweater, which I think she's had since she was twelve, and has on the soft, baggy pants we used to wear for sports at school.

"What do you look like, Vetty?" I say, shaking my head.

She gives a twirl and struts comically across the kitchen to the kettle.

"I know, right?" She flashes me a smile while she fills the kettle with water and places it on the stove. "I'm tired of wearing my tight work stuff. Today I'm all about the comfort!"

For a beautiful girl, she's really good at looking like a mess. I love her for it.

I spend a truly relaxed afternoon at Verity's. We talk about people from school who we've caught glimpses of through the week, and Verity fills me in on some of the nastier girls from school, who have ended up working at the government as admin staff. She's been really enjoying being able to boss them around and seeing their passive frustration build. Only Verity would cope so well with the role reversal. I know if it was me, I would still blush furiously every time I spoke to them, and would somehow end up doing their work for them. I need to go to "be more like Verity" classes. Her boss is really pleased with her and she's been told she can make the move to the Funerary Department. Her eyes sparkle with excitement when she tells me about it. "I'm going to have my own office and *everything*."

When I tell her about my first tattoo, Verity squeals gratifyingly.

"Oh *wow*! Do you think you'll be able to ink me? How amazing would that be?" She pulls up one of the legs of her pants. "I'm starting to think I want my ink to be like a vine, starting here"—she points to her calf—"and kind of showing different fruit as it grows. What do you think?"

"I think you should make an appointment," I say with a smile.

I'd love to ink my friend. If we can't have our marks done at the same time at least I will be able to be there and be a part of her first mark. I can see vines and fruit on Verity. I'll have to ask Obel what he thinks.

Obel. I remember my last moments in the studio and shiver.

"Have you ever seen the White Witch tattooed on anyone?" I venture. Verity's eyebrows rise and she leans toward me conspiratorially.

"No! I didn't know it was allowed, somehow. To have yourself marked with someone so evil—the first blank. What have you seen—was it on some sleazy old man's bum?" She shudders gleefully, clearly excited to hear some gossip from my side of the studio.

"Urgh! Verity! No, nothing like that. I've never seen one, obviously—who would choose it? But her picture was in this book of old marks—tattoos that people used to actually have. Well, it seemed so odd. I can't imagine anyone wanting it, even years and years ago." I weigh up what to say next—I don't want to regret saying too much. "So it's not come up in your work at the archives?"

Verity rolls her eyes. "Nope, nothing that interesting. There's so much to slog through." She hesitates, her eyes distracted, before pulling herself together and smiling at me—and do I imagine it, or is her smile wary? "I'm glad to be moving on. I feel like I'm actually about to start work properly. But I'll tell you if I hear about any weirdos with a White Witch fetish!"

As the light gets dimmer I hug Verity and Seb, and head toward home. My shawl is deliciously warm around my neck and the rain has stopped. I'm relieved that Mom's not downstairs when I get in. I make myself a sandwich and hide out in my room for the rest of the evening. I go to bed early.

And I dream.

. . .

I'm in the inking studio and each of my ancestors is there—in the flesh, not just their papery forms. And they're yelling at Obel and me. They're all saying that they get to choose my first mark and they're all shouting out words that I can't quite make out. Until all their voices merge into one and then I hear what they're saying, and the word they scream is "Crow, crow, crow."

chapter 25

THE WEEKS PASS—ONE, THEN TWO—AND FINALLY my hand is completely better. There will be a scar, but I can use it well enough. I'm thrilled to be back in the studio and getting to work. I've missed it. Plus, anywhere is better than the atmosphere at home right now. Mom's been so quiet, but she won't admit that she's worried, which just makes me more anxious.

I reach the studio early on Monday morning and Obel lets me in. He's been writing in a notebook that he tucks away when he sees me. We both spend time quietly preparing things for the day ahead. I keep meaning to ask him why he made me draw the

White Witch the other week—whether it's my imagination that tells me she looks just like me—but every time there's a chance I lose courage.

I'm absorbed in my thoughts and don't notice Karl come in until he knocks over the inks as he passes me.

"Pay attention, Leora!" Obel calls out crossly. He throws a rag my way and my cheeks burn as I clear up the ink.

Why can't I just say, "It was Karl"? Why do I let everyone walk over me and make me feel like a clumsy child? Karl's mocking smile doesn't help and my fist tightens around the inky rag while I tell myself to calm down. I slow my breathing, forcing myself to relax and rinse out the rag and hang it over the tap.

"Right, you two," Obel says, grabbing his keys and a leather bag from the table, "I've got an errand to run and there are no appointments this morning. We'll open up the shop a little later today. While I'm gone you can give the studio a good clean—that floor could do with a sweep as well." He shoulders his bag and leaves out the back door.

I glance at Karl, who is looking smug and annoying as ever. "I don't think either of us wants to spend more time together than we need to," he says as he opens the store cupboard and removes a few cleaning items. "One of us can clean the studio and the other can do in here."

I shrug in agreement and opt to do the back room; this way, Karl has to clean the bathrooms.

Doing the cleaning feels mercifully therapeutic and I lose myself in it. An hour passes. I stand back to see if I've missed anything. It's looking fine so I decide to carry on with my reading. The shop bell rings; a customer must have come in. I can hear Karl answering the door and the murmur of voices. He must be telling them to come back when Obel is here.

About half an hour later Obel returns, seeming cheerful after whatever his errand involved. The back room is looking beautiful, and it's shiningly clean.

"Thanks, girl." Obel smiles as he hangs up his bag.

He heads to the studio with his keys in his hand and I follow.

I hear the familiar buzzing of the inking machine before I step through the door. Obel stops abruptly and then his keys clash on the slate floor and Karl looks up. With a slow click the machine switches off, and we survey the scene in absolute, chilling silence.

Karl was marking the customer himself, unsupervised. The man lifts his head; he looks pale against the black of the chair, his brow glowing with a sheen of pain-induced sweat. Obviously bewildered by the sudden silence—and perhaps relieved to have a momentary reprieve from the sting, he raises himself to sit. Obel steps forward and takes the machine from Karl's hand.

"I'll take it from here. Step into the back, please, Karl." There's a cold, stony quality to his voice that makes me shiver.

Karl flushes red and walks into the back room with his head held high. Obel turns to the customer.

"I'll be with you in just a moment." He follows Karl into the back room. "Leora, lay out the inks."

I quickly gather the equipment from around the studio and lay it out for Obel without speaking. I hear Obel's voice, low but full of barely controlled anger, as I pass the door to the back room.

"What the hell did you think you were doing? Are you an idiot?" He's whispering, but his quiet voice just makes his anger more electric.

I look at the man waiting on the chair and give him a smile that I intend to be reassuring but probably shows exactly how mortified I feel. I wonder if Karl will still have a job after this is over. There is the sound of a chair being scraped across the slate floor and then silence.

Obel comes back looking completely calm. He has gone into inker mode and is chatting with the man about his mark. He dismisses me with a wave of his hand and I head to the back room.

Karl is sitting in a chair and his face has the embarrassed expression of a naughty toddler. He gets up when I come in.

"You could have stuck up for me." I'm so surprised that I just stare at him. He eyes me with absolute contempt.

"Why should I?" My voice is shaking. "What you did was crazy."

He's still holding his gloves and I can imagine the ink and blood smeared on the fingertips. He shoves them into a trash can roughly.

"Do you fancy him? Is that what it is?" Karl's face is flushed. "You've been his favorite from the start." He looks like he's about to cry or hit me, or both.

"Why did you do it? You must have known he'd be furious."

He shrugs. "I didn't plan it—but when the customer came in I just—I thought when Obel saw what I could do, he might start taking me seriously—"

"Well, I'm sure it'll be OK." I don't know why I'm trying to reassure him, but I make my voice soothing. I sit down at one of the tall stools at the counter. "Just give him some time to cool down." I step past him and get out my drawing things. I sit and with a shaking hand begin to sketch out some marks I've been thinking of, hoping that if I ignore him Karl will leave me alone and calm down. "He likes you," Karl is muttering now. "You could put in a good word for me. I can't lose this job, Leora, do you hear me? My dad would kill me."

I try to think of something to say. I can see he's sorry, and scared, but why would I stick up for Karl Novak?

"Listen to me! Don't just sit there and pretend I'm not here, Leora!" Karl grabs my shoulder, fingers digging into my skin, and tries to force me to turn around. I pull away and as I do the stool slips. I hear Karl gasp and I don't have time to put out my hands to soften the fall.

The last thing I see, as my head hits the slate floor and my vision recedes into black spots, are Obel's boots striding toward us.

chapter 26

"You're sure you don't want to see a doctor?"
Obel frowns his concern at me. "The mark on your forehead is really red."

I gingerly move my head from side to side and rub the sore
skin on my forehead. I can feel a lump swelling up nicely.

"I'm fine. The guy Karl marked is probably in a worse state."
I try to stand up but am struck by dizziness and slump back into
my chair. "Is he still in the shop?"

Obel shakes his head and passes me a glass of water.

"I'd just sent him home when Karl called out. He'll need to
heal up before the next sitting." He smiles and then closes his

eyes, his smile fading. "You gave me a scare, girl. I thought he'd killed you." His voice quivers into silence for a moment. "That *boy*," he hisses. "I knew he was a little rough around the edges, but I never would have imagined this. He's gone, by the way. I told him not to come back."

"It . . . it wasn't really his fault." I can't believe I'm defending Karl. "He was upset and angry but he didn't mean for me to fall. He grabbed my arm and the stool slipped." The necklace from Dad is hanging out of my shirt, and my head swims when I move too fast to straighten it and tuck it out of sight.

"I'm not blind, Leora—it was clear you two hated each other from the moment you both walked in. I should have done more. Getting the two of you to compete for a permanent post was perhaps not the best plan."

"Don't worry about it, Obel. It's happened but he's gone now; it's over."

Even as I try to assure Obel, images of Karl grabbing me pollute my thoughts. Thankfully, Obel leaves me alone, and a moment later I hear the comforting sound of the kettle boiling. I let out a tiny giggle.

"Tea solves everything. That's what my mom says."

Obel looks my way and offers a smile.

"It might not solve everything, but it helps."

I watch him while he pours and stirs. His hands are steady and even; making tea looks like art when he's doing it. Then I realize why I feel so safe with Obel—he reminds me of Dad.

He hands me my cup, then takes a seat opposite. He sips his

tea and sits forward in his chair, looking suddenly very tired. "What a disaster. And he showed such promise. Anyway, I'm sorry, Leora—you're free of him now."

I hold my cup in shaking hands and smile at Obel. A little part of me is relieved; I was right about Karl, right to be wary of him, and now he's gone. He messed this up all on his own. He won't interfere with the one thing that's going well for me, not anymore.

"Well." He goes to rise. "You sit there and recover."

Suddenly I can no longer help myself. "You gave me that drawing of the White Witch to copy on purpose, didn't you?"

Obel turns back to me. "What are you talking about?"

I stare him out. Eventually he shrugs and sits back down.

"Yes, I thought you seemed unnerved—by the resemblance, I assume. But, Leora, of course you look just like her. I thought you would have known. Especially given who your father was."

Who my father was.

"You knew my dad?" I ask, with a voice that sounds shriller than I intended. "You knew my dad, but you didn't tell me?"

Obel shifts in his seat. "Your dad was an important man. He was special to a lot of people."

I try to convey through a hard stare that this isn't good enough. I want more. "Listen to me, Leora. Believe me." Obel moves his body so he can look right into my face. "I did know your dad—from afar, and of course I'd heard of him before I came here. Most of us have."

"*Us?*" I snap.

He presses his hand to his forehead. "So hard to know the right thing to do," he murmurs, almost to himself. Then: "Leora—your father . . . He's the reason I came to Saintstone. I followed him. I listened to him—many did. He gave us all hope that things might change—that blanks might live alongside the marked." I gasp and he stops to look at me. "You're so like her—I thought he would have prepared you . . ."

"What are you saying? That I'm, what—linked to the White Witch somehow? To the original blank? And my dad was fine with that?" My voice rises high and sharp. The idea is so ludicrous that I laugh, but Obel doesn't.

"Why did you make me draw her if you didn't want to tell me more?" I grip the arms of my chair as another wave of dizziness hits me. "You raised all this. If you didn't want me to ask questions you shouldn't have baited me. Why? Do you think I want to be associated with a blank witch?"

I see Obel flinch at my words but I carry on. "We all know the story, Obel. She's cursed, she's strange, she's the one who is *forgotten*. And you're telling me I'm like her?"

He just looks at me.

"Is she forgotten, Leora?" He looks at my face as though studying it for his next line. "Is she really forgotten? It seems like you know enough about her—and I bet your friends do too." I dip my head in reluctant agreement.

"It seems to me that she's one of the most remembered women in our history."

At this, I can't help but laugh.

"You talk about her like she . . . like she matters. It was a long time ago. It's just a fable. She doesn't matter anymore. The blanks are gone—banished just like she was. I'm not stupid, Obel. I am not a child."

Still he looks at me with that cold, measuring gaze. "Tell me something, Leora," he says, and underneath the calm I hear a note of desperation in his voice. "Do you remember that woman who wanted to be marked with a leaf, so she could remember her dead child? Who wanted her child on her family tree?"

"You made me break the law." My anger flares, but Obel just cocks his head as though it's nothing.

"Why did we do that in secret? Why could that child not be openly remembered? I'll tell you why. Longsight is so afraid of the blanks that he refuses to even allow a day-old baby who dies unmarked be remembered. He is afraid that if we remember an unmarked baby we will start to try to remember other blanks too. He tells you all that the blanks are a threat, but he's the most dangerous man I know."

I stare at him. I'm stunned not only by the words he speaks—words I don't recognize, words that deserve punishment—but also by his urgency and feeling. The calm and controlled man I've always seen is gone and he looks pained by the words he's said to me.

"That isn't true," I say quietly. "That woman was grieving. She didn't know what she was saying." My heart is beating so fast I can hardly think straight.

He's speaking calmly now. "Why do you think the

government cares so much about records and marks? They want to know everything about you; they want to control you. They're certain that the blanks are planning a revolt; so certain that they would hurt their own people. And what are they so frightened of, Leora?" He leans in, his face suddenly earnest. "They're frightened of a bogeyman made up to scare children. Have you ever wondered if the blanks are really so terrible? Or are we just told they are?" I close my eyes. They're stinging from tiredness and from all the tears I'm keeping locked away. I want to sleep; I wish I could just curl up and switch off from all this. Go back to before—before the public marking, before I heard Mayor Longsight's warnings, when the blanks were like pictures in a book to me.

"Don't try to make out that the blanks are just misunderstood," I whisper. "You've been to the museum; you've been through that green door. The blanks are monsters." I shake my head at him and find the strength to move.

"Think of your dad, Leora. He wouldn't have wanted you to feel this way."

"I never stop thinking about him." I struggle to keep my voice steady. "I don't know why you think my dad has anything to do with witches and blanks."

"Leora. Your dad fought for freedom, for equality, for unity." He groans in frustration. "One day you'll understand."

I walk toward the back room and then turn around a moment. "Thanks for making today worse. I didn't realize it was possible. You must be very proud."

Blinking away my angry tears I walk into the back room, take my bag down from the hook and wrap my shawl around myself. When I look back through the open door, Obel is still in the studio, sitting in his chair, head in his hands.

I open the heavy door and don't look back when I let it slam behind me.

chapter 27

I'M TOO TIRED FOR ALL OF THIS. I'VE LOST TRACK OF where can I go, of who is safe. These weeks have been the worst of my life. I thought things couldn't get worse after Dad died—I thought I'd had my fill of sadness. But it was just the beginning. I try to look into the future and see light and hope, but there's nothing there. It's all bleak; it's all cursed. It's all blank.

I walk with my head down against the biting wind that makes my eyes water and my face sting. I'm buffeted by people as they walk past. Maybe I don't exist anymore. Maybe I can be invisible.

Less of those thoughts, I tell myself. *Those are the thoughts of a blank—those are the words of the White Witch.*

I'm mostly tired of feeling like the only one who hasn't been let in on some big secret. I feel like my life is being orchestrated by everyone else. A man walks past me with his dog on a leash and I realize *that's* how I feel. Like a stupid dog who thinks it's leading the way but all the time is being held back and controlled. Well, I can change that. I don't have to wait for life to happen. I'm going to be in charge from now on. I know where I need to go.

The government building looms before me. Utilitarian and imposing, the red-brick building hasn't been designed with beauty in mind. It's all boxes, squares, and sharp corners. It's as if the architect wanted the place to be as ordinary as possible, so as not to distract from the truly important work that takes place inside. I've never been inside the admin section of the government building before. They used to offer it as a school trip, but I couldn't think of anything more boring. Of course, Verity went every year. We haven't seen each other for a bit; work takes up more time than I expected. The last time I went to her house Simon said she had a cold and I didn't see her. I've missed her.

The entrance foyer is impersonal and pale brown. Chairs line one wall and people are waiting there. The curved reception desk takes up most of the space and blocks the path so that people must pass it to get to the offices. I see that the girl on reception is one of the popular girls from school; she would make fun of me whenever she sat behind me in class.

I walk briskly past the desk with my scarf still on, deciding that if I look confident enough no one will stop me. She looks at me. I don't know if she recognizes me but she has her usual look of disdain. Maybe that's just how she always looks. I see her open her mouth to speak, and then a person comes to the desk, rings the bell, and claims her attention.

I keep walking.

When the corridor takes me around a corner, I pause and try to get my bearings. There are signs on the walls and hanging from the ceiling pointing the direction to different departments. I remember that Verity is in the Department of Marks and Records and follow the signs.

Walking through corridors with countless wooden doors—hidden rooms full of important people making decisions—I wonder how Verity manages not to get lost. Eventually I reach her department and push through an oak door.

It's quiet in here, with thick carpets and richly paneled walls. Everything feels hushed and secret. I keep my shawl up and head down. Of course I turn a corner and walk right into someone. Muttering an apology, I hurry past. A hand falls on my arm and I freeze.

"Leora? What are you *doing* here?" Verity hisses. She grabs my hand and leads me back the way she came, rather quickly, I think. She opens a wooden door and pulls me in behind her.

I close the door behind me, and Verity and I take in each other's shocked faces and her demeanor changes; she sighs with relief. The room is dominated by a grand desk, ornate carvings on its legs. There are cabinets lining the walls, each with a keyhole, each keeping secrets.

"Is this your office? It's enormous!"

"I know!" She grins at me. "Honestly, what are you doing here? Why didn't you just call for me at reception?" She grabs a spare chair and puts it across from her own larger, more ornate wooden one.

"Yeah, that would have been easier," I concede, sinking into the seat. "I didn't really want anyone to see me." I unwrap my shawl and Verity's eyes widen.

"What on *earth* has happened to your face?"

I put my hand up to where the bump on my head is raised and sore. I sigh and tell Verity what happened. She is furious on my behalf and it feels wonderful.

"I think he just lost his temper. I don't think he would have meant for this."

"There is no excuse for that, none; he shouldn't have touched you." She's pacing around her office, her cheeks flushed with rage. "What a horrible thing to happen at work—and you were loving it so much. Are you going to be OK?"

She comes and hugs me while I'm still sitting on the chair. She strokes my hair and whispers words of comfort about how he's gone now and losers never win.

"I'll be fine, Vetty. It's a shock, that's all."

I give Verity a tight smile. In the relief of talking to my best friend, I've lost sight of what I came for.

I need to find out what she knows. How much she knows.

"Anyway. Distract me. Tell me about what you've been doing." I look around the room. "I didn't realize you were so important—you must have really impressed them."

Verity sits back down. She gives me a quick smile, but I suddenly feel a constraint in her manner. She seems awkward—embarrassed, almost. Worried. Or am I imagining it?

"Well, I know how dull you think my job must be, and it's not the same as making marks, but actually it's been really interesting."

"You're still excited about this new role?"

Verity grimaces. "Well, let's just say it definitely feels like I'm new, but I'm getting the hang of things slowly. Everyone is very nice. Did I tell you that I met Mayor Longsight a few weeks ago?"

I shake my head, eyes wide. "I knew you were hoping to."

"Well, he is *amazing*—exactly how you'd imagine him to be, you know? Anyway, he *spoke* to me—I thought I was going to die—and we talked about me hoping to work here, doing the funerary stuff, and, well, I think he might have pulled some strings."

"That is so cool. I can't believe you met him! You must have made quite an impression."

Verity shrugs, but there's a faint blush on her cheeks. "Well, anyway, I'm just glad to be here. Everything moves at a different pace and there's this big project that has just come in—they need everyone working on it." She tails off and avoids my eye.

I'm feeling pretty terrified about what she might say next. What I might learn. On the one hand it's impossible that my best friend would find out something about my dad and not tell me. On the other, at this point *anything* seems possible.

"So, tell me about what they've got you doing," I say urging her on.

She looks down at the desk, and when she speaks, although her tone is casual, something doesn't ring quite true. I know her too well. "Well, at the moment I've been asked to go through the information and evidence for the weighing of the soul ceremonies that are coming up—working on individual cases. I think that's why they let me join the department early; it's all stuff I did for extra credit last year. Basically, I summarize the evidence so the judges can reach their decision."

"Yes?" I say quietly. "That sounds interesting."

"It's such an honor, Leora. Sifting through people's lives. Getting at the facts. They don't want anything that could be biased by someone's interpretation. That's why I'm only allowed to summarize; I can't make recommendations. It's a huge responsibility. What if I miss something crucial? What if I'm the difference between someone being remembered or forgotten?" She shifts in her seat.

I lean forward. "You'll make the right decisions, Verity. You always have."

She pauses and looks away from me. "Some cases aren't as clear-cut as I'd like them to be."

She gives a sad smile, and right then I know.

"You mean cases like my dad's?"

She nods. "I shouldn't be talking about this. Not to you. Well, not to anyone. But especially not to you." She takes a deep breath. "Still—I can't not say anything. You're my best friend. Lor, I think you should know. They've put me on your dad's case and there are rumors. Rumors that the man who was marked— his name was Connor Drew—that the body he stole from was your dad's. And that the reason he stole skin was that there was something your family wanted removed. Disappeared from his life."

"I—I know about the rumors, Verity." She lets her eyes flick to mine. "And I know about Connor Drew. I know what he did for my dad."

At this she exhales with relief.

"Oh, Lor, I'm so *glad*." She shakes her head. "No—I'm not glad—I'm sorry. But I'm glad you know. I had no idea what to say." I sit up straight in my chair. This has become business. "But Lor, that's all I know. That Connor might have taken some evidence—that marked your dad as . . ." She swallows and I close my eyes. "As forgotten."

Seeing me wince at hearing it said out loud, Verity swears. "You know that too, don't you? I had hoped it was just hearsay. God, I'm sorry, Lor."

"How much do they know, Verity?"

She stares miserably at the desk. I'm forcing her to jeopardize everything—her job that she loves so much. "There are just so many questions. That's what makes this case complicated. They've examined your dad's book and there's unverified scarring, suspicion that maybe marks have been doctored or, in some cases, completely covered over. That, along with the fact that we suspect he and Connor Drew were known to each other through flaying—and the fact that Drew was arrested for editing people's history . . ." Her eyes meet mine. "The scarring is . . ." She lightly touches the back of her head, a fleeting gesture, and I nod. She's told me enough.

"Thank you, Verity—I know you didn't have to tell me any of this. And yes, I've heard . . . things. I've been worrying and keeping it all secret. How—how long have you known?"

"Not long, I swear. His case has only just come up."

"I should have come to you sooner, Vetty. You know I trust you, don't you?" Verity nods reluctantly. "I've been too scared. It gets more real when you talk about it, doesn't it?"

Verity concedes with an incline of her head. "I'm so sorry, Leora."

She's quiet for a while and starts to doodle with the pencil. "So if your dad was marked—what did he do, exactly?"

I shake my head. "I don't know, Vetty. I just don't know."

And because it's Verity, and because I finally can, I let my guard down completely. I tell her I don't know what he could have done. I tell her I saw the mark on his scalp only by chance, when I was small, and that the public marking brought that memory, kicking and screaming, to the surface. I tell her my mother won't tell me anything.

Now that I've started, I can't stop. I tell her about finding out that Dad's book was confiscated at the museum. I tell her that I met Connor Drew's son, and that he thinks he can help me, but that I'm scared I can't trust him. I tell her that he's called Oscar and he has dark eyes and curls and that his glasses are always askew.

She squeals when I tell her that, pulls her knees to her chest and says, "Oh! Tell me more—do you like him?"

I shake my head at her. I need to keep talking. I'm just about to tell her about Obel making me draw the White Witch and how dreadfully alike we look, and how that must just be a coincidence—mustn't it?—when there's a knock at the office door. Verity's eyes widen with panic. "Quick—behind the door!" she whispers.

She opens it a little and stands talking in the doorway. When the visitor is gone she shuts the door and leans her head against it.

"That was close. Seriously, if anyone sees you—if they make the connection, we're in serious trouble. If I'm going to work on your dad's case, no one here can know we're friends."

I nod. The repercussions for her could be huge. "Tell me one thing, Verity, and then I'll leave. Do you think my dad's in danger?"

"I don't know, Leora—I don't think they have anything concrete now, but I know they'll keep digging. They're working hard to find Connor Drew's hidden work. They seem to have really focused on finding *something*." She hesitates, then carries on quickly. "Look, I think you need to talk to this Oscar, ask if he's heard anything new. You contact him, and I'll find out everything I can, and then let's regroup."

"He doesn't deserve this, Vetty. I wish I knew what he'd done to be marked, but whatever it is, he was a good man. You know he is worthy, don't you?"

Verity hugs me and whispers, "I do. I'll help you, Leora. We'll make sure he's remembered."

I leave the office alone, with my scarf pulled up and complicated directions from Verity on how to find my way out. She looks nervous as I leave, and I can't help regretting that I've involved her. But I had no choice.

The corridors all look the same; I guess that's what works here—everything uniform, predictable, controlled. The foyer is busy when I get there and I leave without being noticed; the haughty receptionist is deep in conversation with a broad figure. As I slip past, I notice who that is.

Mel.

Verity's right, I need to talk to Oscar. I walk to the bookbinders where he works. It's late, though, and he's already left for home, but I talk to someone who works there who agrees to pass on a message the next morning. I scrawl a quick note and leave it with him.

Heading home, I see a dirty white feather on the ground and again my mind wanders back to my conversation with Obel and the fable of the White Witch. I can't keep away from her story. Although, it's not *her* story at all, is it? She lurks at the edges of Moriah's tale. She's in the blank space. I should be drawn to the one with words and marks—and yet there she is. The first of her kind. Forgotten, because she has no story to live on.

But not really forgotten. Obel is right, I realize. You can't count as forgotten if your story is told to children every day.

There *are* other ways of remembering, then.

And suddenly I wonder for the first time about all those forgotten souls. What were they like? Can they be remembered? Do they actually live on, through their friends and family? If my father is forgotten when his soul is weighed, then is he truly gone?

These are dangerous thoughts.

. . .

When I get home, Mom greets me with cross words about being late, but when she sees my bruised face she rises without speaking, and leaves the room. A few minutes later I am lying with my head on her lap and she's bathing my wounds with warm water infused with lavender while I tell her about Karl. She carries on long after I've finished talking; the silence is soothing and her gentle touch and the fragrance send me to sleep, right there.

chapter 28

I'M STILL ON THE SOFA WHEN I WAKE AT DAWN, lying under a blanket Mom must have covered me with last night. The sofa isn't quite long enough for me and I'm aching from being curled up all night.

Mom raised me to believe in order, that obedience was the way to a quiet and happy life. When I was at school I quite liked rules. It made me feel safe that I knew what I had to do and knew what it took to be good and to be praised by the teachers. My faith in the system—in our marks and our eternities—has always been ironclad. As long as I stick to the rules, everything is neat and good and safe.

But the rules say that if Dad was marked with a crow, he deserves nothing more than the fire of judgment.

The rules say that his soul has already been marked out for destruction.

In which case, why am I fighting to save his book, if he's already doomed? And if he is—then can one wrong action really damn a good man?

For the first time in my life, I'm doubting my faith, and it terrifies me.

For the first time, I want to change the rules.

For the first time I wonder: Does it matter what it says on your skin when what's at stake is your soul?

Before Mom wakes I walk into town. I arrive at the museum as it's opening and ask for Mel. I wait for a few moments in reception, everything empty and quiet in the hour before the shops open. I'm studying the intricately tiled floor, avoiding eye contact with the person at the desk, and then I'm told to go right down.

I knock and she calls cheerfully for me to come in. When I do, I see that she's with a little girl who has olive skin and deep, dark eyes that watch me closely. Mel greets me and introduces me to her companion.

"This is Isolda." When she sees my curious look, she explains further. "She's my charge—apprentice, if you will."

The girl looks about six and is wearing a miniature version of Mel's storyteller's skirt and chest piece. It looks like she's playing at dress-up. She fixes me with a bold stare and goes to sit under the desk. I look around me with pleasure; the room is cozy and lined with books. Comfortable chairs occupy either side of a cluttered desk. The whole impression is one of warmth and rich detail.

"Do you have time to talk?" I venture.

"Of course. Did you get my cards? I probably should've visited you at work, shouldn't I? I'm sorry, I'm new to this mentor thing." She gives me an irreverent grin. "I'm glad you've come. In fact, there's something I've been wanting to show you, Leora."

She turns to the little girl and tells her we'll be back soon, then leads me out of the room.

"Have you always had a charge?" I ask as soon as the door closes behind us. "She's so young."

We walk up some creaking wooden stairs marked STAFF ONLY. The staircase is narrow and I follow Mel, who turns her head toward me now and then as she speaks.

"Not always, no. A charge is a *receptacle*, for want of a better word, for all that I have learned. I intend to pass on my stories to her." She smiles. "It's the right time, Leora. It's time for me to pass on my stories to the next generation. Isolda needs to know the stories perfectly and will be marked in exactly the right way. Not that I'm planning on going anywhere, but it wouldn't do for me to die and for the stories to be lost with me, now would it?"

I nod in agreement, but I wonder. It's a strange life for a little girl.

"What do her parents make of it all?"

Mel pauses, an odd expression on her face. "She has no parents," she says quietly. And then I remember and blush at my insensitivity; storytellers have no family.

"I'm sorry, I just didn't think—"

Mel shrugs. She carries on up the stairs, her right hand trailing gently on the handrail.

"Don't worry about it. To be a storyteller, you have to be without family. Isolda's an orphan. I was given up at birth. My parents couldn't cope or something." I begin to speak but she waves a hand. "Don't be sorry—it's worked out for the best. I was chosen to be a candidate for storyteller when I was very young. They kept an eye on me as I grew, to make sure I was bright enough, and then when I was about the same age Isolda is now I was placed with a guardian. She was a storyteller and she trained me, just as I will train Isolda."

"Is that why you don't have a family tree?" I ask. As we climb the stairs I can see her back, filled with stories but empty of family. I'm aware these questions might be impertinent but Mel makes me feel like I can ask them.

"I don't have any of the usual marks; I am not permitted to. My skin belongs to the community. I don't have a story: I *am* our stories." She speaks in a totally matter-of-fact way, but I can't help feeling sorrow at the idea of not being able to leave your own mark.

We reach the top of the stairs and Mel leads me through another door that isn't for the general public.

"And here are the storybooks."

She turns to me with her arms outstretched and I see shelves full of books. The room is decorated in gold and red; beautiful images surround the bookcases. They are packed with skin books but the books look slightly different—perhaps they are bound differently from the usual books of the dead.

"Plenty of bedtime stories here, Leora." She walks to a shelf and selects a book, removing it from its place gently. "All these books are the stories of our society. They're exceptionally precious. And I get to be part of this."

She looks at me, beaming with pride. But all I can think is, *We'll remember your stories, but who will remember you? No one will speak your name.*

I spend time walking the shelves, breathing in the scent of wood that has been meticulously cared for and polished with beeswax, pulling out books at random. There are no names on them and I feel uncomfortable that I can't greet the dead and ask their permission to read them, like I do with my ancestors at home. They have no names, just story upon story. It's a curious feeling; a skin book is so intimate, and yet these are anonymous. Mel is obviously energized just being here. I suppose it's a reminder of her purpose. She smiles broadly.

"Beautiful, aren't they?"

I have to ask her.

"Have you ever . . . questioned all this?" I blurt out.

Mel stops abruptly and looks at me. "Tell me what you mean," she says, smiling gently, encouragingly.

"What if . . ." I steel myself, forcing myself to ask the

question that sounds so close to heresy it terrifies me. "What if our marks *don't* matter? What if all . . . this"—I wave my hand around the room at the shelves of stories—"is just a way to try to get us to be good? What if"—I whisper it—"what if there *is* no afterlife?"

"Oh, sweetheart." She puts her arm around me. "Those are big questions. I'm not surprised you're asking them now— death forces our minds to travel to dark places." I don't reply, but she's right. I never thought such things before. "You might be surprised. Most people ask these questions at some point."

I look up at her. "Really? But everyone seems so . . . *certain.*"

Mel lets go of me and runs her hands over the shelves around us. "Because most people are. They question and they doubt and then they come to believe." She smiles sympatheti- cally. "I'm convinced by the evidence, Leora. These stories have been handed down since the beginning. If you compare all these books you'll see that each story is identical. The words I've been taught are the same words used the first time the stories were told. I believe it's our story—our history."

I frown, trying to get my head around my confused thoughts. "So you believe in a real White Witch, a real Moriah, a real Saint?" I can hardly believe I'm asking this, but Mel seems unfazed.

"More or less, yes." She looks at me compassionately. "Every- thing can be misinterpreted. There are some who like to use these stories, to twist them to fit their own schemes. But how- ever they're used, the stories remain the same. One woman who is pure with marked skin. Another who is rebellious and cursed and blank. To the pure of heart, the truth is obvious. Marks show that we have integrity; they show that we know that the secrets of the heart will be revealed even if only on the day of judgment." She looks around at the shelves. "Look to the stories for answers, Leora. You have my permission to come here any time. This is your own history; it can be your way back to sure faith."

She makes it seem so simple.

Mel escorts me out of the room filled with the storytellers' books and we walk down the stairs. At the bottom she gives me a friendly hug.

"I know this is hard, Leora. Give yourself some time. You don't need to force it—if all this is true, and I believe it is, it will be true whenever you're ready to return. Just don't give up on it, OK?"

I nod; I do feel calmed by her reassurance, by all that wealth of history. I take a deep breath and ask her the question I came here to ask. "You go to the weighing of the soul ceremonies, don't you?"

Mel has turned to go, but at my words she stops with a foot on the cold stone staircase. "Yes. I get to tell each person's final story. It's an honor."

"Can you tell me something about it? Have they made the judgment already, or will they discuss it during the ceremony? Are they still gathering evidence?"

Mel sits on a step and pats the stone next to her. There's still space to pass us on the wide staircase, but I'm glad it's so quiet. I feel self-conscious as I sit beside her.

"You're thinking about your father's ceremony, aren't you? It will be coming up soon." I nod mutely. "Well. There will be all sorts of things happening at the moment, Leora. Someone in the government will be studying his book and making copious notes about what they read." I think of Verity. "Then every weighing I've been to opens with a prayer calling on the ancestors to give wisdom and insight. The judge invites friends and relatives to come to the front and share stories and memories about their loved one—sometimes those stories can help influence the judge's decision, if it's hanging in the balance. After that, he will read out the verdict."

"Will I have to speak?" The idea of standing in front of everyone and telling tales about Dad is terrifying. I'd love to hear the stories, but there's not a chance that I'll be telling one.

"No, of course you don't *have* to." Mel nudges me with her knee. "But you might feel you want to say something once you're actually there."

Shaking my head, I smile. "I doubt it. I think I'd die of nerves!"

Mel appraises me. "I think I know what might help. You know that every citizen can choose a story to be read at their ceremony?" I nod. "Well, would you like to hear the one your father has asked for? I think it will give you strength. The story he has chosen is about life beyond death, Leora. Your father's hope was certain." And right there, while we're sitting on the steps, she tells me a tale.

The Lovers

Once there were a king and a queen who ruled their kingdom with wisdom and grace. He was as bright as the morning sun and she was as pure as the full moon. Their love was sure as dawn and beautiful as sunset.

The king had a brother, whose jealousy was hot as fire and sharp as ice. The brother saw how the people loved their king and how the queen adored her husband. He wanted to know how it felt to be treasured, and he resolved to remove the king from the throne so that he could take it and enjoy the adoration for himself.

The brothers were competitive, as brothers often are. They loved to challenge each other to duals and contests. The king's brother knew just how to lure the king into his wicked clutches. He held a banquet for his friends, and invited his royal sibling. After the food was eaten and the wine was drunk, the brother revealed a beautiful chest made from the most intricately carved ebony.

"Whoever fits into this trunk can keep it!" announced the brother.

The king smiled—he had already noticed that his brother's friends were, to put it politely, rather portly, and taller than the average man. *I'll win this easily,* thought the king as he watched guest after guest attempt to squeeze into the box.

Finally it was the turn of the king. He stepped into the box and lay down, curling his legs close to his chest. He fit perfectly—it was as though the chest had been made for him.

"Aha, brother! I think I have succeeded where your friends failed!" the king cried.

Just as he did so, his brother heaved the lid of the trunk shut, and the hefty guests sat on the chest while it was locked and wrapped in chains. The men carried the box outside and threw it into the river. The king floated away—the trunk was now his coffin. It came to rest beneath a tree and, as the tree drew in the goodness of the king, it exuded the most wonderful scent.

Soon, the mourning queen heard about this fabulously fragranced tree, and when she saw it she knew in her heart that this was where her missing husband lay. She found the chest, hidden beneath the trunk of the tree, and brought it home, glad to know her husband could now rest in peace. Of course, the envious brother was enraged to discover that the king had been found and he crept to where the chest was kept, opened it, and chopped the king's body into pieces. He scattered them far and wide and returned to the kingdom, gleefully sure his brother wouldn't be heard of again.

But love as strong as the queen's for her king can't be stopped that easily. The queen put her son in charge of the kingdom while she searched for her husband. As she wandered the land, she would find a foot in some fallen leaves, a shoulder in the reeds, his head drifting on the ocean's tide. Years passed, and she had gathered all but one piece, which had been eaten by a beast. She stopped her search and took the parts she had back to the kingdom and arranged them in their correct positions.

While she had been away, the king's brother had fought the son, trying every day to usurp his royal position. He was a vicious and insatiable enemy, and the son often despaired. Every day, however, the king's son grew stronger.

There is a certain magic that comes with true love—if you've experienced this kind of love, you'll know that this is true. There has never been a love stronger than that between the king and his queen. The magic worked quickly. Before long, the pieces of the king's body joined together and his blood flowed and his lungs filled. Hampered though he was by his missing piece, he was able to return to the kingdom with most of his kingly stature intact. His brother cowered at the sight of him, but the king, in his kindness, did not destroy him.

The king passed his crown to his son and descended to the depths, where he and his queen ruled over the dead with all the justice and wisdom with which they had ruled the living. Their son battled the king's brother—it was bloody and fearsome, but the son won.

And soon the brother found himself in the underworld, once again under the king's rule and never again to rebel.

Mel and I say the adage that ends the tale together. I know it by heart.

"This tale is told to remind us that we will live beyond death. Although our skin must be sliced, and our bodies must be buried, our souls—and our love—will last eternally."

Mel stands, her marks stretching with her long body, and takes my hand. "Your father loved your mother, Leora. But, more than that, when he knew he was dying he chose this story to show his confidence. This is the choice of someone who is not afraid of death, who knows with absolute certainty what will come next. Now good luck, my dear. Don't worry yourself about the ceremony; you'll do the right thing. I know it."

We say goodbye and she heads back to her basement office and her little blank student and I leave.

For a moment I waver over what I am about to do. It's so tempting to think that everything will be OK. That I shouldn't be afraid.

But I don't quite believe that.

chapter 29

OBEL HAS OBVIOUSLY BEEN AT THE STUDIO FOR A
while when I arrive. He looks tired, and I wonder if he slept
here. The look of relief on his face when he sees me takes
me aback. I had assumed I wouldn't be welcome. Really, I'd
expected to be fighting for my job.

"You have no idea how glad I am to see you." He stands
quickly and takes my coat, hanging it up for me. "I know yesterday was a mess. There were things I said . . ."

"Things we both said," I say ruefully.

"Leora, we might have to just agree to disagree for now.
What is undeniable is that you're a very fine inker and I would

like to continue training you, regardless of what we both believe. What do you say?"

I hesitate for a second, then nod. My head is too full at the moment to make decisions. For now, I will just keep working at what I love.

"Good! I need you today," Obel says, passing me a letter. "After the business with Karl yesterday, the powers that be need to come and investigate. He's left me with a lot to clean up, that boy." He gives a wry smile.

Scanning the letter, I see that someone named Jack Minnow is coming to the studio today. The note says he will be helping Obel go through the paperwork that is required after Karl marked a man without Obel there to assist.

"They work fast." I frown.

"Yeah, I only reported it last night. Either they don't have much work to do, or they're keen to check me out." Obel swallows and I see his nervousness just beneath the surface.

We go through our accounts of the previous day and ensure our stories match. I clean the studio and set up while Obel opens up the shop. The inspector from the government could come at any time, so we might as well carry on as normal while we wait for him.

We have a couple of inquiries, and I book a woman for a consultation later in the week. I'm just filling in the appointment book in the reception area when I hear the bell on the door clang loudly. I look up and a tall man in the official black uniform of those high up in the government is letting the door slam behind him.

"Jack Minnow," he says. "I'm here to see Obel Whitworth."

He's bald and tanned, and he towers over me. He must be even bigger than Obel. His shorn hair shows intricate marks on his head and I read what I can see of him in a flash. They are all based around predators. Their meaning is clear. His scalp is a cackle of hyenas and I read that it's his tribute to the banishing of the blanks, with all the violence left in. I read such joy in the gore, it chills me. I try to keep my voice steady.

"Take a seat, Mr. Minnow. I'll just go and get Obel for you. Can I get you a drink?" My voice is too shrill—he will be able to tell how nervous I am.

Jack Minnow closes his eyes and shakes his head. When he opens them he's smirking a little. "Just Mr. Whitworth will be fine."

I go to leave the room but then Obel is walking into the studio drying his hands on a rag. He puts one hand out to greet Minnow, who takes his hand and frowns with disdain at its dampness.

"Well, shall we get started then, Mr. Whitworth?" He wipes his hand on his pants, looking at Obel with open hostility. "Someone's been naughty, haven't they? Unauthorized marks, I believe?" He gives an indulgent chuckle. "I understand the young man was ambitious. I must say, that's a trait I admire."

Obel tells me to do some drawing practice in the back room but Minnow stops him. "I'd like to talk with you both. Sit down, Miss Flint."

He makes us tell him what happened, asking me to go first. I talk with half my attention on Jack Minnow and half on Obel. I'm worried about saying the wrong thing and getting Obel in trouble. Is this visit just about Karl?

All the time Minnow makes notes and asks little clarifying questions. He is being perfectly polite, but I feel like he's waiting for me to trip. His marks are glaring and vivid and I can hardly think straight. He asks Obel the same questions, grilling him about why he left us alone and pressing him for details on what he said to Karl when he fired him. He writes in silence for a few minutes and then passes the piece of paper to me.

"Just check this through, and if you agree with my summary, please sign it." Reading it again feels like living it again and absently I rub my head.

"It all looks fine," I say, sliding the paper back across the table to him.

"Fine or correct, Miss Flint? There's a difference." He says it with a smile, but it's the kind of smile I imagine belongs to a demon.

"It's correct, yes. It's what I told you and it's true." He passes me a pen and I sign, glancing briefly at Obel to check I'm doing the right thing.

"Thank you." He passes it to Obel, who signs above my signature, and then Minnow places our statement in his bag and looks around. He leans back in his chair and stretches a little. "So, how are you finding it here, Miss Flint? All going well so far?"

"It's brilliant. Well, apart from that." I nod toward his bag and the papers. "I'm really enjoying it."

"And Mr. Whitworth"—he looks at Obel—"you're happy with him? He's training you well?"

It feels strange to be asked this with Obel right here, but I try not to look surprised. "He's been excellent. I'm very happy here." I'm not going to say any more.

"Glad to hear it. Well, maybe you could show me out, Mr. Whitworth?" Minnow picks up his bag and he and Obel walk through to the reception area, talking all the time. I leave them to it and am about to head to the back room when Minnow's voice grows louder, and I look up to see him return- ing, undoing the top button of his vest as he walks toward where Obel works. Minnow relaxes into the chair as though he owns it, puts his bag on the ground, and looks my way.

"Seeing as neither of you are busy right now, your tutor has agreed to begin a mark for me. Isn't that right, Whitworth?" I see Obel stiffen. It's clearly not a question. Button by button, Jack Minnow removes his vest and short-sleeved undershirt. As he takes off his clothes, I've never felt so battered by reading someone. The onslaught of violence and rage in his marks is overwhelming. I want to run. I want to cry. I want to tell him I can see through him. But I stay silent, watching this strange dance between him and Obel.

Obel breaks the silence. "We wouldn't normally, sir. Usually we would ask you to come back after a consultation. But of course, considering it's you, it would be an honor." He looks at me. "Leora, Mr. Minnow would like . . . an owl, wasn't it?"

Minnow nods brusquely and his shoulders square. "A great horned owl," he confirms. I know the type he means; Obel's had me drawing so many creatures.

Obel begins his usual patter of questions, apparently as calm as ever. I go to get the equipment ready. When I return with a tray full of instruments I hear the end of Obel and the man's conversation.

". . . phenomenal hunters, yes. Sight and hearing like nothing else. The prey think they've run fast enough, far enough, hidden themselves perfectly out of sight and then—*swoop*. Before they've even heard him the owl has got them. Unstoppable. Formidable."

Obel swallows and turns to me. "Thanks, Leora, I'll take it from here."

I turn to leave, then Minnow says, "Actually, why don't we use this as a training opportunity? I'd like Leora here to make this mark."

My shock obviously shows.

"You've done a mark before, though, haven't you?" I nod weakly. "Well then, this shouldn't be a problem, and Mr. Whitworth is here to assist. I'd like it here, up high on my shoulder. It can watch over my family."

With shaking hands I wipe down my workspace with disinfectant, covering it carefully and arranging everything in an order that works for me. I show him that all the equipment I'm using is new and clean, and I ask some questions about how he wants the owl to look, showing him some sketches I've done before, feeling grateful that Obel has made me draw and practice *so* much. I clean his skin and shave the wispy black hairs. With each touch of his skin his marks roar at me. It's nothing like the pleasant electric shock that I felt when I inked the woman; it's like a murderous crowd screaming for blood. I don't know if I can bear it for a moment more, let alone for the hours it will take to complete his mark. I stall for time by showing him the image as I create a transfer and making sure I've really understood what he wants. I let my eyes flick to Obel, who is, for once, looking worried. But when he sees me looking he smiles his reassurance.

"You've got this, girl. You're a natural, remember?" he murmurs quietly.

I place my drawing on his skin, letting the guidelines leave their clear marks and bracing myself each time we connect, trying to block out the violence that ebbs through his ink. I show him the lines in a mirror and he nods.

As I begin marking him I feel the familiar buzz of the machine and allow it to take over. Each time I find myself slipping into this safe feeling, Minnow speaks. It's like being wrenched out of bed when you're on the edge of sleep, and each time I feel the jolting sense of being disturbed. It makes it hard to concentrate on his words and construct my replies.

"So, what was the first mark you did, Leora?" he asks.

"It was a leaf," I answer distractedly.

"A leaf? Where was it?"

I am inking the owl's talons and think of that brokenhearted woman. I answer without thinking. "It was at the base of her family tree. Her baby died."

I notice his muscles tense at that and it's enough to wake me up a little and put me on my guard. "Oh. And she wanted a mark for the baby?"

I remember her words as if she was speaking them right now. *I know I'm meant to forget them when they die before they're marked . . . He was only two days old.* And I remember Obel's warning. I can't let him down. I need to stop Jack Minnow's questions.

Allowing myself a moment to breathe, I drag the needle a little raggedly over a patch of skin that is already raw. I hear him gasp.

"Oh, sorry!" I say. "I think maybe I need to concentrate a bit more—you know, I'm still learning. I obviously haven't quite grasped the skill of chatting and inking at the same time."

I catch Obel's eye and he smiles briefly out of the eyeline of Minnow. From then on, the only sound is the machine, Minnow's breath as he inhales the pain, and the uncensored bawl of his marks screaming their secrets to me.

Eventually, with the outline complete, his skin is too sore and swollen for me to be able to carry on.

"I think we'll have to let this heal a bit before we do stage two, Mr. Minnow," I say, cleaning away the blood and dressing the beautiful, fearsome wound I've imprinted on his shoulder. I am desperate for him to leave. "It's looking good, though," I say as

I peel off my gloves. "It looks just like the owl's about to swoop down and catch his prey." I do my best to sound casual. "I wonder what horned owls hunt."

"Oh, almost any small, insignificant creature, I think," says Minnow. "But there's one thing they hunt that I think is rather remarkable—it shows how brave and strong the owl is."

"Oh yes?" I ask brightly. "What's that?" My hands are busy breaking down my workstation and removing the plastic covering from the chair.

"Crows. Horned owls hunt crows. Late at night, when the crows roost, just when they feel completely safe, the owl comes for them."

I throw the plastic away and wipe my hands. I try to smile politely as I hand Minnow his shirt and help him put it on over his bandage. He's a hunter.

He catches my hand as I help him and frowns at the wound, still healing. "Cut yourself? You should be more careful, Miss Flint."

I don't speak as he drops my hand. He doesn't book another session but says he'll be back sometime. Just as he's about to leave he stops and turns to me, pulling something out of his pocket as though he's just remembered. He holds it out to me.

"Ever seen anything like this before?" I take in the smudged paper and swallow as I recognize a picture of a feather, just like the one the woman gave to Obel when she came after hours. I shake my head.

"No, means nothing to me," I say lightly, willing my face not to flush. He gazes at me silently as he puts the paper back in his pocket. I see him out the door, and feel a moment of satisfaction when he forgets about his tattoo and puts the strap of his bag over his painful shoulder, wincing as he does so. He walks away without turning back.

When he's completely out of sight I shut the door and lock it. I go into the back room and scrub my hands over and over again, until they're red and stinging. Obel puts his hand on my shoulder and I let him turn the tap off. I dry my shaking hands.

"I'm scared, Obel."

And the worst part is when Obel says, "Me too, Leora. Me too."

chapter 30

THAT AFTERNOON, WHEN OBEL IS WITH A CUSTOMER and I'm working quietly, there's an insistent banging on the back door of the studio. I open it to find Verity, breathless. Her eyes are wide with fear. I step outside into the street.

"They've found it," she whispers. "All the evidence that Connor Drew was hiding—it was located in a hidden space in one of his workshops. I can't be gone long; I'm only on my break. But Leora"—she stops to catch her breath—"they've confiscated it all. Everything is in the department ready to be itemized, starting tomorrow. You don't have long; you've got to find your dad's skin before they do." I nod. She passes me a folded piece of paper and a key. "This should help. You need to do it tonight." Her eyes are wide and frightened. "Please be careful, Leora. There's too much riding on this."

And she leaves before I can say goodbye or thank her.

I pray that Oscar got my message. I pray that he will come. I suggested the museum as our meeting place. It's warm and doesn't cost money, plus it's busy and public enough that no one would suspect us of doing anything untoward. I didn't expect us to be planning a break-in, but this is as good a place to talk as any.

When I see that he's waiting for me in the reception area, I nearly cry with relief. Composing myself, and without speaking, we walk through the atrium, which houses the books of our old leaders. We stop now and then to look at a piece of artwork or an archaeological find, but mostly we walk.

As we walk, I pass him the paper Verity gave me; it is a plan of the building and instructions for where we can find the confiscated evidence. I murmur to him the news that Verity gave me. He nods gravely, looking less shocked than I thought he would—he must have been expecting this moment to come, or at least preparing himself for the possibility. He slips the paper into his jacket pocket and we're silent for a while as we gaze through the glass. Then he turns to me and gently, so gently, brushes my hair out of my eyes to reveal the bruise on my forehead. He frowns when he sees the red and blue marks.

"Are you all right?" he asks, his voice low. "Every time I see you, you have some new injury." He takes my hand and examines the healed cut. I'm suddenly aware of how warm and strong his hands are; I can feel rough skin on his fingertips as he runs them over my age marks. "Do you think you might need a bodyguard?"

I laugh and pull my hand away. "Are you offering?"

"Well, we bookbinders are renowned for our intimidating physique." He laughs, and I just grin at him.

"What do you want to be remembered for, Leora?" he asks suddenly. "What are you going to make sure gets inked onto your skin?"

I frown a little. The question catches me off guard; it seems odd, a little morbid. But when I look up into his face I can see he's serious. I close my eyes and think. What will it be, this first mark? What do I want my children to read on my skin? What do I want to be known forever for? What will matter enough to be there for eternity?

And I can't come up with a single thing.

I think of things I'd like to do—reach the highest grade of inker, get married, have kids. But are those things worthy of remembrance? Does it really matter that someone remembers me beyond my days, when my life is just one spark in a great fire? On skin, my life won't look so different from anyone else's.

And then a treacherous thought comes into my mind. Perhaps you can't know someone by reading their book. Not really know them. I banish it and try to concentrate on Oscar.

"I don't know," I say. "I guess I haven't given it much thought. What about you?"

Oscar laughs incredulously. "Seriously? You haven't given it much thought? This is what we're supposed to be living for, and you've not given it much thought?"

I shrug and he shakes his head in an exasperated way. We walk farther around the room, taking slow paces, trying to look like ordinary visitors.

"I have one mark—it says I've completed my first year of bookbinding training. And the mark on my tree deleting Dad." He shrugs. "I just want to live long enough to have more than this on my skin . . ." His voice peters out.

"I know," I say.

"Maybe that's all I want," he says quietly. "The chance to honor Dad's memory, to be remembered enough for the both of us." His voice is distant and I can tell his mind is somewhere else.

We look at each other and that's when I know what I want to be remembered for. I want to be remembered for fighting for my dad. Oscar and I both have tears in our eyes. He rests his forehead on mine.

"It's going to be OK, Leora." My breath shivers as I look up at him.

When a curator passes us, guiding a group around the central exhibit, we break apart. The guide frowns our way so Oscar takes my hand and we hurry through the nearest door, past a guard, hiding our smiles. I stand still while my eyes grow accustomed to the gloom of this new space and Oscar takes a step back, knocking into something with a dull smack. We pause, and as my vision sharpens I see Oscar's smile slowly fade, and we realize where we are. We have gone through the green door, and the tank where the blank man floats is rocking ever so slightly from when Oscar bumped into it, the liquid sloshing lightly while the man's elbows squeak against the glass. We are surrounded.

On every side are pictures of how it must have been before. These alabaster tombs of people with their blanched white skin and their secrets. Some of them have swollen stomachs, as though the lies and evil they've hidden have filled them up and are ready to burst out. They all have eyes that see too much, know too much, hide too much.

I shudder at an image of a blank cutting off the hand of a marked man—taking his years, taking his marks, taking his life. The room is heavy with the evil that seeps off the pictures and writings in this room. There are the written accounts of the horror faced by families tormented by the blanks. It's all too easy to think that this is part of the fairy tale. But it's real and we mustn't forget it.

They look like skeletons—no, like ghosts. We're only haunted by their memory now. I remind myself that they're gone. We're safe. But my fear feels real and their power feels all too strong.

I turn to Oscar and whisper, "I hate it here."

He squeezes my hand and murmurs something, patting the pocket that contains Verity's instructions. I'm not certain of what he says, but it sounds like, "But we all have secrets."

. . .

When I get home a little later Mom calls out to me. "Leora, are you back? I'm coming down!" She clatters down the stairs with a piece of paper in her hand. Her face is an odd mixture of fear and relief.

"The letter came today. We've got a date for the ceremony."

She hands me the slip of thick, official paper and I read it. Dad's weighing of the soul ceremony is just weeks away.

I don't have much time.

chapter 31

WHEN I WAS SEVEN I STOLE A COOKIE.

I stole it from the bakery—the one where Seb works now. I knew that if I asked Mom for one she would say no, because she always did. They were stacked at my eye level, tempting me, taunting me. So, I waited until the baker's back was turned and Mom was leaning forward asking for the bread to be sliced, and I slipped a round, pale, sugar-dusted cookie into my coat pocket.

I hadn't thought far enough ahead to figure out how to eat it without my parents noticing. For the rest of the day I tried to figure out how to get to my coat, hung on its hook near the door, without Mom or Dad becoming suspicious. The mixture of guilt and desperate longing consumed me. The only solution was to creep downstairs in the middle of the night, shivering in the darkness. I fumbled my way to my coat and found the pocket, my heart racing with fear of being caught and excitement at being able to eat my cookie. But in my pocket there were only crumbs.

I was much too afraid and ashamed to ask Mom in the morning. Had she found it? Or maybe it had fallen out of my pocket on the walk home. I was certain she could read the guilt on me, or perhaps smell the sugary vanilla-fragranced worry I wafted wherever I went. I never have plucked up the courage to ask what happened to that cookie. But I've never stolen anything since.

Until tonight.

Maybe this isn't really stealing. After all, he's my dad. His story belongs to me. Still—breaking into a government building at night feels very, very wrong. And there's Verity and Oscar too; they're risking so much for me. We could all be forgotten if we're found out. But it's the only way. If I don't try to rescue Dad I will always wonder if I could have saved him.

Verity, *lovely, amazing* Verity, has mapped out our path through the government building. We have to get in through a window that leads into a locked storeroom. She's written that they keep a spare key on a shelf and that the key she has already given me should open the door to the room where Connor Drew's confiscated work is being kept. I have no idea how she's doing this, but I just hope she's been careful to make sure that not too many signs point to her.

Preparing to sneak out of the house in the dead of night, I feel the same guilt and fear as I did when I was seven, slipping downstairs to find my stolen cookie. It's so cold, all I really want to do is snuggle back into bed, pretend this isn't happening. Dressing in my darkest clothes, I'm distracted by the marks on my skin; the stretch mark on my breast is darker and more jagged by this half-light, and there is a patch on the front of my shoulder where the injury from Karl's fingernails remains. At this rate I'll have more marks from stretch marks and scars than ink. I lace up my soft boots, creep past Mom's door, and ease the front door closed. The key that Verity gave me is heavy in my pocket.

The square is lit by lanterns at night, so Oscar and I have arranged to meet around the back of the government building, where it's dark and no one walks. I nearly walk right into one of the large trash cans as I turn the corner, and I hear a muffled laugh.

"Well, that was slick," Oscar whispers. I peer into the darkness and can just see the glint of his glasses ahead of me.

"Shhh!" I ease forward, nervous that I'm going to trip. Reaching out my hand until I feel his rough coat, I step toward him and he pulls me closer. We both shiver and I tiptoe to whisper to him.

"Now, where's this window we're meant to climb through?"

Oscar's smiling at me; I catch the flash of his teeth in the darkness. That makes me think of his dimples. *Not helpful, brain.*

He gestures for me to follow him and leads me down the side of the building. "I think I found it just along here." He stops at a frosted window, which sheds enough light from inside for us to see the catch Verity told us about.

"If we slide a knife or something between the two pieces of the sash window we can ease the catch open and get in," I say.

Oscar reaches into his bag and takes out a metal ruler. "I'm not getting caught with a weapon." He grins at me. He wedges the ruler where the two sections of window meet and pushes it up through the gap. Paint falls in crusty puffs as he wriggles the ruler in the tight space. I keep looking around, hoping that I would see anyone coming near. A couple of times the catch nearly slides open and then snaps back with a *clack*. Oscar wipes his hands on his pants while the ruler stays stuck in the sash and tries again. At last, the catch slides and Oscar tugs the ruler free. He eases the window open; it groans and hangs wonkily while Oscar gives me a hand getting through. I drop down onto the floor and stumble on a bucket, which clangs loudly. I hope Verity was right about there being no guards at night, because I would have just alerted them. I clear some space for Oscar and I try the door, relieved when the key works smoothly and the door into the corridor opens easily. But now we're in, my heart is beating too fast, and when I try to remember Verity's instructions my mind is blank. I close my eyes, take a deep breath, and peer down the corridor. It's empty and eerie. I remember now.

"She said to turn right, then left at the end, then it should be the third door on the left." Oscar nods at me, hitches his bag over his chest, and we walk slowly and quietly down the corridor. The smell of the heavy wooden doors and polish gives it the feeling of walking through my old school. There is dim lighting along the corridor that gives everything a greenish tinge.

I keep looking back, expecting to see someone ready to pounce.

But everything is just as Verity said it would be. It's almost too easy. The door is closed but unlocked and it creaks heavily as Oscar pushes it open. There are no windows in this room— nothing that can change the temperature too much in here. There are boxes and boxes piled all around the small room.

"Looks like they've not started the inventory." We ease out boxes one by one. "Remember where everything was; we need to put it back just as it was." Oscar nods and opens the box nearest to him. There are more than I expected.

"Are these all people your dad has . . . edited?" I whisper.

"Mostly," he replies quietly.

"Why did he keep it all?" I've been wondering this for the last couple of days. "Why didn't he just get rid of the evidence, burn it or something?"

Oscar looks at me sideways. "It's still people's skin, Leora." He handles the items in the box he's looking through so carefully. "You can't just get rid of it. It's part of who they are."

I think about it and he's right. As offensive as Dad's missing mark is, I would feel more heartbroken to think it was lost forever. Skin matters too much. Oscar moves to the other side of the room and we work in silence, just our breath and the shifting of folders, papers, and skin making sound.

"Here!" Oscar says, gently brushing off a folder as he pulls it from a box. "This is him, right?" He passes me the folder, and I read Dad's name on the front, JOEL FLINT, in careful script. I ease the cover open, and a small fragment of skin slips out. I pick it up carefully, as though it were a living thing. I take a shuddering breath, relieved to have found him. It's not like last time, when we saw his whole book. The hope and pleasure in seeing him then is replaced by nerves and a sense of horror at seeing that mark again. You can tell where his scalp was shaved, tiny hairs still showing. The scar from the injury that Verity's Mom sewed up is a pale line, but the mark is there, black-winged and unmistakable.

Oscar must notice my reticence because he steps over the open boxes and puts a hand on my shoulder.

"Shall I take him?" He puts his hand out and I give him the folder containing Dad's skin. We had already agreed that he be the one to keep it safe. Oscar said they've searched his house so many times he knows the places they'd never look.

"He deserves this, Leora." Oscar slides the folder into his bag. "Let's get these boxes put away, hey?" I nod and help him.

We work in silence and soon everything looks the way it did when we arrived. I'm confident no one will suspect we've been here.

Unless someone knows about the mark already, a nasty voice whispers. I shut it out.

"Ready?" I turn to Oscar, who is fastening his bag. As he does, I see a second folder has been shoved in it. I'm sure he has slipped something else in there. He catches me looking.

"This wasn't in the plan." My voice is loud in the silence.

"It's nothing." I reach for his bag and he stops me with a hand on my arm that feels suddenly hard and unyielding. All of his warmth and humor is gone and his eyes are cold. I'm about to argue when I hear it. It's the noise of a door being shut carefully, the sound of someone who doesn't want to be heard.

Without speaking we slip through the door and, half walking, half running, we hurry through the darkened corridors. We reach the storeroom and I lock the door behind us, relieved to see the window catch is still open. Oscar lifts the window and gives me a leg up; my arms are on the window ledge when we hear the storeroom door handle rattle.

We freeze and I close my eyes—a childhood instinct, trying to make myself invisible. My heart is beating so hard and so fast I think I'm going to faint.

"Move!" urges Oscar, and I hurl myself through the window. I stumble and bash my knee on the ground. Oscar drops softly next to me, pulls the window closed, and neatly latches it again.

We run down the alley and then when we reach the square Oscar stops and catches my arm.

"If there is someone in there, they'll see us running across the square."

"What do you suggest?" I say desperately.

"Take off your hat, try to breathe steadily, and walk with me as though we've just been for a moonlit stroll." He removes his own hat, opens his jacket a little, and walks ahead with a relaxed demeanor. He turns, holds out his hand. I shake my head, amazed at his calmness, and take it.

When we're partway across the square I glance back at the government building. In one of the front windows I see a pale figure standing, watching us. I think I recognize his broad silhouette.

We're being hunted.

But some prey escape. Don't they?

chapter 32

*IN MY DREAM I OPEN OSCAR'S SATCHEL AND IT'S
filled with crumbs. I turn and see them both there: Mom and
Oscar, eating the page we stole, licking vanilla-scented crumbs
from their fingertips. I try to stop them and all I see is Oscar, finger
to his lips, smiling at me.*

. . .

I see Verity on Monday evening and she tells me there has been
no mention of a break-in. I try to feel optimistic; perhaps we've
done it. But I can't stop thinking about the figure at the window.

Everything carries on as normal, the rest of the world
unaware of my Dad's ceremony looming. I daydream at work and

I'm too agitated to draw. I spend every moment of spare time thinking through Dad's case. If they can't prove that he was marked as forgotten they can't use it as evidence against him. His skin—what they have—can speak for him and show what a good and worthy man he was. The judge will find it impossible to cast his book into the flames.

That's the theory anyway.

In just over a week it will be over. And I will never have to think about it again.

Or see Oscar again.

The problem is, Oscar's more of a distraction than I imagined he'd be. When I'm not with him my mind is going over the times we were together—remembering every word, every smile, every touch; remembering the cold look in his eyes. What was he putting in his bag? And then I wonder if I should have been more cautious from the start. I tell myself over and over again that I can trust him. I must. And then my imagination plays and creates new memories, memories of things that haven't happened but I wish would. And yet I don't know that I really want my daydreams to become reality.

Something seems to have changed between Mom and me; we're talking properly for the first time in ages, talking about our memories of Dad. Sometimes, like when I do an impression of Dad's face when he would try to be cross, Mom even laughs. It's a good feeling. We've danced around each other in the last few months—too scared to disturb the healing wounds, too afraid that what makes one of us happy will break the other's heart. But we're trusting our own scarred souls a little more now, fearing that if we don't remember him now, we never will. If he's forgotten in the ceremony next week, we will be forbidden from speaking about him again. His name will be removed from our trees—inked over with dark crows pecking away at the corpse.

One evening I notice that my grandfather's book, wiped clean of coffee, has been moved to a higher shelf, where I can't reach it. I try, that night, to get Mom to open up about how she and Dad met and why Granddad hated my father so much. About my father's early life in Riverton. About what she knows of his life before us. She won't tell me anything, though. I realize I am searching for clues: for a reason why a man like my father would have been marked as forgotten.

I let myself believe it can't matter. I know how good he was. Nothing can shake that.

It's been a while since Mom and I last did our speaking of the names duty, and it has come around again. We set off in darkness to meet Verity, and the ground is icy underfoot. I'm already getting a little tired of the cold, even though I know there's a couple more months of it to live through. I've had enough of the dregs of autumn and the wintry season of death, and I'm ready for the new life to spring up. Winter looks a lot like a graveyard, bleak, cold, and lifeless, but the green shoots are getting ready and they give me hope.

There's something about leaving the house when you would normally be going to bed—wearing cloaks and shawls instead of nightclothes and slippers. There's something about walking through the darkness and entering the candlelit hall. There's something about the silence of nighttime with just our voices piercing it.

Tonight as we stand in the hall, lit by flickering candles, I am struck by how different I feel. Nothing has changed here; this beautiful space has rung with voices speaking names all the time I've been working at the studio, all the time I've been worrying about Dad. I'm not the same person and I can't go back. This evening, we read a familiar name on the list. I listen to Verity as she reads it out and spend silent minutes trying to remember who it is. Then I realize it's just the name of one of the books in the museum that I've read before. No one special. But of course, she is special; she should be. If nobody really knows the person anymore, does it matter?—does it still count as remembrance? My mind murmurs doubts and heresy even as I'm reading the names. What if it doesn't work? What if all this is for nothing and there's no such thing as an eternal soul? What if it doesn't matter and we've wasted our lives on this? What if it's nonsense but it's all we've ever lived for? I try to quiet the rebellious voice in my mind by reading out each name more loudly, more clearly when my turn comes. But each time I do, the voice just asks, "Who? Who? Who?"

I look over at my mother, calmly reading. And I'm grateful for this moment of just being mother and daughter and of doing the things we've always done. If I pretend, I can imagine everything else is unchanged too.

chapter 33

IT'S SO MUCH BUSIER AT THE STUDIO WITHOUT KARL there, and when I'm at work it's possible to forget everything else and to get lost in the routine. It's oddly soothing, and is the only time I don't feel like my hands are shaking. The week passes. The nights are bad—hours of tossing and turning, interspersed with vivid dreams—but the days are calm enough. I manage not to think about Monday.

But on Friday as I hang up my apron, my anxiety about the ceremony returns. I just can't believe it will be that easy; that all we needed to do was remove that one sliver of skin. I can't bear the thought of the whole weekend stretching ahead: a weekend of uncertainty and doubt. My heart races as though I've been running. I breathe deeply and, on my way home, take a detour; it's late, but I want to see if Mel's still there.

I'm in luck. She's at her desk, while Isolda sits on the floor reading a book. I can see that they've not marked her yet—I wonder when she'll be told her first story.

Mel gives me her usual warm smile, her eyes creasing up in pleasure at seeing me.

"I'm glad you came in; I had a feeling you would." Mel gets out of her chair and turns to the bookcase. "I thought you might be worrying still—about Monday."

"I'm trying not to think about it, but I'm ready to have him home with us."

Mel looks at me thoughtfully, sympathetically, and reaches up to get a book off one of her shelves. It's bound in blue leather and I recognize it as one of the storybooks my schoolteacher used to read from when I was little.

"I wanted to lend you this before the ceremony. I thought some bedtime reading might be a nice distraction. Plus, it's got the story your father requested in it, in case you want to look at it again before Monday."

She hands me the book.

"I bet you've hardly slept in weeks. You should rest, Leora."

I concede her point with a dip of the head and thank her for the book. As I go to leave she whispers a traditional benediction.

"*May your ancestors go before you; may they make your path straight and light your way. May your descendants follow you, praising your name as they walk in your footsteps. May your feet not grow weary; may your heart not fear. May your name be remembered and your soul live eternally."*

Her touch warms me and, despite myself, in spite of all my fears and dread, I am comforted.

Mel was right—I haven't been sleeping, and tonight is no exception. My thoughts bounce around my mind, building more and more momentum, until I switch my lamp back on and notice the book Mel lent to me. I pick it up and spot a bookmark. I open the book at the marked page, expecting it to be at the story of the lovers, but it's a different tale. Mel's writing is on the bookmark.

I always loved this one when I was little. You're more like the sleeping beauty than you know. Good luck. Mel.

chapter 34

The Sleeping Princess

Sleep is a wonderful gift. A good night's sleep solves most problems, heals most ailments, and sweetens most sour moods. Sleep is a fragile gift, though; nights are easily broken by wailing infants, noisy neighbors, and worrisome thoughts. No one would ever imagine sleep would be a curse.

Of course, no one knows the preciousness of sleep better than parents of newborns. They fantasize about sleep. When they do get a snatched moment to doze, they dream they're awake and have forgotten to feed the baby or to put her in her cradle.

Little wonder, then, that when the sleep-starved king and queen had their first child they forgot one or two people when they sent out invitations to the banquet celebrating the birth of their daughter. Most of the people who were forgotten were much too polite to complain—after all, who were they to expect an invitation to the palace? But there's always someone who thinks a little too highly of themselves—and it's always that person whom you accidentally offend.

When the guests were laying their gifts at the foot of the baby's cradle, no one noticed the woman who crept in, the one whose name wasn't on the guest list.

The king and queen were lucky to have friends who knew the secrets of magic, and their daughter was bestowed with virtuous qualities fitting for a princess. One gave beauty, another charm, another riches, and still another intelligence. As the last guest approached the cradle, there was a sudden chill in the air. Those assembled murmured in embarrassed fascination as the uninvited woman strode up to the thrones.

"I see I'm just in time for the gifts," she crowed as the king and queen shifted awkwardly in their thrones. "I'm so glad I haven't missed my chance."

It's fair to say that this magical creature was piqued. She was angry to have been forgotten and had decided to make sure the king and queen would remember her every day from here on.

"My gift is to be saved for her sixteenth birthday," said the woman with a smile, baring her white teeth.

"The day this child turns sixteen, she will prick her finger on the spindle of a spinning wheel and she will instantly die."

The queen fainted and the king begged her to change her mind, but the forgotten woman walked away unhearing, taking a slice of cake as she left the castle.

As the horrified shouts and screams faded, one final magical guest—who had been waiting to give her gift—spoke up.

"I can't undo the curse in its entirety, but I can change it. Instead of dying, this child and the whole kingdom will sleep for one hundred years, after which time, a kiss from a prince will awaken her."

The shocked and sleep-deprived king thanked the guest and secretly felt that one hundred years of sleep was the best gift anyone had given that night.

The king commanded that all spindles and wheels be destroyed, and his daughter grew in safety and peace all through her childhood. No one is sure why people weren't a little more watchful during the princess's sixteenth birthday party. But somehow she managed to wander into a secret part of the palace. There she met a woman spinning, there she pricked her finger, and there she fell into a deep, accursed sleep. At that moment everything and everyone in the kingdom froze. Time had halted and would only begin again in one hundred years' time.

During the one hundred years, many princes tried to reach the sleeping princess, but it was only when the apportioned time had passed that one young prince beat his way through the thornbushes that had grown up around the castle. He found everyone as still as statues and the princess gently snoring where she had fallen. He kissed her and she woke.

When you're asleep it's hard to know how much time has passed. But it was clear to the princess that this had been no ordinary nap.

She woke to see a stranger looming over her and she ran away, out to the throne room to find her parents. She saw everyone easing themselves back into wakefulness and wondered what strangeness had occurred. Before long, her parents told her the full story. The princess was enraged. How could they have kept such a secret from her? If she had known, she would never have been so foolish as to prick her finger on a spinning wheel. Wondering if she could ever trust them again, she rode away with the prince. She told him that he shouldn't kiss sleeping girls, and that she would think about his marriage proposal in a few years.

chapter 35

I GET THROUGH THE WEEKEND SOMEHOW. MOM looks as tense as I feel, but I can tell she's decided to be optimistic; her mouth is set in a calm smile that looks utterly false. Late on Sunday evening, the night before Dad's weighing, there's a knock at the door. Verity stands there, her hair plastered to her head and her teeth chattering in the biting rain.

I catch her arm. "Come in! You'll freeze out there. Where's your shawl?"

I hang up her sodden coat and pass her a towel for her hair. It's only then that I notice she looks ill. Something's wrong. Really wrong.

"What's happened? Is everything OK?" She shakes her head slightly and looks dazed. "Is Seb all right?"

"He's fine. It's not Seb." She catches my hands in hers. "I heard something on Friday at work, Lor, and I need to tell you. I should have come earlier, but I didn't think—at first it didn't seem important. But the more I've thought about it—I don't know if it matters—but I have to tell you."

I pull out a chair for her and we sit down. "What happened?" I dread asking, but I have to know everything before tomorrow morning.

She rubs the ends of her long hair with the towel. "It's probably nothing, Lor. It's just that I bumped into Karl." She makes a face as though she's tasted something poisonous. "I tried to keep walking but then he called after me. He said . . . he said, 'See you on Monday.'" She sees my face and laughs shakily. "I know—you'll tell me I'm overreacting. But it sounded—as though he meant something by it."

"You think he's planning to come to Dad's weighing?" I ask in disbelief.

Verity shrugs. "I have no idea, Lor. I thought he was just winding me up—he knows it's my first ceremony case. But the more I've thought about it, the more I've wondered if he knows something."

"He's not that clever, Verity—not clever enough to have found out anything. He just loves annoying people." *Do I believe that?*

"But still, Lor. He knows we're friends, and he knows I've

been working on your dad's case. Will you be careful? He could try to ruin everything."

My heart sinks, but I keep my voice light. "He doesn't know anything," I repeat. "Does he?"

Verity shakes her head. "I don't think so—I think I've been careful enough for people not to make the link, and the summary of your dad's book that I've written for the judge is neutral—no one could suspect me of favoring him. But I wanted to warn you." She gives me a weak smile. "Not that you can do much about it between now and tomorrow, I suppose. Just be on your guard tomorrow, OK?"

I lean forward and rub her knee.

"Thanks, Vetty. It's going to be OK. I've got a good feeling—it's really going to be all right."

She smiles again—her old hopeful smile. "You're right. I'm sorry, I'm being silly. He just makes me nervous." I wipe the tears from her cheeks and we hug.

"Listen, it's getting late and we could both do with a bit of sleep tonight." I give her my coat, as hers is still soaked. "Here, take this. Get home before your Mom worries."

Verity nods. "Mom and Dad will be there tomorrow. You know we will all be asking our ancestors to uphold justice tomorrow. I'll light a candle in remembrance of your dad before I leave for the trial."

We're both crying now, but trying to smile and sniff our way out of it. I open the door, and the wind makes the coat and shawl billow around Verity's slim frame. She reaches into the pockets and pulls out two dead leaves. She frowns and lets them drop onto the sodden ground.

"Thanks, Verity—you're the best friend I could ever imagine." I mean it.

I watch her walk away until the rain is all I can see. Eventually I hear Mom call from upstairs, "Is there a window open, Leora? It's freezing!" and I shut the door.

chapter 36

M OM AND I ARE BOTH AWAKE EARLY, WE EAT HOT
toast with butter in a nervous silence. I stir the tea and
the only sounds are the spoon hitting the side of the pot
and the scrape of the lid as I replace it. We are both dressed
formally—with our finest shawls draped over the backs of our
chairs, ready to encase us with their power and protection.

We light candles for each of our ancestors, and one for my
father too. We speak a short prayer, asking them for guidance
today whatever the outcome. But these are only my mother's
ancestors; will they care? Still, I must trust my ancestors to be

good, to be just. I even ask Granddad to have mercy and call for justice for Dad.

Mom is crying as she blows out the candles. She gets to Dad's and shakes her head. She walks away, hand over mouth, shoulders quaking with sobs. It's down to me to blow his candle out. It's never felt so wrong.

"See you later, Dad," I whisper. And I extinguish his flame.

chapter 37

I N SPITE OF ITS EVER-BURNING FIRE, THE HALL OF judgment feels cold. The stone arches of the outer walkway are whipped by a cold breeze from the open doors. The entrance doors are always open to remind us that this is where we all will enter sooner or later. The fire is always lit so that we don't forget the threat of eternal destruction.

The bench Mom and I sit on has flattened cushions running along it; stitched, I expect, by earnest devotees years ago. They offer no real relief from the shallow seat and hard wood. Even the fabric has absorbed the chill, sending it through my muscles into my bones. Nothing here offers any comfort to my anxious heart.

Being inside the hall feels like being inside a witch's hat. The ceiling funnels upward, and the colored stained glass panels that slant inward toward the chimney bathe us in their watery glow. The full spectrum is displayed in the leaded shards that look down on us. The sun's position illuminates the indigos and violets, making the room look bruised and drenched in wine.

Two men in the leather of our traditional dress stoke the fire, adding more cherry and apple tree logs to it, which gives the air an incense-sweet fragrance that combines with the scents of the cold benches, musty stone, and tangy metal columns. I always thought I would come here feeling hopeful, feeling joy beneath the grief of death. I never imagined I would sit here with even an ounce of uncertainty about the outcome of the judgment. I wouldn't have considered that I'd need to be praying that my own father would escape the flames.

I read a fable once about three men who were put in a furnace for treachery. The onlookers saw that the men weren't burning up and that another mysterious figure had joined them. The men were freed from the furnace unscathed, not even smelling of smoke. I pray that my ancestors would shield my father, that they will be with him to protect him from the fire. Surely we've done enough. Surely he will be saved.

I look up at the sloping ceiling, its beams and panels making it look like a cobweb. The great metal columns lean in toward the chimney; we sit at the base of one of the legs like flies hiding at a spider's foot. The chimney hangs down, the stamen of a carnivorous plant, an insect tongue sucking the smoke away.

People arrive and sit themselves on the tiered benches that curve around half the room. Some come and touch our hands and whisper consoling words. I wish they would just walk by. I look out for the people I really want to see, and spot Simon and Julia, who give me encouraging smiles. Julia blows us a kiss. Verity will arrive with the judge in the procession that walks from the government building with Dad's book. I spot Obel across the room, sitting on one of the benches farthest away, his face pale and set.

And there's Oscar. He is pulling his shirt straight, combing a hand through his messy curls. He looks uncomfortable in the formal surroundings, and I remember that he's been where I am now. He knows what it's like.

Closing my eyes to block out everyone else, I try to go through the order of the ceremony in my mind. First the judge will speak, then Mel will tell the story Dad requested, then the floor will be open to anyone who wants to speak and share stories and memories about Dad.

And then it's the summing up. Verity was sure she had written the summary of his book clearly enough for the judge to make the right decision. She had been neutral, she said, but everything about my dad's life shouted out to be remembered.

My feet are cold and I tap my toes on the stone floor to wake them. The hall is filling up now, and that's when I notice him by the door.

Karl.

He is looking right at me. Why couldn't he leave me alone just for today? When he sees that I'm looking his way he looks over his shoulder and raises a hand. He beckons to me from across the room, urging me with his eyes to follow him as he walks out the door.

The judge still isn't here, and neither—as far as I can tell—are any members of the government offices.

I decide I have no choice but to see what he wants. I tell Mom I'll be right back, then stand and walk through the doors Karl just went through. He's waiting, and now I'm up close I can see he too looks worried, anxious, sweating a little. He gives me a brief snarl of a smile and I follow him as he walks farther down the corridor. He stops under an arch between the pillars—it's a space tucked away from the main concourse, shaded by the huge stonework, out of the gleam of the leaded windows.

"What do you want, Karl?" I ask, my voice cold.

His body sags as he sighs. There is something in his face I have never seen before, and then I realize—he looks frightened. "Look—I want to help you. And to apologize," he says quietly. "I didn't mean to hurt you the other day." His eyebrows furrow. "Everything's just such a mess," he says, almost to himself. "I'm sorry." He looks smaller today, a little crumpled.

"This isn't the time, Karl. Don't make this about you." I resist my instinct to pity him. I need to set my mind on Dad, not get distracted.

"I know, I know that." His voice comes out strained and he's fiddling with the buttons on his shirt. "Look. There's something I need to tell you."

My patience is running out, and I don't have time for his games. He's playing me like he always has. I look behind me and see a flurry of movement—the judge must be about to come in. "I've got to go," I say, and begin to walk away. Karl grabs my wrist and I turn in fury. "Don't touch me," I hiss. "Do you hear? Don't you ever touch me again." He takes a startled step back. I head back toward the hall, cursing myself for letting him get to me.

"Leora! Just . . . just be careful who you've put your trust in." I stop, but don't turn around. "All this work you've done to save your father, they've known all along—they're . . . they're just playing with you." His voice trembles. "You're doing exactly what they want you to do."

I shake my head and carry on walking, hearing him groan with frustration as I make my way back to the hall. But a tiny voice in my mind whispers: *How does he know unless they've told him?*

chapter 38

I STUMBLE BACK TO MY SEAT. A CLUSTER OF PEOPLE are in my way and I step around them and sit down next to Mom. She pats my knee.

"Just in time," she whispers.

There is nothing I can do now. Nothing I can do to change what will happen.

The judge enters then with the representatives from the government in procession after him. Verity is right at the back, carrying some papers. With them is Mel, who shoots me a reassuring glance, and I shiver when I recognize the broad figure of Jack Minnow. The judge has a wooden box; he walks to the front of the dais, where the lectern is, and opens the box. He places its contents on the wooden plinth next to the lectern and sets it up. It's the scales. They are copper-colored and marked with age. He places a weight on one of the dishes and it drops to rest on the base of the scales. The other dish is empty, waiting for Dad's book.

The scales that tell the truth. Or is it all part of the ritual, all part of the show? I don't know anymore.

I feel like I'm listening to the proceedings from underwater. The judge's voice honks importantly but I can't follow what he is saying. I've been waiting for this moment for so long that I can't really believe it's happening.

When the judge introduces Mel, I chew my thumb hard in a desperate attempt to jolt myself into the present moment. During the story the conniving brother's tale interests me most. Deception is always discovered. Good always triumphs. Who is good in my father's story?

People who knew him come to the stand and talk about my dad. Mom is crying and she reaches to hold my hand. Wonderful father, loving husband, masterful flayer. Eventually people stop coming and there's a pause. The judge begins to sum up.

"This is an unusual case. At first glance, it is clear that Joel Flint was a model citizen—a good husband, a loving father, a hard worker, and an honest man. But there are irregularities that have caused us some headaches as we prepared for this ceremony." He clears his throat and Verity fidgets in her seat. I look at the back of Oscar's head and see his jaw tense.

Mom grabs my knee. "We've done everything right. We've done all we can, don't worry," she whispers. I don't know if she's reassuring me or herself. Her fingers feel like talons.

The judge gestures to one of his assistants, who brings the box containing Dad's book to the table. The judge removes it from the box and gently places it on the empty dish of the scales. They wobble and sway and for a while I wonder if they will ever still, and then they halt. The balance is perfect.

I gasp. *He will be remembered.* The people are on their feet applauding, cheering, hugging one another. I stand too, an uncertain smile beginning on my face. Mom has her hands over her mouth, sobbing in relief.

But the judge isn't smiling. An assistant bangs a gavel and calls for order. We bustle into silence, confused. We've seen the outcome; what more could they have to say?

The judge clears his throat.

"As you can see, Joel Flint's book weighs true. It tells us he should be remembered." He gestures to the scales. "But it has come to our attention that there is more to this man's story. More than has been told here today. Something is missing."

I see Verity look up at that, alert and afraid. Her fear is catching and spreads heat through my chest. I cling to Mom's hand.

"Let me hand proceedings over to the esteemed Jack Minnow." The judge turns and Minnow steps forward. His face is a picture of serene malevolence. He clears his throat and begins, his voice resonating through the silent room.

"Try as some might, it is hard to keep the secrets that are written on the body." He glares around at us all. "There are those who would try to slither into our society, to worm their way into our lives and then inject their poison. They don't look like snakes, but their bite is just as deadly." Minnow's shoulders draw back and I see the hyenas on his head looking as though they are barking with delight. The fire crackles and I think I hear them cackle.

"What we have here," he taps my dad's book with disdain, letting the scales clang as they swing, "what we have here is a book of lies."

I can hear Mom's breath, ragged and fast. Jack looks to his left and nods; an assistant leaves the hall and returns a moment later with a smartly dressed man wearing the same uniform as Minnow, but in a deep blue color.

"This," Minnow moves to one side to let the man have space next to him, "is Tom Page. A government representative from Riverton, the town where Joel Flint grew up." Mom exhales and I look at her face. Her eyes are wide. Mr. Page takes center stage and reads from a sheet of paper in his hands. His voice rings out.

"Mr. Minnow contacted me after an examination of Joel Flint's book revealed hidden scarring and potentially doctored marks. Joel Flint, or the man who called himself Joel Flint, was once a resident of Riverton and we were asked to examine our archives to see if we had any information as to what might be missing. We had to dig deeply, we had to make inquiries—but in the end, we found what was required." The man looks across at Minnow, who nods and crosses his arms over his chest.

"Our records show that years ago, a man matching Flint's description but whose name was Joe Elliot was discovered to have links with"—he flinches as he reads—"the blank community. In fact, more specifically, he was found to have given shelter to a blank."

I swallow, not daring to look away, to see the faces of the people I love frozen in horror.

"The records show that Flint was arrested and marked with the sign of the crow, which, as you know, means he was a forgotten."

Mom is whispering, her clammy hand clawing into mine. I hear her voice hissing, "No. No. No." The rest of the room is talking, shouting, crying out, and the gavel sounds again.

"Not only this, but our records show that he had been colluding with the blanks for some time. He left Riverton and hearsay tells that he went to live with the blanks, even . . . marrying one of their kind." He spits the words out, disgust leaching into his bland tones. "Unconfirmed rumors claim that he had a child with this blank woman, and that when his deviant wife died, he brought this half-breed baby with him to Saintstone. To live among us." His eyes flick up and he looks straight at me. The whole room looks straight at me. "To live as one of us."

Blank.

This can't be true. It can't be right. Not my father. He couldn't.

But then I look at Mom, and she's silent. I want to shake her, make her get to her feet and tell them. *Tell them it's not true; tell them I'm your baby. Tell them he wasn't that man.*

I see Verity flash me a look of concern—*doubt?* Then she rises and resolutely steps toward Jack Minnow. He inclines his head to listen to her; she has to get close to be heard above the cacophony of the room. Simon and Julia are standing, watching Verity with naked fear on their faces. Eventually Minnow stands tall, looks at Verity with his head to one side, and shrugs a little, conceding some ground. He turns to face the throng and raises his hands to quiet them. When everyone has stopped and is seated once more he speaks again.

"I have been reminded by Ms. Kohl that at this ceremony we can bring in other evidence—evidence of records and other testimony—but that everything must come back to the book. So in order to continue in this vein, I need the proof that is Mr. Flint's own skin. Evidence that is missing: the mark of the forgotten, which was so glaringly absent from Mr. Flint's book." He glances back at Verity, who returns his gaze calmly. "Of course, I have no desire to wrongly convict a man." He looks so relaxed I can hardly bear it. "And without that mark, this lady is correct; we have no evidence of his crimes."

I look at Verity and want to run and hug her. I look across at Oscar but he's not sitting on the bench anymore. I scan the room and see him stepping toward the dais.

He has something in his hand.

"Thank you, Mr. Drew." Minnow says smoothly. "I think this is what we were looking for."

The heat from the fire makes his outline blurred and gleaming. He speaks to the judge, who nods; then he reaches out and drops something onto the scales on top of Dad's book. I know what it is.

The added weight shifts the balance and the book slams down.

And my hope is outweighed by ink and skin that proclaim to the room that my father was not the man I knew.

Minnow turns to me and calls out, "Leora Flint, I call upon you. Is this your father's skin?" His eyes bore into mine. "Do you recognize this mark?"

My father. Who was my father?

I can feel the beating warmth and hear the spitting of wood splitting in the heat. I'm blinded for a moment by its light, and the smoke stings my eyes. The fire roars in my ears and I think of Dad. Dad at the flayers, Dad teaching me to draw, Dad joking at the dinner table, Dad kissing Mom, Dad on the sofa with stitches in his head, Dad dying, Dad under the embalmer's cloth.

I open my mouth to speak but I can't raise my voice loud enough. I wipe the sweat from my hot brow and look across at the book slung low on the scales. I clear my throat.

Who was Joel Flint? My father: the protector of the blanks. He was a traitor. He was married to a blank and hid the truth every day of his life in Saintstone.

Joel Elliot. Joel Flint.

Joel Flint the forgotten.

Father of Leora Flint, the blank.

My stomach twists with revulsion and hate, and with the smallest nod, I condemn him.

Looking right at Minnow, feeling all eyes on me, I speak loudly. "Burn him."

I'm aware of my mother's desperate cry and her hand ripping from mine. I see Minnow nod, and then watch him advance toward the pyre, look as the fire keepers stand aside. With all the strength that comes from his hatred of my father, Jack Minnow hurls his book into the flames. I watch each page curl, melt, and singe. I watch my father burn.

In the shouts and shoves after Minnow has done his duty I take in the glow of justice being done. I bask in the warmth of my father's fiery reckoning. I never thought it would feel like this. People shout at me, someone tries to save him from the flames but is held back. There's a person calling my name. The sunlight shines through the rainbow glass. The hall is bathed in red.

But all I can do is stand there. Hating this whole sick business.

And most of all, hating my father.

chapter 39

SOMEHOW, I ESCAPE FROM THE PANDEMONIUM AND run back to the house. Hurriedly, I pack a bag, hurling things into it. I can't stay here. I'm trying to figure out where I can go, but I can't think of anyone to run to. Maybe I don't need anybody. It's best not to love anyone; they only betray you. I don't want to be the one standing there lifting my heart up in my hands for all to see, just hoping they'll accept it. No. Hearts are for keeping inside—you can't keep it safe if you give it away.

I grab my coat in the hall but before I can leave the door flies open.

"What have you done? You could have saved him. Just one word, and you could have protected him. How could you?"

Mom is screaming, crying, coming at me looking ready to kill. Her hair is wild and her eyes are red.

Simon holds her back. They're all here—here to pull me apart, I expect. I can just imagine them sitting me down to tell me what a terrible thing I've done. That one nod that broke everything. Maybe I should be feeling bad, at least feeling sad for how they're hurting. But I can't cry, I can't scream; I can't feel.

"You knew everything, didn't you?" I hiss at her blotchy face. "You manipulated me—you manipulated it all. His blood is on *your* hands, not mine. You're as guilty as he was."

I try to walk past with my bag on my shoulder but Mom grabs me. Verity's dad breaks us up, stands between us, and speaks calmly.

"Leora, wait. You will come to regret what you've just said—I think you should apologize to your mom, don't you?"

I laugh at the strangeness of his calm and the madness of his words. I shake my head.

"No, I don't think so. I don't think I will apologize. And anyway, she"—I nod my head toward the ragged-looking woman in front of me—"*she* is not my mom. Or didn't you hear? My real mother was a blank."

I walk out of the house, and no one calls for me to come back.

I go to the museum. I creep into the room of stories that Mel showed me, and when it's closing time I hide myself among the shelves. I sleep with my head on my bag, my shawl covering me and the guardians of the fables looking down on me. When morning comes I wait until the place is busy enough for me to leave unnoticed and I head to the government building. There's no point putting it off.

I sign the forms at the government inker's and let him scrape away my father's existence from my family tree. I am left with a cuckoo roosting on my back. I wanted him to get rid of Mom's name too—maybe I should just call her *Sophie* now—but he needed to cover it with someone else's name and I don't know who the woman is—*was*—who should take her rightful place at the top of my tree. The usurper will have to dwell there a little longer.

While I'm there the inker receives a message. Someone who ranks higher than him has instructed that he is to add a mark to my already throbbing skin. I assent. So I get the mark of an eagle, to show that I stood for the truth, even when it meant forgetting my own family. He also touches up the marks that were botched by the scar on my hand.

As I go to leave the building a familiar voice calls my name. I turn and see Mel. Her face is sad but she's smiling and has her arms out ready to embrace me. She beckons me into a plain and tired-looking office room and offers to make me a drink, which I accept gratefully. I've not had anything to eat or drink today.

"I heard you were here and I came down. I wanted to see how you are. Well, how are you, Leora?"

I can't answer her. She hands me a steaming cup of coffee and I take it in silence.

"Not too sore, I hope?" She's looking at my new marks. "I saw the tattoo you gave Jack—it's a beauty. It seems your instincts were right; you're a gifted inker." She takes a sip of her drink and looks at me with a whole world of worry and affection in her gaze.

This feels good. I still have someone. Someone who knows—who knows the truth but doesn't hate me. "I still think you would have been an incredible flayer, though." I can hear the regret in her voice and I frown as I look at her face. She looks sad. She looks tired.

"Where's Isolda?" I ask.

"She's having some lessons." Mel sips her coffee and smiles that sad smile again. "There are some things that even I can't teach her." She sighs and looks right into my eyes. "You were brave yesterday, Leora."

I shrug. I don't feel brave—I feel angry, I feel like a fool. I feel betrayed.

"What else could I do?" I look down into my mug and quietly admit it.

Mel's voice is gentle. "You did the right thing, Leora. I knew you would, remember? It's awful to find out the way you did, but you did the right thing. Your father may have been a good man in some ways, but he did not lead a good life."

I look up at her. "Did you know, then? Did you know about my father?"

Mel nods. "I did. But Leora—I couldn't tell you. And I didn't have to. I knew you would do the right thing. You've impressed me. You really have." I look at her, trying to read her face. "Now." She puts a warm hand on my knee. "I have a confession of my own to make." I force myself to look curious. "The government has been interested in you since your test results came back. You could have had your pick of the trades. In fact, I think there's only one thing you lack: If you had confidence—if you knew how good you are—you would be the full package."

I flush and shake my head. "Why would the government care about me?"

Mel laughs at my confusion. "Why would the government care about someone with such talent? Someone who could do so much for the sake of our community? Don't be naive, Leora; your potential was obvious. We were certain of that. There was just one thing that we weren't so certain of. Your loyalty."

She looks right at me. "His time living with the blanks seems to have consolidated his already deluded beliefs. He came to Saintstone, not to work and begin again with a clean slate, but to intercede for the blanks. He wheedled his way into the hearts and minds of vulnerable and foolish men and women, who trusted him. He told them he was a freedom fighter: a warrior for peace and equality. But of course, he was trying to prepare the way for war. You know that's what the blanks want?" She pauses, checking my response. "So yes, Leora, we knew all about your father. And your mother—your *real* mother."

The coffee cup is starting to burn my hands as I grasp it tightly. But I need to keep holding it, I need something solid, I need to feel something.

"With your background there was no guarantee you would dedicate your skills to serving society. You have rebel's blood, Leora." And just for a moment her face betrays her; she's disgusted by my blankness. "We couldn't know what seeds your father had planted in your mind. We needed to wait and see where your allegiance lay."

"We?" I try to smile. My voice sounds hoarse. "You've known this all along? You've just been testing me?"

She shifts in her seat and leans back. "I've been mentoring you. Supporting and helping you." She searches my face for a response.

"Is that why you wanted me to read that story? 'The Sleeping Princess'?"

Mel tips her head. "Sometimes parents think they're doing the right thing. But some secrets shouldn't be kept hidden." She smiles gently. "I knew you would understand."

"Mel, I've lost everything." My voice shakes and I have to remind myself of my vow to hide my heart—let nothing in, let nothing out.

"I know it must feel that way, Leora. Believe me, I know what it's like to have nothing except for the community. It's worth it, Leora—what you gain outweighs the cost every time." She reaches out to rub my knee again. "I promise.

"Leora, the people are so afraid. They fear a blank uprising; they know they've lost their way." Her gaze is fixed on my face. "Your father stood for everything that we fear and most despise. But now that they know where your loyalty lies, the government is ready to give you a prized place in society. A role custom-built around you and your myriad skills. A half-blank girl, shown mercy by the benevolent Mayor Longsight, turning her back on all that is dark and evil and embracing all that is good and open."

I shake my head. "But I don't want to work at the government. I . . . I want to be an inker. Or wanted to." My dreams and ambitions feel like a lifetime ago.

Mel laughs as though I've told a joke. "Oh, Leora! This wouldn't be a desk job. For you—well, for *you* we could offer a most remarkable post. One that uses your skills so perfectly it's as though you were born for it." She tilts her head. "As perhaps you were."

chapter 40

AS I WALK THROUGH THE BITINGLY COLD STREETS I try to make some kind of decision about the offer I've just received. Is that what I am now? The perfect member of society, the ideal candidate to uphold our values?

Your father stood for everything we fear and despise. I think of Obel suddenly, about what he said to me about knowing my dad, and I wonder if he knew it all too. He must have. Hot anger rises in me, and I change my course and head toward the studio.

I walk through the shop door and the bell rings. Obel is inking a customer—business as usual. He looks up at me for the briefest moment and then studiously finishes the section he's on.

It's an anticlimax after all my righteous anger. The minutes tick by. He cleans up the client and sends him on his way. All without speaking to me. He removes his gloves and puts them in the trash can; when the bell of the door signals that the customer has gone, he sighs and puts his head in his hands.

"What were you thinking, girl?" He says it gently. "What on earth were you thinking?"

He walks over to me and I see his hands flex—what's he going to do to me? And then he pulls me to him in the tightest hug. I hear him whispering curses, feel his tears hit my head, and he sniffs.

"You knew," I try to shout into his chest. All my anger dissipates, in spite of myself. "You knew it all."

Obel releases me from the hug but holds my shoulders as he gazes seriously into my eyes. "What I know about your father is only good."

"No." I shake my head, trying to find the words—trying to work out how to make him see. "He protected blanks. Lived with them. Helped them. Fathered a child . . ." I break off as another sob rises in my throat.

"I think it's time we talked." Obel starts walking toward the back room. "Come on, I'll make us some tea. Solves everything, remember?"

I sit at the familiar wooden table and feel a pang of sorrow at all that I'll miss. Before the ceremony, as complicated as life felt, things were good. This studio, this career—this was my place. I could be me. But now I feel like a stranger in my old life.

The back door bangs open and there's Oscar. He looks as shocked to see me as I am him. I don't know whether to fight him or thank him. He betrayed me—but justice was done, wasn't it? And what's one more betrayal?

To my surprise, Obel ruffles Oscar's hair and gestures for him to sit down.

"You know each other?" I ask incredulously. Obel looks a little ashamed. "Sorry, girl."

Oscar shakes him off, but eventually, reluctantly sits down as far from me as he can manage to be. "If I'd known she'd be here I would never have come." I can't tell if he's angry with me or ashamed.

Obel takes another mug from the shelf and sighs. "I didn't know she was coming either. It was the last place I thought you would come, Leora. But you're here now, aren't you? And you always have surprised me. We might as well talk—we may never have the chance again."

He pours the tea and hands a mug to Oscar while putting the other mug in front of me carelessly, spilling a little as he does so. That carelessness feels so unlike him. "Let me tell you a story."

Oscar and I both look up but avoid looking at each other.

"Once upon a time there was a woman whose skin didn't have any marks on it."

"Yes, we know how it goes, Obel," I sigh. "She was banished by the prince and was never heard of again. Blah, blah, blah. I'm not here to be told fables; I'm here to be told the truth."

Obel smiles ruefully. "All right, maybe I shouldn't have started it that way." He sips his tea. "Leora, your mom—your real mom—was beautiful."

My chair falls as I stand. I can hardly get the words out. "*Don't* call her my mother. She was not beautiful. She was a freak. She was evil. She was disgusting."

Obel doesn't move; he doesn't even look at me. "She was none of those things. Your mom was a beautiful, exceptional woman."

"Obel!" I'm screaming at him now—my throat burns with it. "Shut up. You shut up now. She was blank—she was nothing. She's nothing to me."

I hear Oscar let out a breath. I turn to him, rage making me shake. He drops his gaze.

"You can't even look at me, can you?" I speak slowly, spelling out the horror of my situation. "My mom was a blank. He married a blank." I feel nauseous even saying it. I can't believe I have her blood in me—her deviant heart begat mine. I turn to Oscar. "Did you know, and that's why you betrayed me?"

Oscar stands up and I think he's going to leave, but he's just getting his bag. "They threatened me," he says so quietly I can hardly hear. "Before we broke in they came to my house at night. They told me they knew everything about your dad, about my dad—everything that we had done." He snatches a glance at me. "They gave me an ultimatum: give them the skin and they would let my dad go. Why do you think it was so easy for us to break in?" He sighs and begins to unbuckle his bag. "And if I didn't do it, they said I would never see him again. I'm so sorry. I didn't dare tell you, but I did have a plan." He reaches into his bag and removes something, and slides it across the table to me.

It's Dad's skin. The mark, the scar, it's all there. "How?" I gasp.

"In the archives, I took a backup piece. Just in case." He looks down at his hands. "That was the piece I gave them."

I can't bring myself to touch the missing piece of Dad's book. The one part of him that remains. I slam my hand on the table.

Obel clears his throat. "Leora, there is something I have to show you, and we don't have much time."

I look over and it's only then I notice what Obel's doing. He has the flask of alcohol we use to clean skin before we ink. He holds a rag over the neck of the flask and tips the liquid onto it. He carefully places the bottle back on the table and begins to rub his arm with the rag.

I see the smudge of color on the white rag. He folds the cloth over and uses a clean piece to keep on rubbing his skin. And then the images fade, and beneath the beautiful, intricate layers of ink, his white skin shows.

Empty.

Blank.

chapter 41

"I COULD NEVER READ YOU," I WHISPER.

Obel looks up from his arm and smiles gently. "Sorry about that, girl."

"How long . . ."

"Before I moved here. I had to, didn't I?"

"So what, are you some kind of blank spy, sent to watch us?" I shudder. Up until now I'd never seen a blank in real life. And yet, I've been working with one all these weeks. The sickness rises within me and I hold on to the table to counter the dizziness. I look over at Oscar and am relieved to see that he looks as shocked as I feel. "Don't you have a soul?"

"Leora," Obel pleads, putting down the rag. His skin is beginning to look red where it's been rubbed with the pungent liquid. "I'm just like you."

I laugh darkly.

"Hear me out, Leora. I wanted to be something—to have something that was mine. I wanted something to be remembered for." He looks at my unimpressed face. "Blanks want it too, you know, girl—you don't have the monopoly on wanting to leave a legacy. I knew I could be a great inker. Why should I be invisible just because I'm blank?"

"But why didn't you just get marked, Obel? Why go to all this trouble to decorate yourself when you could have just done it once and been one of us?"

Oscar's moved closer to Obel now. He's touching his skin, examining his marks. Obel holds out his other arm for Oscar to look at.

"Because I choose not to. Because I demand that choice." He smiles at our faces. "Yes, it's been a disguise that's hard to maintain. I've been painting myself with this ink for years—topping up the faded patches each day, checking for smudges and mistakes." He lets Oscar turn his arm. "But your dad needed me." He looks at me. "And yours did too," he says, nodding toward Oscar. "They needed one of us to be here, to help the cause." I grit my teeth and shake my head. "They were fighting for us. Us blanks wouldn't be able to survive without people like your dad sending us resources: fuel, food. They saw the injustice and they fought. You mustn't believe what Longsight says—it's not about war or land or any of that; it's just about survival. And I was a link between the worlds—their contact."

I don't believe it—it can't be true. "What are you saying? What was my father doing?" I turn to Oscar. "Did you know? Is that why you talked to me, that first day at the museum?"

"I didn't know about this"—he gestures to Obel's arm—"but I knew your father knew mine. They've been working together for years, like Obel says, making sure the blanks are getting what they need. They'd starve otherwise, Leora." I scoff. As if I care. "My dad wanted to make sure the legacy your father built wasn't lost. The blanks still need us—need you. He told me Joel Flint's daughter would be a powerful weapon. I just didn't know why." His face is hard and sad.

So this is what's been happening in the background of my life. Did everyone know? All the things I've been taught, everything I've believed has been dragged from under me. It used to be so neat: You get more and more marks until one day you die. And then you're either a book or you're burned. But now it all seems like a tangle. I can't take it. I can't manage any more of this.

I look at them both: Obel with his calm, sad face; Oscar, his expression mirroring my confusion. I remember his hands on mine and his grin in the dark.

There have been too many lies.

I grab my things and leave, and neither Oscar nor Obel tries to stop me.

chapter 42

WHEN I REACH THE HOUSE (IT'S HARDLY HOME anymore, is it?), I peer through the windows to see if I can see her—*Mom*—Sophie. There's no sign of her, no lights on, and I can't see her coat hanging up. I try the door and it's locked. I use my key, open up, and go inside. I'm confronted by all those smells that you usually don't notice—the amalgam of scents that make up home. It should be the most comforting thing in the world and yet it turns my stomach.

I call out, ready to run if I hear her reply, but everything's quiet. I head to my room and repack my bag. I'll need another change of clothes, and I find some bandages from the bathroom that I can use if I need to change the dressing for my new marks. Mustn't forget my notebook—the one with all my sketches in it. It should be under my bed. My fingers close on something hard and papery. I edge it out and, while I'm half trapped under the bed, I hear footsteps coming up the stairs.

When she comes into my room and finds me I feel like that girl from one of the stories Dad used to tell. The one that wakes up in the den of a family of bears. The one who runs for her life when she sees their ferocity and the mess she's made. *She'll kill me*, I think. *She'll eat me alive*. I wriggle out from under the bed.

It's too late for me to run away—the bear's got me. She comes right at me with a menacing silence. A roar would be better than this. Her hands reach out—her fingers like claws. I cower close to the bed, but there's no escape. She grabs me. She snarls; her words bite.

"You stupid, stupid, stupid girl. You stupid, idiot girl. What have you done? What have you done?"

I flinch and try to break free but she's stronger than me. For a moment my body goes stiff—I brace myself for her attack.

But she's not devouring me, she's stroking me. She's not growling her wrath, she's weeping and whispering. I go limp and my tiredness rises to the surface. I can't fight a bear and I can't fight her. I let myself be embraced and spoken softly to. Tears rise, ready to drown me. But I'm cocooned in her arms. She keeps me safe.

"You stupid, stupid girl," she whispers with tearful tenderness. "I'm so sorry, Leora, my little light—I'm so sorry. I should have told you, I should have trusted you." She strokes my hair—as though I'm a wildcat that might bolt any second and needs to be soothed. That's not too far from the truth.

I move from her touch and switch on the lamp on my bedside table. We both squint in the glare and look at each other blinkingly as our eyes adjust to the brightness.

"Wait here," she says, getting to her feet. "Please, just let me get something, I'll be right back."

She returns a minute later with a papery package and passes it to me. I sit on my bed and untie the string that is keeping the paper wrapped tight around whatever is inside. The knots are tight and I have to use my teeth to ease them apart. Eventually the string comes away and I toss it to the side; it clings to my blanket for a second before falling down the side of my bed. The paper is thick—bent rather than creased as it encases whatever treasure Mom has hidden. I let it unwrap itself—the parchment pings back as though exhaling after having its belt loosened.

Inside is a book. Of sorts. It's more of a notebook—no inscription on the cover, nothing on the spine to give away what's inside. The front is like the back is like the front; I try to guess which way round it goes. The suede-like texture of old paper is soft under my hands. I open the cover—nothing, so I turn the book over and upside down and try again.

And then I see the beautiful blank face of the White Witch and I throw it down. "I don't need another book of fairy tales, Mom. What good is this to me?" I'd hoped it would be something—anything—that would make sense of all of this. I wanted something that would right my upturned world. But no, here I am with another book about the White Witch.

"Please, love, just look," she says gently. "This isn't a fairy story."

For a while I just stare at the book—sending it hateful messages with my mind. But eventually I pick it up again. I flick past that first picture of the witch and find that I'm not reading fables—there's no "once upon a time"-ing or "happily ever after"-ing. It's a journal—no, it's a letter—a message.

I read until my eyes are tight and blinking with tiredness. All the while Mom is there, sitting in silence next to me, watching me read the story of my life before.

"This was hers?" I ask. Mom nods. "Was this what she looked like?" I show Mom the drawing at the front of the book.

"It's her, yes, a drawing your dad did of her and kept. He was a talented inker as well as a flayer. He showed it to me so that I could see the likeness between you. He told me the blanks believe your birth mother was a direct descendant of Moriah and the White Witch. You see the likeness, surely? So yes, it's his picture, but it's not his handwriting, it's hers. Her story." She looks over my shoulder. "I've never read this. I was keeping it for you, for when the time was right." She sighs and tucks my hair behind my ear. "The right time just never seemed to come."

I turn the pages of neat slanted handwriting. "She wrote this bit when she was pregnant, Mom." I'm excited in spite of myself and show Mom the passage I've found.

You're moving all the time, little one. You're getting so big! I love to hold my hands on my skin and feel your bony limbs slide beneath my touch. I think you can feel me too. I'm getting so tired, but you're worth it all.

But a few pages later the handwriting stops and another hand picks up the story. "But look—here, the writing changes toward the end."

I don't know who it was who wrote the end of her story, who filled in the gaps. I wish I'd had this sooner. Before Dad died, before everything. I think I wish that. Maybe I don't—maybe it's been for the best that Mom felt like my Mom through all of the mess of the past few months. I don't know what we'll be to each other now, but we needed each other then.

And anyway. They (whoever it was)—they don't know the ending. That's not where I finish—it's not the end of my story.

I wonder how much of my birth mother's story she knows. There's no way of telling from looking at her face—she just looks tired and concerned. And sad. She looks terribly, awfully sad.

"Tell me, Mom," I whisper. "Tell me everything."

"Julia introduced us," she says, looking at the patterned surface of my bedspread. "You and me. She had been given the task of getting rid of you—there were regular raids on blank strongholds and babies were taken. You were dangerous; blank blood in your veins."

"You don't mean that—?"

She smiles bleakly.

"But she couldn't do it. She wouldn't do such a terrible thing. She came to me, Leora. I'd read for her before she became pregnant and we'd formed a friendship. I lived on the outskirts of town. There she was on the doorstep with you in a bundle resting on her own belly."

I hear her sigh then—the relief of telling her story without having to lie anymore.

"You were beautiful. Perfect. No one could know where you came from—if they knew who your mother was they wouldn't have let you live. And so I was going to name you and you would be mine."

She risks another glance and strokes my arm. I don't turn to her, but I don't move either.

"When I took your blankets and clothes off that first time, I saw it. Leora, you were marked already. But it wasn't the usual black mark—it was purple. This tiny baby I'd been told was a blank was just like Moriah. You were born marked—born ready named. I knew it must be a sign that you were good. Just like Moriah," she says again, thoughtfully. "We had your mark covered over in black ink so no one would know. And you were my little girl."

I look at her then. Can this be real?

"You had been with me for six months when your father showed up demanding I give you back. He'd spent all that time trying to find you, to find out if you were even alive." She rubs her hands over her skirt and shakes her head. "Oh, I read it all straight away—what he'd done—and I hated him for it." She rubs her hands over her skirt and shakes her head. "Oh, I hated him. He was worse than a blank. He had betrayed us and gone over to their side. He was polluted, barely human."

She gently pulls my hand into her lap and plays with my fingers.

"I wasn't going to turn him over to the authorities—he was your father, after all—but I wasn't going to let him within a mile of you. But he kept coming and one day—just to shut him up—I let him in. And I suppose you can guess the rest. We fell in love. He agreed to make a new life with me in Saintstone. I vouched for him, approved his marks at the government building. I lied for him. By the time we moved to this house we were just another married couple with a charming little baby. No one knew, no one guessed. My parents didn't approve. Dad has the gift of reading too, and he could tell that something was wrong. When I wouldn't tell him what, he and Mom disowned me." She looks sad. "But by then I had my own family. You were our perfect secret. You were even a secret from yourself."

I flinch at this and finally look her way.

"So everything about me being sick, about me and Verity at the maternity unit together—it's all made up?"

Mom nods.

"So I wasn't really born on the same day as Verity?" She shakes her head.

"No, love. You're almost nine months older than her, give or take. But we can't be sure when you were born." I laugh coldly and try to wriggle away.

"So I don't know my real mom, I don't know where I was born, and I don't even know my birth date? And at no point did this seem like an awful, cruel idea—keeping all of this from me?"

Mom gives my shoulder a placatory rub.

"My love—it was the hardest, worst thing I've ever had to do. Every day I wanted to tell you—to tell everyone."

I raise an eyebrow.

"But you were also the best and most beautiful thing that had ever happened to me. Try to understand. If they marked your dad with a crow back in Riverton simply for helping save a blank, imagine what they would do if they discovered you were the child of a blank? The descendent of the White Witch. Just imagine if they found out you had survived?"

She sighs heavily, tears and regret in her breath.

"I know it's not right, Leora, and I know it's not much, but your life was in danger and every day I kept you safe. I think Dad wanted to tell you. I think that's why he gave you his feather pendant, a sign of allegiance to the blanks."

I take my necklace out and examine it. Not a leaf, then. A feather. Mom gives a timid smile and shrugs.

"How come I've never been able to read this on you?"

"I've often wondered why you didn't see; I thought our marks would give us away. Your dad's marks were covered over, of course. I never imagined you would be a reader too—I never dared hope you would grow to be anything like me. My guess is that sometimes we see what we need to see—that sometimes the truth is wound too tight for us to unravel."

I frown, trying to take it in.

"But also, it's not a lie—you're on my tree because you're my daughter. You may have arrived in an unconventional way, but you're mine—you made me a mother the moment I held you in my arms. You know that, don't you? I'll understand if you can't see me that way any longer, but you will always be my girl—the one I took in, the one I raised, the one I've adored every single day you've been in my life. I would still do anything for you, even if you feel I can't be anything to you."

It's dark now. My head is aching and I climb under my bed-covers. I'm out of emotions—I don't know how to respond or what to feel. I can't fit all of this into the puzzle of my life.

Mom leaves me then. She tucks me up like she used to when I was a child and she goes. I lie wide awake trying to decide what to do. I don't want to stay here and pretend everything is how it's always been. Everything's changed. Everyone else has been keeping my life a secret from me. Now, I want to own it and see how I do.

"But," I whisper to myself, "there's no point leaving in the middle of the night and wandering the streets when there's a perfectly good bed right here."

I take my own advice and settle down to sleep in the early hours. I'll make a decision in the morning. As I sleep, the words from the notebook entwine with my dreams.

I dream of a man, branded and banished from his own people.

I dream of a woman, who looks like the White Witch, falling in love with the marked man.

I dream of the disapproval from her family.

I dream of her tight white stomach growing and blossoming.

I dream of her tiny baby and her weakening body. All her strength gone into bringing this life into the world.

I dream of the baby, marked at birth.

I dream of the death of the witch and the wailing of the marked man.

I dream of the screams of father and child.

I dream of his walk through the woods.

I dream of a woman who hides the baby.

I dream of the one who holds the baby to her chest as though her soul is now complete.

I dream of nothing nothing nothing.

When I wake, Mom has already left for work. I'm not sure where we stand with each other, but my mind is clearer; I understand more. I'll stay here while I work out what to do next; there's water in the kettle and tea leaves in the jar. I'll make a pot of tea—tea solves everything, right?

There's a knock on the door when I'm just pouring my second cup.

"Sophie?" Verity calls, "Are you in? I've got a letter for Leora."

I take a deep breath, stand up, and open the door.

If there was one person I didn't want to hurt—if there was one person who was totally innocent—it was Verity. She looks at me openmouthed, an envelope in her hand. She tries to speak but she has nothing to say to me. She just shoves the letter in my hand and walks away, turning back once to give me a look that says more than her words ever could.

And I don't go after her.

I watch my best friend walk out of my life.

I sit at the table looking at the government seal on the envelope. I smack my fist on the table and scream with sadness and anger and frustration. There was so much I wanted to say: I wanted to apologize, to find out what happened to her after. She must still have her job, or she wouldn't be delivering letters from the government. But is she OK? I guess it was easier with Obel and with Mom—we all had things we'd hidden, we all had things to forgive. But Verity has been nothing but good, nothing but brave, nothing but on my side, always. I don't deserve her. I betrayed her.

I leave the letter on the table and keep an eye on it while I go to tip the rest of my tea down the sink—I can't drink it now, I feel too sick. I don't turn my back on the letter—as though it's a poisonous insect that might scuttle away.

There's only one thing worse than having a venomous bug on your table, and that's having it run away to hide so that it can bite you when you're least expecting it. I don't know what I am expecting from this letter. I've learned some things I wish I didn't know since I last saw Mel. I've lost more than I ever imagined. I've found some things too. Maybe this letter will make sense of it all; maybe things will start to fit into place.

I step toward the table, pick up the letter, and break the seal to see what's inside.

There's a story of a girl who was given a box and told never to open it. Everyone knows that a gift you can't open isn't a gift at all, but a test. She fails the test—she opens the box and in doing so unleashes every kind of evil into the world. We shake our heads when we're told the story—stupid girl. *All her fault.*

I break the seal. I read the letter.

> *Dear Leora,*
> *Do you have an answer for me?*
> *Come to the government building at 10 o'clock*
> *tomorrow. I've booked you in for a truth-telling*
> *and then we can talk.*
> *Mel*

That's it? That's what warranted hand-delivered mail? I drop the letter on the table and go upstairs to get dressed. The red marks that feather down my neck, that have been there since Karl attacked, still haven't faded.

I wonder for a moment whether Obel is expecting me at work today. I wonder if he's expecting me ever again. Would I still have a job if I went there? Shuddery nausea rises every time I think about Obel.

I love him. I love his kindness and how he's welcomed and taught me. But I know his existence is an affront to our community. I should feel that his trickery is worse than a betrayal. I think about my real mother's blood in my body and wish I could open a vein and let her polluted legacy drain out of me. I wish I could change it all and rewrite my story. Begin all over again.

chapter 43

I BARELY NOTICE THE COLD WHILE I WALK TO THE government office for my truth-telling. It's only when I'm struck by the heavy heat inside that I realize how chilled my body had become. I take a left into the truth-telling waiting room, knock on the door, and let the man with the machine know I've arrived. The first time I was here I was so afraid. I was scared, but Dad was with me. Now he's gone and I don't care about the test. I'll give them answers; let the alarm sound. Let it catch the lies, if it can.

The man gestures for me to sit on the chair at the wooden desk, and I place my hand on the metal dome. I breathe deeply and wait for the questioning to begin. I know what he wants to hear.

"Is your name Leora Flint?"

"Yes."

"Have you had any contact with blanks?"

All my life.

"No."

"Have you committed any crimes that require marking?"

Broke into the government building, stole skin.

"No."

"Do you know of people who are not loyal to our leader?"

Where do I begin?

"No."

"Are all the marks on your body an accurate representation of your life?"

My marks are just the visible bit of the iceberg.

"Yes."

With each reply and every lie I wait for the alarm to sound, but it stays silent. Just as it did when Dad was tested. The system relies on our fear, I realize. We have to be so afraid of death and being forgotten that we will obey. We have to be so terrified of being marked as unworthy that we dare not lie. But if you don't care anymore, they can't scare you and they can't catch you.

It's just a show.

When I'm finished I walk out of the truth-telling section into the reception of the government building. The usual surly girl is there when I finish, and she tries to give me a scornful look. But I'm beyond feeling intimidated so I ignore her smirk and tell her who I'm here to see.

"She's in a meeting," the girl says, checking a book.

"She'll want to see me."

The girl sighs and wanders away slowly, but when she comes back to the desk she looks sheepish.

"I am so sorry to keep you waiting, Miss Flint. Come this way; the storyteller will see you in just a moment."

Her politeness looks like it almost kills her and I relish the pain it seems to bring. For all I know she might have been the one to help Karl get a job. A flush of fear runs through me then, while I follow her to the office. What if I see him? Was he really trying to warn me?

"How funny, Leora," Mel says as I walk into a small, hot meeting room with brown upholstered chairs. Isolda sits next to her, looking at me, her little shadow. "We were just discussing you in the meeting I was in. The mayor has been very interested in your case."

"Mayor Longsight?" I stare. I hadn't expected this. "He knows who I am?"

"Of course, Leora, and he's very keen to meet you when you start your work here."

"*If* I start work here," I correct.

Mel just smiles. The door opens and the light is almost blocked by the man who enters. "You've met Jack Minnow, of course."

The heat is beginning to make me sweat. I shake his hand clammily and feel like the room is shrinking.

Mel goes on. "I was quite open with you, Leora. I have never lied to you. The role the government is offering you is tailored to your unique skill set. They're keen to make the most of your remarkable reading abilities. You will be changing lives—offering hope for the living and the dead." She smiles. "You will be joining the ranks of a new role, as an editor."

"What's an editor?" I ask, after a startled pause.

"The job is as it sounds. You would alter marks as we see fit, for those we feel are deserving. It would involve a combination of skills: reading, inking, flaying . . ."

"But . . . isn't that deceptive?"

Mel smiles patiently and tousles Isolda's hair. "I sometimes forget how young you are." She lifts Isolda onto her knee. "When we're young, we see the truth in black and white—true or false, right or wrong. But, as we grow older, we see the nuances—we can't always put things neatly in our black-and-white world."

"So you prefer gray?" I ask, trying to mask my confusion.

She laughs—really laughs.

"Oh no, Leora! I love black and white. I love our society. I love fighting for the truth and for our stories to be told. But sometimes people need a little help." She sits back in her chair. "We all make mistakes, Leora."

I nod—and I think of Mom's lie, Dad's wife, Obel's skin, Oscar's dad. I think of me at the weighing and I don't know where I belong—black or white? Right or wrong? True or false?

"Sometimes it would be cruel to let those mistakes dictate our future, don't you think? You wouldn't edit just anyone. It would be in specific cases, when someone is particularly good or worthy. Someone on whom society depends. Surely there is room in our world for forgiveness, for hope, for redemption?"

Slowly, I nod again. "So we can cover up people's mistakes—remove them if need be. Let their goodness show through?" I ask.

"*Exactly*—and you will be the one to do it! You're an exceptional reader. You can know their hearts—you can know what their marks truly mean, you will know if they deserve to be remembered, and, if they do, we can make a little tweak here, a little snip there . . ."

I think of Oscar's dad. Of the cruelty and finality of his public mark. I think of my dad. There was no mercy for them.

"Who gets to decide who's edited?"

"Obviously the process will be stringent. Society's values need to be upheld. But we must be willing to do what it takes to keep the peace and to honor those who are most valuable to our community. There will always be those who have nothing to offer. People will always be forgotten."

"What if I say no?"

I hear Jack Minnow shift as he stands in the corner and I remember the owl.

"This decision, like all the other big opportunities in your life, will be marked on your skin." Mel's voice is smooth. "Who knows how this will look when it comes to the weighing of your own soul?" The threat is obvious.

"And if I say yes?"

There is a pause. "There are ways of resurrecting the dead, Leora."

For a moment I don't understand. And then I realize. "Dad?" I ask.

"We can make one book look much like another in the hall of judgment, Leora. It's theater. You just assumed that the correct book was burned."

I'm being offered the chance to save him still. If I want to. "I will give you until the end of next month to make your decision. It gives you just over four weeks. I'm being extremely generous. Think carefully, won't you?"

The cold slaps me this time—the heat of the government building tricked my body into comfort. My eyes prick with tears from the icy wind.

I sense rather than hear someone behind me. What if it's Verity? My heart is pining for my friend. I step back toward the building and call out her name.

"Do you even know what Verity means?" Jack Minnow steps out from the doorway he was sheltering in. My heart sinks with disappointment. "It means *truth*. And look what you made your poor friend 'Verity' do. She lied for you; she hid the truth for you. And you threw it all into that fire."

He walks close to me. Too close. His hand closes on my wrist.

"Oh, and don't be too hard on Karl if you see him again, Leora. He did want to help you. All he did was tell you the truth. And you know what they say: The truth will set you free."

chapter 44

I DON'T WANT TO GO BACK TO THE STUDIO BUT I FEEL I must. I need to apologize, for one last thing.

I enter through the back-room door. Obel is with a client and I decide to wait. I go over to the shelf where he has placed the *Encyclopedia of Tales*: the book of fables with the beautiful, blank White Witch at its heart. I touch its spine. And then I give in; I heave the book off its shelf, sit at the table, and read.

I don't notice when Obel comes in. I am jolted into alertness when he turns on the tap to fill a glass with water. He gulps it down while he looks at me. I have time to notice that he's touched up the marks he had erased yesterday—so perfect, so silent.

"I'm sorry I ran off yesterday." I break the silence. "And I'm sorry I didn't react better."

Obel puts the empty glass in the sink and continues to regard me.

"It was such a shock. It's all new to me." I close the book carefully. "It's hard to change what you've believed all your life, Obel. I truly am sorry, though."

I walk toward him and he just stays there. The image of his arm yesterday flashes from my memory and I see him there, in my mind's eye, completely blank and empty. Everything I've been taught whirs in my mind and tells me to retreat, to protect myself from him, from his kind. But my heart is breaking and I reach out and touch his beautifully empty painted skin. I trace my fingers over his marks.

And finally, finally he smiles at me, holds my hand, and draws me into a hug, which reminds me so much of my father I'm laughing and crying all at once.

We talk then, for a long time. Obel's mom knew my birth mother before she died, before I was born.

"You know, Leora, people still remember your dad."

"Well, they're not allowed to anymore," I say. We shouldn't even be talking about him.

"You can't stop memory, though, can you, girl? And anyway, *we* don't live by your rules, us blanks. We choose what makes someone worth remembering. He was brave, you know? He left everything because he fell in love. And then gave it all up again because he loved you. He loved Sophie as well, you know—it wasn't pretend."

"Was it you who put the feather in my pocket on my first day?"

Obel gives a rueful nod. "It was supposed to be a clue. I wondered how much your dad had told you about what he'd been doing, so I wanted to send a message in case you knew already. I'm sorry if I scared you."

"I'm frightened, Obel." I blow my nose on a handkerchief and put it in my bag. "There is so much wickedness."

"You still think we're bad, don't you? You still think you all have the last word on truth and on goodness."

"Mel says it's black or white—you're good or bad, no gray," I say, and Obel raises his eyebrows at me.

"You know what the real alternative to black and white is, don't you?"

I look at Obel, confused. He goes into the store cupboard and gets out the paints we sometimes use when we're designing marks. He does a quick picture of me, all black lines on the white paper. It's a pretty good likeness. He smudges over it with white paint until all that's left is a gray shadow of what he'd first drawn.

"Leora. Things don't have to be black, white, or gray."

He cleans his brush and begins to paint. The picture is of me again, but this time he puts in every detail—every bit of shade, every line. Every splash of light is rendered in brilliant color. The picture is so vibrant it's almost breathing.

"We're all a bit bad, Leora. We all have things in our lives that bring us shame and regret. Things that have hurt our souls or hurt the people we love. But we're all a bit good too. I reckon we're mostly good, actually. And life is about trying to learn the balance, plot our place on the continuum. We're a little bit good, a little bit bad—but that's not gray. It's this." He gestures to the painting. "We're not just made up of good and bad—we're everything else too."

He points at me. "For instance, you're a little bit moody, a little bit creative, a little bit funny, a little bit in love with Oscar."

I look up at that one, mouth open, ready to deny it, but he stops me with a smile and I just shake my head.

I tuck the idea away to think about another time. I wonder if I'll ever see him again. "But how can you know any of that if it's not marked on someone's skin?"

"This isn't the real me, Leora." He brushes his hands over the marks that are on display. "This isn't my real story. And aren't you more than your marks?"

I sigh. "I only have official ones."

"Even if every inch of you was covered and every word you have ever spoken was written on your skin, would it be enough? Would it be all anyone needed to truly know you?"

I close my eyes and imagine what that would be like. I think of my words and actions over the last week. "It would be enough to condemn me, I think."

"That's true for us all, isn't it?" Obel rubs my shoulder. "We can't live life hoping we'll never get it wrong. We're not made for this world of ink. We're not made for a place with no fresh starts."

I look at him, confused.

"Show me your scar," he says, and I hold up my hand. He raises his eyebrows at the amendments the government inker made. "You made a mistake, right?" I nod. "And here's your scar—it will be there forever to tell the world that you can't even wash up without being a danger to yourself."

I laugh and rub my hand—it's still tender.

"But have you ever broken a bone, girl?" I shake my head. Obel holds up his arm. "I broke my wrist when I was nine. Mom told me not to climb the tree, so I did it. She was right."

He smiles at me.

"You can't see it anymore can you? But it's there. My body doesn't tell tales on me for every single mistake. Our bodies heal, our bodies repair. Our bodies are built with redemption running through our veins. We don't consist of the failures and mistakes. We are made new every morning. The past doesn't have to define you, Leora. Your mistakes don't have to be forever. There's redemption. There's always redemption."

I'm crying now; the broken pieces are fitting back together, and I think I know what I need to do.

chapter 45

"HOW LONG WILL IT TAKE?" I ASK OBEL.

"Two, maybe three sittings. With healing time in between. You'll be ready in a month at the fastest."

"Well, in that case, we'd better start."

. . .

In the darkness as I leave the studio I hear her call my name and I think I must be dreaming.

"Leora. Don't walk away."

I turn around and it's really her. She looks freezing, as though she's been waiting for me for a while.

"Are you coming for a walk, then?" she says. And she turns away. I scamper over to catch up to her and walk with her, trying to keep in step with her long paces.

"Did you think about me at all, Leora?" She turns her head for just a second. "For so long everything I've done has been about you. You realize that, right?" I nod, but she doesn't see me. "I believed in your dad." I try to reply but she turns a corner and my words are lost.

"We were in it together. I would have fought for you till the end. But then at the weighing you just—gave up."

I interrupt, "No, Verity . . ." But she shakes her head and continues.

"You just let them destroy everything that we had worked for." She stops and turns to me, hands still in her pockets, her cheeks pink and her eyes shining with angry tears. "*Burn him.*" She mimics me, spitting the words out. "You might as well have burned my entire career that day. Do you know how much I risked for you? Do you have any idea how close I came to losing my job?"

I reach toward her but she takes a step back. "You're right. I wasn't thinking about you," I admit. Verity raises her eyebrows, challenging me to say more. "There was no space for anything else in my mind except what he'd done and all that he had hidden. I'm sorry."

She just looks at me coldly. I'm losing her.

"I've hurt everyone who loves me and everyone who loved him, Verity. Everything broke when they threw him in the flames, but at the time it seemed like the only thing, the only possible thing to do."

Verity turns and starts to walk again and I call after her. "They knew anyway." She stops, her back to me. "The government fed you information to pass on to me to see what I'd do. They even knew when we were stealing the skin."

Verity turns to me with a rueful smile. "I know. They were testing me as much as you. You passed, though," she says pointedly. "I just look like a rebel. You know, they thought I knew you were half blank?" Her mouth twists in revulsion. "Anyway, you ended up doing what they wanted you to. You're a hero." She exhales this last word as though I'm everything that makes her sick. "I'm on probation. I've been chucked out of my office and I'm back working with all the other trainees."

"I owe you so much. I know I do. I *always* do."

A tiny smile almost reaches Verity's mouth. "Understatement of the year, Lor. Is it true you've been offered a job?"

I nod.

"What will you do?

"I'm not sure." I rest my hand on her arm and she doesn't move away. "It depends on whether I've still got anyone left."

Verity frowns. "You've always had me," she murmurs. "But do I have you? Are you here for me? Would you fight for me?" And she stands there, freezing hands held out to me.

"I'd like you to let me try," I whisper. "Let me try to show you I can be as good to you as you've been to me."

Verity doesn't speak but she doesn't stop me from walking next to her as she makes her way home.

. . .

The next few weeks pass at once slowly and unbearably fast. I spend time with Mom—Sophie—finding out as much about the gaps in my history as I can. Julia comes to see us and I quiz her too. She's my rescuer, really. I owe her my life.

I want to be able to resurrect everything I've destroyed. I want to bring my broken friendships back to life, but if they rise again I'll still be able to see the scars. I want to bring Dad back from the dead, but do I really want to know the real him, the one with the past that I can't read and I still don't know if I can forgive? Sometimes I wish I could follow this thread back to where I started, rolling it into a neat ball. But if there's no going back, maybe I can knit these events into something new and beautiful.

. . .

My skin is itching. It's nearly time.

chapter 46

The Box

There was once a girl who was cursed by her own beauty. She had been created to be irresistible—to bewitch men and women with her looks and to make almost everyone fall in love with her. When the time came for her to marry she had no lack of suitors; they lined the streets outside her house, eagerly hoping for a glimpse of her face.

One by one she saw them—each one was handsome and full of charm, but she knew by now that beauty was deceptive—she was looking for something special. She hoped for love.

The girl waited and waited but love never came. The men who visited her thought of her as a prize to be won, a fortress to be breached, a wild garden to subdue. No one noticed the tender heart that she would so readily have given to a true lover. Her hopes dashed, she settled for the one who seemed kind, who had wealth to share and honor to bestow. She married the king and the people celebrated.

On their wedding day, when the festivities lulled, the king whispered to his bride that he had a gift for her. He ushered her to his chamber and presented her with a beautiful, ornate box. She let it rest on her lap as tears came to her eyes. Perhaps, perhaps he could love her? Perhaps, perhaps he had seen beneath her warm skin and noticed the quiet, wild soul that ached for love. She stroked the box and her fingertips played at the lock. She gazed into her new husband's eyes and smiled.

"The box is yours on one condition, my bride. You must swear never to open it."

Her tears of joy became bitter and she knew his love was like the contents of the box—out of her reach. She nodded, thanked him for the gift, and locked her heart as tightly as the box.

They lived together in companionable estrangement. The king was not cruel, but his neglect of his young wife soon broke her heart. Her skin grew pale, her hair lank, and her body became bent and guarded, as though she expected at any moment to need to defend herself. Now and then she would take out the box her husband had given her and gaze at its intricate carvings. Soon she lost sight of the box's beauty and saw only its forbidding lock.

When the king went on his next voyage to a faraway country, she formed a plan. She entered his chambers and searched and hunted until she found the key to the box hidden in the depths of the forever-blazing fire in the hearth. The embers singed her dress and the key burned and blistered her hands, but so determined was she that she carried the key straight to her box and inserted it, still smoking, into the lock. With one twist the box was open and, with scorched hands, she raised the lid.

Out of the box flew everything evil, everything venomous, everything malevolent, everything ugly, everything vile and repugnant. Into the world crept those pieces of poison and they devoured all that was good in the world. Because of one box the entire world was polluted.

All that was left was hope.

chapter 47

I PREPARE FOR THE SPEAKING RITUAL AS THOUGH it's my wedding day.

I look at my new mark—the one begun by my own body and finished by Obel. I dress in my traditional garments. It's the first time I've worn them since the party. I rub scented oil over my skin and cover myself in orange and gold. The robe, cloak, and shawl hide me. I close my eyes and prepare myself for the evening ahead. Mom and I walk to the speaking of the names in companionable silence. Our arms are linked. The cold is piercing enough to numb your lips and freeze your tears.

The hall of remembrance is misted with wafts of incense. The candles flicker as we close the door. Verity is already in the hall; she didn't wait for us this time. Mom and I walk to the front and check that the book is on the right page for our evening's reading and we light some more candles. I get water for each of us in case our voices grow tired.

We look at each other and Mom nods and gives an encouraging smile. We'll all speak the names even if no one attends to hear them. Verity goes first and I sit at the side of the room, eyes closed, listening to each name—relishing the sound of the syllables. I inhale the incense and feel I'm breathing in the souls of the long-passed. I feel the temptation of sleep, enjoying the way it lures me in the warmth and dimness of the hall. I open my eyes and wait while my vision adjusts to the candlelit gloom. I notice a couple of figures sitting down now, but it's no one I recognize. I move closer to the front in an attempt to stay awake—I need to be alert tonight. It's too important.

I hear Verity's gentle but clear voice chanting names as though they're liturgy or perhaps poetry. I guess we're re-creating tales of old here as we revive the dead and let them dwell with us in this room for one evening. I can almost feel them here tonight; all of us gathered here, souls entwined.

Candles flicker as another person comes in. It's Obel; he looks over at me and sits down. Mom changes places with Verity and her soft voice echoes around.

While I'm sitting I think about that girl. The one with the

box. She shoulders the blame—it was all her fault; she was the silly girl who gave in to temptation. She was the one who unleashed the evil. But she didn't create it, did she? She didn't ask for the box; she didn't intend to change everything. Sometimes evil is just waiting and it doesn't care who lets it loose.

I wonder what she did after it all went wrong. Did she try to gather all the badness—scooping it up in her hands and cramming it back in? Did she give in and accept that all the hate was released and join it? Did she try to fight? Did she just open a window, let the darkness out, and hope no one would notice, that no one would realize it was her?

I like to think she kept that box and took it with her wherever she went. And that when she glimpsed evil hiding in the corners of her life, she would gather it up, speak softly to it, and tame it. I like to imagine she coaxed the evil back into the box and tended to its sorrows. I like to think she didn't give in to the evil. I like to believe she didn't give up on hope.

With a shaking breath I ascend the steps and find my place in the book. The names are beautifully penned—handwritten letters, bones joined by sinews, combining to become a real person. I take a sip of my water and start to read.

Taking my time, I turn the page. As I breathe in I look up, to acknowledge the people sharing these names, these moments, these lives. And I see them there: Oscar and Verity, Obel and Sophie, Mel and Jack Minnow. But I can't look at them for long. I must focus on the names. As I read, I take a piece of paper from my pocket. I hide my hands behind the pulpit and unfold the sheet. I lift it onto the book and smooth it out across the page. Here is a new page of the book and it's my duty to read it.

Connor Drew—Oscar's father.
Mel—storyteller.
Miranda Flint—my birth mother.
Joel Flint—my father.

I look up and see them there. Everyone, sitting, watching. I see them smiling—the ones who matter. And I read all the names. All the names of the forgotten Verity grudgingly found for me in the archives. All the names of the blanks Obel gave me. All the names of dead and gone and never mentioned again.

I pause. There's a murmur in the hall; people are moving, someone's coming to the front. I take another sip of water and add one last name to the list.

Leora Flint.
We remember you.

As Mel strides up to where I stand, I close the book. I shut my eyes to the chaos that is beginning to unfurl and I unwrap the shawl from my neck. I remove my cloak and unbutton my robe.

I drop all my outer layers to the ground and stand in my breastplate and skirt. Leaving my robes and my old life at my feet. There are gasps as I walk down the aisle away from everyone and everything. I hear the shock as they see the mark Obel has given me across my chest, skimming my shoulders. The talons clawing at my breast, the tips of its wings fluttering down my arms.

A crow. A crow. The mark is a crow.

I walk outside. Snow falls like feathers. The whole town is blank.

Acknowledgments

I really never thought this would happen. I am the happiest writer in the world, and it is all thanks to this astonishing lot:

Genevieve Herr (UK) and Mallory Kass (US) for being wonderful editors and amazing encouragers.

Jo Unwin, my agent. Thank you for helping me to be brave— you are a treasure to me.

Thank you to all those at Scholastic US and Scholastic UK who have worked to make this book exist.

Dr. Gemma Angel, your work inspired me and this book, and I am so grateful to you for your wisdom and input. Thank you for sharing your creativity and awesome mind.

Emma Kierzek at Aurora Tattoo Studio in Lancaster: thank you for letting me watch, learn, and ask *stupid* questions.

To the Broadways: Mum and Dad and Ruth and Hannah. You are the best; I love you so much. It is a bit impossible not to be inspired by you, and you make me want to be a person of peace in the world. Blimey, you're a great family to be part of.

Oh, and Mum: From you, I learned that books could switch off the rest of the world and that they could be a safe tent or a dangerous adventure. Thank you for letting me wallow in books as a child. Thank you for showing your pride in my writing. Thanks for dealing with my phone calls about spelling and grammar even though I am a grown-up and should know these things by now.

Dave, remember that time you gave me a rapper name? We should have known then that it was destiny: Fatal & Danger 4eva (idst). I love you and your dreams and your goodness. You still make me laugh until I can't breathe. Thanks for fighting those frightening demons with me. Having you in my corner is my joy. Buckleys stick together, yo.

Mikey, Dan, and Jemima, you chumps are the best kids in the world. You make me want to be braver, funnier, stronger, and sillier. I love you. Thanks for all the sleep (smh).

About the Author

Alice Broadway is a former theology student from England. She wrote *Ink* as part of NaNoWriMo and now writes full-time in Lancashire where she drinks more tea than necessary, cheers on her husband as he wrangles their three children, and enjoys brainstorming new stories in her yellow camper van.

There are no secrets in Saintstone.
At least, that's what Leora thought until she
discovered that the marks can lie . . .

The adventure continues with *Spark*, the thrilling sequel to *Ink*!